D1411591

"Simply enchanting. There is a quiet kind of magic in this poignant novel. Ad Hudler's prose swoops effortlessly between the voices of two brilliantly conceived characters, between past and present, between loss and triumph."

—BEV MARSHALL, author of *Hot Fudge Sundae Blues*

"One of the freshest voices in women's fiction is coming from a man.... (*All This Belongs to Me*) is funny, moving, insightful, sweet, and immensely satisfying." —SUSAN ELIZABETH PHILLIPS, *New York Times* bestselling author of *It Had to Be You*

Praise for
Southern Living

"Warm and engaging."   —*Dallas Morning News*

"With sharply drawn characters and pitch-perfect dialogue, this tragicomic entertainment makes fine reading for the Fannie Flagg crowd."   —*Booklist*

"One helluva good read.... both hilarious and horrifyingly accurate."
—*The Albany Herald* (GA)

man of the house

Also by Ad Hudler

All This Belongs to Me

Southern Living

Househusband

man
of the
house

a novel

Ad Hudler

BALLANTINE BOOKS

NEW YORK

A Ballantine Books Trade Paperback Original

Copyright © 2008 by Ad Hudler
Reading group guide copyright © 2008 by Random House, Inc.

Published in the United States by Ballantine Books, an imprint of
The Random House Publishing Group, a division of Random House, Inc., New York.

BALLANTINE and colophon are registered trademarks of Random House, Inc.
RANDOM HOUSE READER'S CIRCLE and colophon are trademarks
of Random House, Inc.

LIBRARY OF CONGRESS CATALOGING-IN-PUBLICATION DATA
Hudler, Ad.
Man of the house : a novel / Ad Hudler.
p. cm.
ISBN 978-0-345-48108-5 (trade pbk.)
1. Househusbands—Fiction. 2. Naples (Fla.)—Fiction.
3. Parenting—Fiction. 4. Domestic fiction. I. Title.

PS3608.U33M36 2008
813'.6—dc22   2008025986

Printed in the United States of America

www.randomhousereaderscircle.com

2 4 6 8 9 7 5 3 1

Book design by Mary A. Wirth

1

Linc

Let me tell you about the screwed-up state of things in our house these days. We have no kitchen. We haven't had one for eight weeks and four days. The refrigerator is standing where a bathroom shower used to be. I am boiling my pasta and making my oatmeal on the grill on the patio. Our kitchen table changes weekly. Right now it's the new stainless-steel dishwasher, still in the box.

Midnight peeing has become a hazardous endeavor because someone inevitably has left something in the middle of my memorized, sacred, eyes-closed path to the toilet. Nails, screws, wood splinters, gobs of caulk and Sheetrock dust litter the floors, and shoes must be worn at all times. Bathrobes, too, for the girls. We have strange men coming and going in and out all doors of our house for most of the day.

The renovation at 363 Jacaranda St. has been systemic, to say the least, and I know now that we should have moved out for the project. Jo says we still should move out for the duration of the renovation, but how much longer can it take? Staying in this war zone has become somewhat of a badge of honor with me. If we can weather this, we can weather anything, right?

We are gutting all three bathrooms down to the studs. For the time being, we shower in one bathroom, pee in another, brush our teeth in a third, and this configuration changes with each week.

We are redesigning the kitchen and great room. We are replacing all forty-two windows and five doors.

But the biggy is this: We are literally raising the roof—okay, not the roof but the ceiling—of the entire house by eight inches because at six-foot-four I feel like Gulliver in this 1952 ranch home. To do this, we are knocking out the existing ceiling and robbing some space from the attic. Can you say "old crumbling plaster"?

Have I mentioned yet that we're living here while all this is going on?

Oh, and did I fail to say that hurricane season is just around the corner? Last year's was the most active on record, and this year promises more of the same. As Violet would say, "Oh, joy!"

I hear the door of Rod's truck shut outside, and I go to the window to peek out and see if my contractor has parked off the grass this time, as I asked him to do last Thursday.

Yeah, he's good. The pickup rests an inch or two from the edge of green. His wheels are straight. Everything Rod does always looks solid, angular, sensible. I can always count on Rod. Wish I could say the same of all his subcontractors.

Rod rings the bell on the back door and comes on in, unannounced, as I've told him to do. I meet him in the hallway.

"Sure hope you're a good drywaller," I say.

Rod grimaces, then scratches at his beard. "I take it Bud didn't show."

"Yep," I answer. "That guy's allergic to punctuality if you ask me."

"Damn."

"Yep."

"I wanted to get that tile started in the guest bath. Carlos is set for tomorrow."

"Carlos?"

"My tile guy—and he's busier than Santa Claus these days. . . . Damn!"

"What?"

"I don't know when I can get him down here again. That Sheetrock's got to be hung today."

"When could you get him here if not tomorrow?"

"You don't want to know."

"Can't you do it?" I ask.

"Well I sure hadn't planned on it. I've got to be on Marco Island at six."

I look at my watch.

"That gives you eight hours, Rod."

He frowns in concentration, purses his lips, then looks at his watch, which is the coolest watch on the planet. You can tell it's as old as the hills, an analogue model with Roman numerals, the rounded, crystal face smudged with scratches accumulated over the years, all held on by a brown-leather wristband stained with sweat and speckled with paint. If the designers at Abercrombie weren't asleep they'd already have come up with a "distressed" model of Rod Hayden's watch.

"I've got a consolation prize," I say. "You smell it?"

Rod puts his hands on his hips and lifts his nose in the air as Tillie, our cat, does when she's trying to detect some foreign odor.

"Cherry pie?" he asks.

"Blueberry," I answer.

Ah, my new weapon! I had been told by a friend in Rochester that the secret to getting subcontractors to show up at your house is to time the serving of aromatic baked goods with the predictable human blood-sugar crashes of midmorning and midafternoon. (Since I have no working oven right now I have to run over to Mrs. Artuzi's house to use hers.)

I have found this to be especially true between nine and ten in the morning. Up to this point it's worked well on Bud The Drywaller, but now he has gone AWOL. I'm guessing it has something to do with the fact that the game and fish commission lifted the ban on grouper fishing in the Gulf this week. I know he owns and loves a new twenty-four-foot Sea Ray with two four-stroke Yamaha engines. He talks about it 24-7.

As I do with all the subcontractors, I listen and pretend to be interested and ask questions and give comment—"Yeah, man, I hear ya . . . Cool, very cool . . . How fast can that go again?"—knowing that their wives couldn't give a damn, and if I prove to be a hospitable sounding board they'll return more often and finish their damn jobs so my family's normalcy and happiness can be restored.

We sit down at the ersatz bar in the kitchen, an old door atop two sawhorses. I pour Rod a cup of coffee, which he likes black. I've always liked half-and-half in mine, but I've been trying it black lately and like it.

He takes a bite and leans back in the stool and closes his eyes as he chews.

"Man, is that good," he says. "Almost as good as that peach cake-thing. Did you always cook like this?"

"You mean bake," I say. "This isn't cooking. There's a big difference between cooking and baking."

"Yeah?"

"Yeah."

He chews and says nothing, shrugs his shoulders.

"Cooking is fluid and organic, more impromptu, like finger painting," I say. "Baking is more exact. More like science. Or like construction. I actually like cooking better. I think it takes more creativity than baking because in baking you have to do everything exactly as the recipe says, and in cooking you're more your own boss. You'll be making this sauce, and you might taste it and say, hey, it needs some white wine, or some dried basil might add another dimension to this. . . . I mean, that's not to say it's easy. God, no, it's not. Cooking requires some science as well. Like if you're using cardamom pods, for example. I mean those little bastards will release their flavor only after a certain point, and then there's a difference between the green cardamom pods and the black ones."

Rod nods as he chews.

"And then there's gravy. I mean that's temperamental as hell. You've got to choose flour or cornstarch, and if you use flour you've got to make sure it cooks long enough to get that floury taste out of it, but if you cook it too hot it'll scorch on the bottom, and then you've got to time it right, and let me tell you with my wife's unpredictable schedule I don't make much gravy, because once it's reached boiling point it's never the same, and I just won't serve something past its prime. Oh, it goes in the fridge, sure, and Jo always eats it. She couldn't care less if the food's lost its integrity. She'll eat anything. That may sound good, it may sound like it makes my job easier, but it's also kind of degrading. I mean if she has no standards then why do I try so hard to make incredible meals? You know what I mean?"

I notice that Rod has accelerated his eating. His bite-size has grown as I continue talking. His plate is nearly empty.

"Do you want some more?"

He strains to swallow one last, large bite. "No, thanks. Was real good, though."

"You sure?"

"Yeah."

He disappears down the hallway, wiping his hands on the back of his thighs, and as I put the dirty dishes in a tub to take outside to the hose I am wondering why I feel so stupid and vulnerable right now . . . exposed in some way, as if I've been caught standing at the curb in my underwear.

Which reminds me: *Add toilet paper to grocery list.*

Which reminds me: *Get clothes to Goodwill.*

Which reminds me: *Buy copy of* Goodnight, Moon *for the Weiss's new baby.*

Which reminds me: *Trim bougainvillea bushes on trellis by drive-way.* (See the connection? Remember that line, "In the great green room," from the book? See it yet? Green? Outdoors? Yardwork?) Stay with me here.

2

Linc

The mothers at Violet's school park in the exact same spot every day as they wait for the bell to ring. I always thought it was just a creature-of-habit thing, but then I heard two of them talking one night when I was sitting behind them at a junior-high performance of *Merry Christmas, Charlie Brown*. One woman was complaining that another mother, obliviously new to the Collier Academy family, had been getting there earlier and taking her spot.

"What's Katie going to think when she comes outside and I'm not in our spot?" she asked her friend. "I want her to feel secure."

During intermission I saw her standing by a table in the foyer, choosing from an array of sushi and chocolates.

"Excuse me," I said, expecting—and getting—a look of surprise that quickly morphed into tethered disgust masked by a smile. What is it about me that these prep-school moms find so egregious?

"I couldn't help but overhear your complaints about the woman who's taking your parking spot."

I sensed her frozen persona instantly begin to melt around the edges. For the first time, she looked at me squarely in the eyes.

"Yes! So you've had the same problem with her?"

"Well, no," I answered. "I wanted to say that I don't think you're doing your daughter a favor."

Her eyes began to flit like a nearly expired fluorescent lightbulb coming on, and she looked away from me, then back again, away, then back again. I knew she was searching for an escape hatch or wondering—correction—*hoping* that none of her friends were seeing her talk to this man who drives the usually dirty Toyota van with the *Cat Lovers Against the Bomb* bumper sticker on the back window. Her reaction was so cliché I just wanted to pat her hand and say, "I'm sorry you've been so heavily influenced by the characters in pop culture." I don't even really have to describe the look because you've seen it on countless horrible TV sitcoms and movies that star·Young Blond Girl and Cute Hairless Boy-Man.

"Excuse me?" she said.

"I'm sorry," I said, and I held out my hand. "I'm Linc Menner. My daughter's playing Lucy tonight. . . . As I was saying, I think it's best for your child if you throw a wrench into her predictable environment now and then. After all, humans are hunters and gatherers, and the successful humans will be those who learn that their environments will change with the day. Do you understand what I'm saying?"

She stood there, frozen, so I took the opportunity to wrap it all up. I told her how this whole land-o-plenty, grand-buffet style of living, with all the choices lying in front of us 24-7, does nothing but make us softer and more endangered as a species, how it's another of those well-intentioned but ultimately destructive parenting techniques that bring us one step closer to extinction.

"Dorie!"

It was a woman's voice, coming from somewhere behind me.

"Lisa!" Katie's mother stretched her arm out, reaching beyond my shoulder, as if her friend had just thrown her a life preserver, and she was going to grab it and hold tight as she was pulled from frigid, shark-infested waters, back to some safe place.

As Hillary said, it takes a village. Over the following days I started to take matters into my own hands. I began arriving early and stealing one of their spots.

My victims of commando parenting would generally coast past me, glaring through two shields of brand-name armor, a pair of Chanel sunglasses, maybe, and the tinted window of some high-end import. I would smile and wave and sometimes roll down my window and try to engage them, but not one had the balls to speak to me.

A few days ago one of them in a shimmery-ivory Cadillac Escalade shot me the finger after she motioned for me to move and I shrugged my shoulders. To piss her off I showed up early again the next day, but she, too, came early and got the spot.

The next day I arrived at two o'clock, an entire hour before dismissal. I never saw her that day, but she must have come in and turned around because I got a call that afternoon from Mr. Burkert, headmaster of the school.

"Mrs. Daniels likes to park there," he said.

"So do I."

"She has parked there for quite some time, Mr. Menner."

"Are you saying there are specific parking spots for specific parents?" I asked, feeling somewhat empowered because I'd just learned that Violet had earned the highest verbal score in the eighth grade on the Stanford Achievement Test.

"Well . . . no," he said, and then, "But . . . how do I say this? There are some unwritten exceptions, I suppose."

And then it hit me. There is no possible way that $21,500 in annual tuition per pupil can even begin to pay for everything this school has—the "smart" blackboards in every classroom (a teacher or student can compose something on a computer, and it automatically goes up on the blackboard, which is actually white); the seventh-grade trip to the Outward Bound school in Key Largo; the top-gun lawyers hired to coach the mock trial team.

No, in every private school there is this hungry monster called the annual fund drive or, in Collier parlance, The Collier Drive for Excellence, and we parents are reminded just how benevolent (or, in my case, irresponsible) we as a collective community have been that year by a professionally made sign in the grass outside the main entrance. Each 10 percent participation milestone is marked by the silhouette of a green head of a panther, the school's mascot. We are told in the letters sent home that it doesn't matter how much we give, that even one dollar is important because it shows commitment. Some, of course, give more than others. For the record, I have not sent in my dollar for the past two years, largely in protest of the ridiculous roving rent-a-cop they hired after 9-11 and the school board's refusal to observe water restrictions during the dry season. I wrote an e-mail to Mr. Burkert about it, explaining that although the restrictions were voluntary it would send a good message to the community that we were being responsible shepherds of our natural resources, and that it made us look nouveau riche to water all that thirsty St. Augustine grass during the dry season in the subtropics. (While I was at it I also suggested they don't plant thirsty annuals, that I knew image was everything to a private school, and planting impatiens and pansies made us look more Madonna and Michael Jackson and less Nature-Conservancy-Old-Money, and it would be best if we xeriscaped with native plants. He never replied.)

"Ahhhh," I finally said. "Daniels. As in the Reston C. Daniels Dining Hall. I assume there's a connection there somewhere."

"That's correct," he answered. "The new dining hall was primarily funded by her father-in-law."

"But there's no sign saying that spot is hers, right?"

Pause.

"Yes."

"Yes what? Yes no sign or yes that's correct?"

Pause.

"There is no sign."

"Then I guess anyone can park there, right? I mean, I'm sorry, I don't want to put you in a spot, but what kind of message does that send to our kids? That if you give a lot of money to the school you can trample anyone else's rights?"

The next day there was a new sign erected in the grass adjacent to that very spot. It is quite professional-looking, like all the signs on this campus. They love their signs at Collier Academy. Perfectly level, the square post is made of immaculate PVC-pipe material on which is affixed a white metal plate with green letters, matching all the other signs on campus. It says, *Reserved for Daniels Family.* The maintenance guy even replaced the sod that had been torn up in digging the hole, giving us the impression that the dear Daniels family had been parking here since the days when fish had legs.

I don't know if it's prep-school moms I don't like or wealthy mothers in general, but I've discovered the feeling is mutual. Maybe they're just afraid of me. I'm a big guy, and I often wear a bandana on my head because I sweat so damn much. I'm never asked to help with anything at school. I checkmarked every volunteer box on the parents' association questionnaire that came home with Violet. I even said I'd help organize the fund-raiser fashion show that they put on with Saks every year. But I have heard from no one.

I will admit that it's made me a little bitter.

3

Jo

They're not answering the phone again. I know they're home—it's 9:35 on a school night. They always do this to me, they do it to everyone. The only consolation is that we don't have caller ID, so I can't feel personally rejected. Lincoln refuses to get caller ID. He says it's a scam of the phone company's that preys on people's paranoia. I see it as a tool to help avoid conflict, preserve salespeople's dignity, and maintain privacy, although I will say it is indeed superfluous when you never answer the telephone anyway. Five rings and then—always!—the roll into voice mail.

Actually—and he would deny this, I am sure—it's a control thing with him. In a telephone conversation it is the caller, not the recipient of the call, who is in control. Each caller wants something, and she has electronically summoned another human to satisfy that need. In essence, the caller holds up the hoop through which the person on the other end is supposed to jump.

Ah, but if the recipient of the call does not answer, well, then that puts him in charge now, doesn't it? It is a brilliant form of passive-aggressiveness . . . or would it be aggressive passiveness? I know that after Linc is finished doing the dishes or folding some laundry or surfing the Net he will retrieve messages and return my call *when and if he sees fit.*

Violet, a full-blown teenager, should at least be answering the phone. She should be jumping for it at every ring. I know I was at that age. She should be thirsty for social contact, going to the movies and shopping at the mall. But she doesn't even want a phone in her room, and she always seems startled and slightly peeved when she gets a call. Not long ago I heard her blurt, "Why did you call me?" after the person on the other end had tried to engage her in idle chatter for a few minutes.

I worry about Violet's overly serious nature. Lincoln is a great father, but I fear he has been too strong of an influence on her. I think it would have been different if we had had our second child—maybe he wouldn't have treated the second one so much like a miniature adult. I thought I'd get a second chance when I got pregnant again, but after I lost the baby I just gave up and had my tubes tied.

Of course, I love my daughter, but she is just not the happy-go-lucky kid I imagined having. Instead, she's a Linc-clone. I guess I have that coming, being the parent who is never home.

The other morning I came down to the kitchen when she was eating breakfast, listening to *Morning Edition* on NPR. Lincoln has it on every morning, probably an indoctrination of sorts—now how might he say this?—to "create in our daughter a thirst for knowledge and an ear for intellectual syntax." Something like that. For the record, yes, I do like National Public Radio, but it suffers from self-conscious, acute seriousness, much like Unitarians. And I don't like the idea of broadcasting it at the expense of eroding our child's lightness and innocence.

I can't forget how irritated she was when I changed the station one morning to 96 K-ROCK. She looked up from her pancakes and raspberries and said, "Mom, do you mind? Adam Hochberg's in the middle of a story about the tobacco farmers of North Carolina."

I am lying on the bed and staring at the ceiling for no particular reason. I've got so many e-mails to read and answer that I don't even want to begin the task. The air conditioner at the window rattles and buzzes. I can hear The Weather Channel through the wall by my head, some other Road Warrior probably checking the temperature back home. I touch the new zit on my forehead. There are four on my face now, including two on my chin and another on my right temple. I always break out when budgets are coming due.

Then it dawns on me: I forgot to tell him I was leaving town for the night. Or did I? God! This is how crazed my life has been these days.

My BlackBerry chirps. I reach over to the bedside table, pick it up, and look at the screen. It's Lincoln.

"Did you need something?" he asks.

"Did I not tell you I was going to be in Jacksonville tonight?"

"No," he answers.

"I am so, so sorry."

"It's fine," he says, "don't worry about it."

"Well, I'm sorry. I really truly am. You cut me so much slack, Lincoln, you really do."

"I said 'it's fine,' Jo. . . . Did you get a healthy dinner tonight?"

I look over at the empty candy-bar wrapper on the dresser top.

"Yes," I lie. "What did you guys eat?"

"Grilled some chicken outside. I miss my kitchen. Violet wanted Linc Pasta tonight, and there was no way in hell I was going to make it on the grill."

My husband is famous for his on-the-fly pasta concoctions. They usually involve some sort of leftover meat from a previous meal, fish or lamb or chicken, and if there's no meat he uses a can of beans or tuna fish. He mixes this with whatever pasta he has on hand, throws in roasted vegetables or sautéed spinach or something, and always garlic, lots of garlic. I quite often can't tell what's in it, but it's always good, and we have it a lot.

"I'd kill for some of your food right now," I say.

"You didn't eat dinner, did you?" he says. "You're lying about dinner. . . . Jo?"

Linc's obsession with my diet both infuriates and comforts me. I'm glad he worries about my health, but he can be so controlling about it. When he thinks I've been eating poorly he slips a Ziploc bag of cut-up raw vegetables in my briefcase, and when I get home at night he often checks to make sure they're gone. Sometimes I have to drop them in the trash can on the way out of the office. I like vegetables—I just forget they're there. As I've said: busy, busy, busy.

He gets downright preachy at times, and I find myself rebelling in his absence; hence, the Twix bar as a meal substitute. When we're going through a rough patch, as we are now, I find I begin replacing vegetables and fruits with comparable levels of processed sugar and preservatives. Childish, I realize, but it feels good, nonetheless.

"What did you have for dinner?" he asks.

"Subway sandwich," I say, as I always say, because for some reason, it's always the first answer that comes to mind, my default lie. In reality I eat at Subway maybe once a year, but I learned early on that it was one of Linc's more acceptable choices in the Fast-Food Axis of Evil.

"Jo, you eat too many of those things. They're loaded with sodium. Did you at least get the multigrain bun?"

"Of course."

"Those processed meats are really toxic."

"I know," I say, "but I did get extra tomatoes. . . . I had extra tomatoes."

I'm a horrible liar. I get nervous and repeat things whenever I lie. I hate lying, but sometimes it's necessary with Lincoln . . . especially when he's in one of his extended funks, and this has been a long one.

The move to Florida has been tough on him, largely because I'm working more hours than ever. He is basically a single parent right now, and he resents me for it, I'm sure. The bomb scene that is our home is not helping matters. He is so negative these days, and though I know he needs me now more than ever I find myself avoiding him because I fear he will drag me down into that dark hole with him.

"Violet and I have to get to the mall," he says. "She needs some bras. God, I hate buying bras. I thought you did that last weekend. It's just asking too much. I mean, pantyhose and tampons, fine, but not bras and panties. I feel like a pervert when I have to loiter in the lingerie department."

"You didn't ask me to buy bras."

"I did so. You were probably on your Crackberry. You never hear me when you're on your Crackberry. I specifically told you."

Most successful marriages have a beneficial constant that we lack in ours: a silent sufferer. It is usually the caregiver, but my family's caregiver is a man, and we all know that men are incapable of being silent sufferers who will gulp down sacrifice upon sacrifice with no complaint, and fake being wrong in an argument for the sake of harmony in the household.

That night, in the moments before falling asleep, it hits me: Of course he doesn't like shopping for bras. It is clear evidence that his little girl, his main companion, the person on this planet with whom he has spent most of his time for the past thirteen years, has started her walk down the path toward womanhood—and he must stay behind. Despite being one of Violet's two moms, he is not allowed.

A necessary separation, indeed, but it doesn't seem fair.

4

Linc

I'm parked in a different spot today. This one "belongs" to Miss Navy-blue Lexus SUV. After passing me and glaring she finally finds a suitable location in the turnaround by the tennis courts. There aren't too many cars left. Violet is usually among the last ones out. It takes her longer than others to get her things collected. She's very methodical and thorough, I'm proud to say.

I tried for a while to fix this, mandating nightly one-on-one at the neighbor's basketball hoop, hoping that the speed and randomness of the game would bleed over into real life. I gave up after a few months; it didn't seem to be working.

There she is. And I can see by her bounce and suppressed smile that something funny and/or good happened today. Thank God.

Violet opens the side door of the van, turns around and sheds her heavy backpack onto the rear passenger seat.

"Oh . . . my . . . gosh, Dad!" (I'm not religious, but I'm a stickler about that G word because I'm so sick of hearing it come out of kids' mouths every sentence. I've caught her saying it to her friends at times, but as long as she can astutely edit her language for her audience I will not say anything. Pick your battles, parents. Pick your battles.)

She climbs into the passenger seat up front.

"You're not going to believe what happened today," she says.

I put the van into drive and ease forward. Again, I wave to Miss Navy-blue Lexus. Again, she ignores me.

"What?"

"Ms. Hutchinson? The head of middle school? You're not going to believe what she said. We were in gym, out on the field . . ."

"What are you doing in P.E. this week?"

"Lacrosse."

"I wish I knew lacrosse. You're gonna have to teach me some-day."

"Anyway," she continues, "a group of us were standing around, talking, waiting for Coach Bivens to get back from the office, and Ms. Hutchinson comes up to us in her little golf cart, and guess what she said? Oh, Dad, you're not going to believe this. This is classic Collier Academy."

"What? What? Come on, man, you're killing me."

"She says—oh my gosh—she says, 'Girls, I see that you're standing in a circle.' And we said, 'Yes, ma'am,' and she said, 'Well, by nature of its design a circle is exclusionary. It excludes everyone who is not in the circle, so that's why circles are not a good thing.' "

"No way," I said.

"No, no, it gets better. She zips away on her little golf cart and then does a circle and comes back to the group and she says, 'You know, as a matter of fact, girls, let's not stand in circles anymore. Let's just say that circles are against the rules at Collier because they exclude others. So no more circles, okay?' . . . Dad, isn't that hilari-ous!"

"Oh, honey, please tell me you said something."

"Of course I did. Oh, you would have been proud of me."

"What did you say?"

"I said . . . Are you ready for this? I said, 'Certainly, Ms. Hutchinson. Would you prefer a lovely oval instead?' "

"You're horrible."

"You would have said the same thing."

"No, I would have said . . . hmm . . . what would I have said?" I was faking, of course, I knew exactly what I would have said in that situation.

"You would have said, 'It is not your responsibility to protect the meek, Ms. Hutchinson.' "

"I don't get it," I say.

"As in, the meek wouldn't be in the circle in the first place. You know, you can't force social interaction?"

"Oh, as in 'You can't force someone into being an alpha? You are what you are?' "

"Yes. You know, Darwin and all that."

Oh, it is a grand day! It's like the old days of preadolescence when my daughter was confident and happy and didn't care what her peers thought of her. So often nowadays she exhibits no pride, no confidence. After years of having great posture she now walks with slumped shoulders. Jo thinks it's because she's so tall, and she's trying to shave off a few inches so boys won't be intimidated. What bullshit is that?

Puberty has changed everything. It's as if she's been injected with some serum that alters her behavior, colors her moods. Where is that outspoken, confident girl I raised, the one who addressed the Pittsford Board of Education when she was eight because her school's art teacher position was getting cut? Where is the girl who wrote and faxed a letter to the governor of New York because she didn't like how they were cutting down the trees along the Thruway? Has she vaporized, or is she simply hiding? Hibernating? Has all my parenting been for naught?

But here she is now, at least for the moment. I look over at her and swell with pride. Honest to God, I tingle from the top of my scalp to my toes. I love this girl so much! I love having such a good companion who knows me so well. She is so bright. She says things that surprise and enlighten me.

I so need this today.

DATE: Friday, May 20
TO: RHutchinson@CollierAcademy.org
FROM: LincolnM@AOL.com

Dear Ms. Hutchinson: Violet came home today and told me that you outlawed circles (as in students-are-not-allowed-to-stand-in-circles) today during her gym class. She says you said circles exclude people and therefore should not be allowed. I do not believe it is proper or smart to legislate the everyday social interactions of children. There will always be dominant individuals, and it is up to each child to learn how to navigate around these people.

Oftentimes, children are excluded from a circle for good reason. They might be snotty or mean or shy. In each case, the child, after being excluded, will have to examine what he or she needs to do to gain approval of their peers. I am certain Bill Gates was one of those children who got left out of circles, and he made the best of it. Instead of being Mr. Social he turned inward and focused on the development of his own creativity, and, of course, went on to change the world.

In legislating social interaction, in trying to preserve every single child's self-esteem—and how TIRED I am of hearing that phrase—I fear we are creating a generation of soft children who will be ill-equipped in growing and adapting in an increasingly competitive world.

Please let me know if you ever want me to participate on a panel about parenting.

Sincerely,
Linc Menner

5

Jessica

When I don't have hall-monitor duty I go to the dining hall and watch him from the window. He drives a van, which I think is real interesting. I know he calls it the "man van." I learned that from one of Violet's essays. It's a white Toyota Sienna and it's got a bumper sticker on the back window that says *Cat Lovers Against the Bomb*, and if that's not strange then I don't know what is. I mean what does that mean: Cat Lovers Against the Bomb?

He's got curly reddish-blond hair, and he's a big guy, like he really likes his barbecue. He looks a lot like Marvin Treadwell, one of the boys I grew up with in North Carolina. Sometimes he's got a beard and sometimes he doesn't, and he's always got sunglasses on, those wraparound-mirror-kind, like the ones the soldiers wear in Iraq.

She looks real down today. I've asked the kids to read the next fifty pages of *Brave New World* so I can sit here and pretend to be doing something at my computer—read my e-mail, mainly, and shop for some shoes on smartbargains.com—because I don't feel like leading a discussion, it's just not in me this morning. All we're doing is coasting into finals anyway. I don't think Violet's even reading the book. I haven't seen her turn a page in five minutes.

I get up and walk over to her desk.

"Are you okay, Violet?" I ask her. "You feel okay?"

"I'm fine, Miss Varnadore," she answers.

"You sure?"

"Yes, ma'am."

"You've read this book before, haven't you?" I ask. "Have you read this book?"

She looks at me like I've caught her in a lie.

"Yes, ma'am," she answers. "Actually, my dad read it to me."

"Your daddy reads to you?"

"At the breakfast table. Every day. Or at least until about a year ago."

"That is so sweet. What kind of books?"

"*Little Women. Grapes of Wrath.* Stuff like that."

"Tell you what," I say. "How about you write me an extra essay and you don't have to read that book?"

"What do you mean?" she asks.

"An essay. And I know what I want you to write about. I want you to write about the most influential person in your life."

Of course I know it's gonna be her daddy because he sneaks his way into just about every assignment I give. My favorite was the story of how he and Violet stopped and picked up a homeless lady and took her to Perkins for breakfast and then drove her to the grocery store and filled up her grocery cart with food. Now you tell me: How many men would do that?

Violet starts shaking her head, so I hold up my hands and shake my own head to protest.

"No, no . . . Now I know it sounds kind of fifth-grade-ish, but I'm real interested in what you have to say, and besides, I didn't have you in fifth grade. You're a unique young lady, Violet, and I wanna know how you got that way. Really, I do."

"Is this extra credit?" she asks.

"No, ma'am, it most certainly is not," I answer. "It's supposed to replace you reading Mr. Hemingway."

"Do you mean Mr. Huxley?"

I bend down closer to her so I can whisper.

"He's so boring anyway, don't you think so?"

"Miss Varnadore!"

"Well, he is. Is that a stupid book, or what? . . . So do you wanna write that essay for me?"

"Yes, ma'am."

I love it when she says ma'am. This girl, she intimidates me sometimes. There's always some student that intimidates you every few years, and this year it's her.

She's got her daddy's big brown eyes.

6

Violet

He's on the patio, which, these days, is our kitchen. I can always find my dad in the place where meals are made. One of my friends calls him Marge behind his back, as in Marge the mom in *The Simpsons* who's always wearing an apron and doing something mom-like.

He's always been a really good cook, but lately we've been eating the same kind of food that all my friends eat, stuff like canned soups and macaroni and cheese and lots and lots of grilled meat.

We've also been eating out a lot more, which we never used to do. I hate eating out with my dad. He critiques the meals in restaurants as we're eating, like he's some sports commentator. He says he's convinced there's a secret spice called "restaurant spice," because the food all tastes the same in chain restaurants.

Dad says this is all temporary, only until he gets his kitchen back. Same with my school lunches, which he's stopped making, and I miss them. He makes the world's best egg-salad sandwiches. He puts garlic and a little bit of sun-dried tomatoes in it.

I see that he's slicing carrots and parsnips for tonight's meal. I think this means we're having those stupid hobo suppers again. Oh, joy. These are the weirdest things. You take a piece of tinfoil and fill it with some kind of meat and vegetables, and then you fold them shut and put them on the grill for a while. They taste the same every time. I actually like parsnips, especially when he cuts them up in small sticks and roasts them in olive oil and garlic and salt. He calls them "Menner fries." We haven't had them for a long time. No oven.

"Dad?" I say.

"Yes?"

"There's a Comcast truck in the driveway?"

"Good."

He sets down the knife and looks at his watch. "Their three-to-five window was closing in two minutes."

"Comcast?" I ask again.

"We're getting cable," he says, like it's no big deal, and it is. You need to know that the chance of this happening is about as likely as my mom taking up crocheting and joining the Daughters of the Confederacy. What a crazy group that is. I learned about them last month in English. Ms. Varnadore, my teacher, actually belongs. She is so random! But her weird Southernisms amuse me. And she's not making me read *Brave New World*. All I have to do instead is write some stupid essay, which will be a breeze. I can write essays in my sleep.

I follow Dad around the side of the house, hustling to keep up, to the driveway where the Comcast white van is parked.

"Dad . . . What's going on?"

"I told you. We're getting cable."

"Why?"

"The hurricanes."

"You're joking, right?"

My dad hates TV. When we go on vacation and watch in the hotel room all he does is go crazy and rant, talking to the TV like it was some child who's misbehaving. Dad says 90 percent of TV programming insults the average American's intelligence. I watch TV at friends' houses, and I have to agree there's a lot of worthless, random stuff, but I do like *The O.C.* and *Project Runway*, though I'd never tell my dad that because he'd probably think I was stupid and shallow, and he'd try to have me hypnotized or something. I've had to subscribe to three different magazines just to keep up with pop culture so I'm not laughed at at school.

"Oh, my gosh!"

I must say it loudly because Dad and the Comcast guy stop talking and look at me.

"Does this mean we're getting high-speed access?"

Dad looks quizzically at the Comcast man, who nods his head.

"Yeah," says the man. "Comes with it. Everything's bundled."

"Yes!"

We must be the last family in North America to be using dial-up AOL, definitely the last at Collier Academy. I've been bugging him forever to get DSL through the phone company, but he has refused.

Dad starts shaking his head.

"I don't want it bundled," he says. "I don't want it, period. I think this high-speed crap is creating a hugely impatient generation. I think it's responsible for all the road rage."

"Got no choice," the man answers, to my glee. "They come together."

"How long will it take to get it up and going?" I ask.

"An hour or so. This house used to have cable. That gray box over there by the air conditioner. See it?"

We leave the man to do his work, and Dad takes me out to the patio to give me a snack. We still have a working refrigerator, it's in the master bathroom right now, but Dad has basically given up on cooking inside, and I can't blame him. It looks like a tornado hit our house. Really.

Instead, we have some coolers on the patio. This way he doesn't have to run inside all the time for ingredients.

It's not that my dad is one of those over-organized anal types like Jen Bischoff's mom, who lays Jen's socks out in the drawer like fallen dominoes. (Honest, she sorts them by color from white to dark, I've seen them.) He's not that way at all. I mean, he keeps an orderly house, but I remember when I was little, I don't know, maybe six or seven, and he and my mom were having an argument one time about my toy drawers. Mom was disgusted with how the disorganized drawers were filled with little odds and ends, rocks and plastic toys and pieces of rubber food and chopsticks and little bottles of hotel shampoo and stuff like that . . . all just thrown in with no thought.

I saved everything, I still do. Mom wanted to go out to Target and buy Rubbermaid containers so everything could be sorted and stowed, but Dad stopped her. I guess he thought it was good for my creative development to leave the drawers all crazy, so that when I played make-believe I would pull things out and improvise.

One thing about my dad: He always has a motive behind his actions.

"What did you eat today?" he asks me.

"Not much. It was Swiss steak. Why do they call it Swiss? What's Swiss about it?"

"The Swiss are horrible cooks."

"Well it was awful. I couldn't eat it. I tried."

"So you're hungry."

"Very."

He throws together a snack of fresh raspberries and two chilled dill pickles, each rolled up in a piece of sliced chicken breast that's been slathered with cream cheese. At first they look like pigs in a blanket (which I have never been served in this house, I want you to know; the same goes for sloppy joes and Hamburger Helper, which I love) and then he slices them so they look like little stepping stones.

We sit on the chairs and look out at the bay. A line of four pelicans glides along the surface of the water, which is choppy at the moment.

"Dad, how high is our house?"

"Five feet above sea level."

"Has it ever flooded?"

"I'm not sure. Why?"

"I was wondering about hurricanes. Some girls were talking at school about last year when Willard came through. They didn't have school for ten days because no one had power. There's one boy in the seventh grade, Anthony Manassa? They lost their roof, I mean their whole roof, and they were there when it came off."

"That's why I want to get cable," he says. "So we won't be surprised."

We haven't even lived here for nine months, and already Dad is obsessing about hurricanes. He's already changed our homepage to a map of the Caribbean. I guess it's supposed to automatically track tropical storms.

"We have the radio, Dad."

He shakes his head. "Not enough. I want visuals. Know thy enemy."

I look out at the water as I eat.

"Are those windsurfers or sailboats?" I ask.

"Can't tell. Just a minute."

He goes inside and returns with the binoculars. He walks across the grass and stands on the seawall to get a closer look.

"Windsurfers," he says. "I think they're boys from Collier."

"What?"

"Here. Look for yourself."

It's Jason Lambert and Robert Fugate, and I have to admit they're pretty good on the sailboards. Unlike most of the kids at my school who wear clothes from Hollister and PacSun so they can look like surfers, these two guys aren't posers. They are true hard-core water rats. There are no waves here in southwest Florida, so if you want to really be a part of the surfer scene and not a poser you have to either skimboard or windsurf, and these guys do both.

"Yeah, I know them," I say. "They annoy me."

"You say that about everyone, Violet."

"Well, everyone's annoying."

"Why do they annoy you?"

"What are they doing there, anyway?" I say, looking at them again through the binoculars. "They don't live around here."

"Do you want to take the kayak out and go see them?"

"Sure, Dad, and why don't we invite them in for tea?"

I go inside and into my room and lie on my bed to read. Although my dad and I have read it before, I'm having to reread *To Kill a Mockingbird*, and for the life of me I can't understand what the big buzz is all about. It's not that well-written, the characterizations are fine but not great. I'm guessing it was a huge hit because at the time no one had written so honestly about race relations. I think Scout is annoying. I mean, I just want to shove her in a dark closet and leave her there. She just won't shut up, and she never does what she's supposed to do. I think the reason Harper Lee is so reclusive and won't give interviews is because she's a little embarrassed for pulling off the biggest scam of the century.

I take a shower, and when I get out I hear voices in the backyard. I run to the window to look.

Dad is talking to Jason and Robert! They are standing in the water at the seawall with their windsurf boards bobbing beside them.

Dad! Stop it! Don't say anything! I will honestly kill you if you do.

I crank the window so it's opened just a crack and try to listen to the conversation. He's telling them about his surfing days in California, which are a lie because I know Grandma Carol would never have let him surf. Jason and Robert are just saying stupid things like "cool" and "awesome, dude." I just know my dad is loving being called dude. It probably hasn't happened for six centuries.

I've got to get him to shut up before he tells some story about me, which he always does, but I can't go out there like this. My hair is wet and flat. So I just lie there, praying to the gods that my friends do most of the talking.

Twenty thousand years pass before I hear them say good-bye and my dad comes inside. I confront him in his bedroom.

"Why did you engage them in conversation like that?" I ask.

"I knew you were listening," he says. "Why didn't you come out?"

"Why did you talk to them?"

"I really didn't have a choice, Violet. They were surfing so close and looking at the house. It was obvious they came to see you."

"But why?"

"Didn't we have this talk three or four years ago?" he asks. "Should I get the books out again?"

"He does not like me, Dad."

"Who doesn't like you?"

"Robert."

"You're wrong—he likes you."

"He does not *like*-like me."

Dad throws his hands up in surrender.

"Okay, Violet, okay! I don't know anything about boys and how they might act around a girl."

"Well at least you're admitting it."

"Admitting what?"

"That you don't know about these things."

"I was joking, Violet."

I dip my head down and unravel the towel that's been riding atop my head.

"You're not a usual guy, Dad."

"Meaning what?"

"Meaning you're more like one of the girls."

"And what is that supposed to mean?"

"Dad . . . You cook better than any mom I know. You find the cool stores in the mall before anyone else does. I benefit from that,

I realize—thank you. You don't watch sports. You're not stupid and out-to-lunch like most of the dads I know. You're just . . . different. You act different."

Oops. Should have stopped before that line, and I wish I could take it back. The second I say it his eyes seem to sink into his head, like he's trying to look inside himself, and I know that's exactly what's going on right here. My dad is always the one who mercilessly holds up the mirror so others can see themselves, but I have managed to make him turn it around and look at himself.

Big mistake.

Linc Menner's Handy Hints for Caregiver Sanity

Hint #28

I swear that someday they will find in cabbage the anti-aging formula humans have been searching for for centuries. If you haven't already noticed, the rubbery, green vegetable lasts for months in the bowels of the refrigerator. Even when it gets a little black, all you have to do is slice off the old part and, voilà, new cabbage.

Cabbage is your friend when you don't have time to get to the store. Simply slice some off, and toss it in with the pasta during the last two minutes of cooking. Coated in the spaghetti-sauce-from-a-jar, it will no doubt go undetected on the palates of most kids.

7

Linc

I judge a book by its cover, especially when it comes to people.

It comes from being a minority, shut out of the world that you rightfully live in because you are different (read: caregiver with penis), always on the outside, looking in, gauging people's reactions to you, wondering how you can get inside and how you would act once you get there. I don't care. I make the most of it. I compile Judge-a-Book-by-its-Cover lists. I'm very good at this.

Percentage of prep-school moms who assume you know who their husbands are and what company or practice they own: 92.

Percentage of prep-school moms who have had needles or scalpels penetrate their skin in the past six months for reasons other than true illness: 63.

Average number of meals these women cook from scratch at home each week: 1.

Percentage of prep-school moms who wear cute little tennis outfits but don't actually play tennis: 28.

Number of times these women's ponytails bounce in thirty seconds due to fake-exuberant head-nodding while chatting with another such woman: 8.

I've added these last two as I wait for Violet in the pickup line. It seems like I live in this van. Okay, while I'm at it: Number of hours

Linc Menner spends in the Man Van each week, transporting Violet to and from school: 11.

I'm looking at my to-do list in my Daytimer, planning the trek home. Jo needs her shoes dropped off at the cobbler's. I need some kimchee starter at the Asian grocery on Airport-Pulling Road. And Violet is down to one pair of jeans that she will wear. Today I've chosen the Marshall's on U.S. 41 as the site to stage the next battle in the never-ending War of Finding Clothes That Violet Actually Likes.

Finally, I see her. She is staring at the ground as she walks, sullen, and I'm surprised she doesn't run into a boy in a pink polo shirt who is strutting down the covered sidewalk like some chicken, poking his head to the rhythm of a song playing on his iPod. His pants hang on his waist as low as they can go without dropping the rest of the way. He's obviously one of the "wiggers" Violet has told me about, rich white boys who act black because they think it's cool. He seems to know her—he says "Hey, Violet," almost unconsciously. I'm happy for a moment that someone has tried to connect with my little girl, wigger or not, but she ignores him.

Suddenly, Violet hears something, someone yelling behind her shoulder, and she stops and turns around. She recognizes Kami Knapp, making a beeline toward her. Violet turns again and continues, this time faster, on her path to the van.

Kami runs after her, and as she grab's Violet's shoulder and pulls her around I instinctively throw open the car door and plant a foot on the ground, but then I remember all the times my daughter has yelled at me for fighting her battles, and I stand there, simmering and listening to as many words as possible.

The crowd has parted to give them room. The girls have started yelling at each other, but good breeding and rearing has made this an unfair contest. Violet is hugging her notebooks to her chest in perfect Sandra Dee posture as Kami is provocatively shoving at her shoulders like some ignorant Matt Dillon character looking to pick a fight. It takes everything I have to restrain myself, and I remind myself again and again: It's just a girl, it's just a girl, she can't hurt my daughter.

Oh, but words most certainly can. And when I hear "fucking whore" spew from Kami's volcanic mouth I bolt from my van, the door left hanging open, and bound up the line of cars in my flip-flops, toward the sidewalk where the girls are fighting.

"What did you call her, young lady?" I ask, trying to catch my breath.

Kami stops short and looks up at me, startled.

"Did you say what I thought you said?"

She appears to falter for a minute and then, aware that she has an audience, unconsciously puffs out her chest and says, "I called her a whore because that's what she is."

I see Ms. Hutchinson, the head of middle school, marching toward us and another woman, this one talking on her cell, struggling to walk on her toes across the grass so that the stiletto heels of her sandals don't aerate the soil. Obviously, Kami's mother.

I look at Violet. "And the reason she would be calling you this?"

"Dad," she says, "this is none of your concern."

"I said, 'And the reason she would be calling you this?' "

Violet scowls at me then replies, "She says I'm trying to steal Jason."

"Jason? As in Model U.N. Jason?" (I am familiar with his name. He's on the Burkina Faso delegation with Violet this year. He's been to the house to research on the Web with Violet and to practice their speeches, more than any normal boy would want to do unless it was an excuse to spend time with a girl he likes.)

By this time Ms. Hutchinson has joined the fray.

"Girls! Girls!" she interjects, but everyone, including myself, ignores her. The other woman also arrives on the scene, her cell phone now shut.

"What the hell's going on here?" she asks.

"Are you Kami's mother?" I ask.

"Yes."

"Well, your charming daughter just called my daughter a whore," I say. "That's what's going on here."

She looks very confused, glancing at Kami, then at me, then at Violet, then at me again. What to do? What to do? What would a good mother say right now?

"My daughter wouldn't say something like that," she finally says.

"Oh, she sure as heck did. I heard it myself, and maybe you would have heard it, too, if you weren't chitty-chatting on your cell phone."

"You have no right to correct my daughter."

"I do when she's wrongfully abusing mine."

She lifts her shoulders and attempts to look down her nose at me, which is difficult because I'm six-four and she's more than a foot shorter.

"I don't even know who you are," she says.

Ah, yes, the Collier Academy hierarchy game. She's mad because she's being dissed and put in her place by someone she hasn't met, someone unworthy, because he has not been invited to the headmaster's private thank-you dinners for large donors. This is supposed to put me in my place.

"Listen," I say. "My daughter doesn't steal boyfriends. She doesn't have to. Look at her."

I've never been one to idealize or romanticize my daughter's appearance. Frankly, she was born into this world an unattractive baby, with a face more pinched than most. She had to get glasses at age four.

In the years that followed few people would say, "What a beautiful daughter," though they would remark on her good manners or diction.

Yet in the past several months, even though she's gotten moodier, Violet has blossomed, finally shedding and escaping the bookish, beanpole persona that has dominated her personality and appearance since she was five. Though she still has braces, she got contacts for Christmas. She rarely has a zit—you can largely thank healthy diet at home for that—and her lips are so red on her fair skin that she never wears colored lipgloss. I call her the Ralph Lauren poster child. If I were Kami Knapp, with boobs, yes, but no chin to speak of and black eyeliner so thick it makes her look like a comic-book character, I, too, would be threatened by Violet in the boyfriend department.

"I want to see both you girls in my office right now," Ms. Hutchinson says.

"That won't be necessary," I say. "Because I was here and saw the whole thing, and my daughter was walking to the van, minding her own business, when this little delinquent comes up and starts pushing her. In fact, I'm thinking of filing assault charges. Give this little sweetie here a nice police record."

"You!" the mother sputters. "Who are you?"

"Someone you'll never know," I say, looking down at her feet. "Because I don't have any friends who have tacky French pedicures or wear ankle bracelets."

She looks down at her feet.

"This a diamond bracelet!" she yells.

"It's tacky," I say. "You should know these things. Has your subscription to *Town and Country* expired?"

We get in the car, and Violet refuses to talk all the way home. In fact, she doesn't talk to me the rest of the night. It's a good thing Jo's in town because, hours later, Violet hears her come in and summons her upstairs, where she relives the horrific scene to her mother.

"So she's pissed?" I ask Jo when she comes to bed.

"You're kidding, right? Of course she's mad. Why did you do that?"

"Because I had to right a wrong."

"You're not Superman, Lincoln."

"I'm her father."

As Jo takes off her blouse a smile spreads across her face.

"What?" I ask.

"If it's any consolation," she says, "Violet did enjoy you dissing the ankle bracelet."

8

Jo

It's the strangest thing—Linc is actually quiet around Rod. Oh, if some subcontractor fails to show up for work Linc will have something to say about it, but for the most part he sticks to Rod's shadow like some seven-year-old boy infatuated with his baseball coach.

I never thought I'd see the day when Linc Menner is the gofer and not the giver of orders. He patiently stands at Rod's side and hands him his tools, or he runs out to flip a switch in the electrical box. He asks him questions and quietly absorbs the answers, which is very un-Linc-like.

Even Violet has noticed how different Linc is around Rod. "Mom, I swear he changes his voice when Rod's around," she said the other night. "What is that—a cowboy twang or something? What's that all about?"

That said, I have to admit that even I am a little in awe of Rod. I find myself growing quiet and shy in his presence. He is almost a caricature of manliness. We've never known anyone like him.

Rod is a big man, as tall as Lincoln, but what is fat on my husband is muscle on Rod. I'm certain he works out somewhere; he's got the most beautiful arms I've ever seen on a man, not obscenely large in that Arnold way, more like Russell Crowe in *Gladiator*. He usually wears T-shirts, tucked into jeans with a thick brown belt. I think he's about thirty.

He wears black work boots, the kind you see on firefighters, and these match his hair, mustache, and beard which are all fastidiously trimmed the same short length.

Rod lives on an acreage out on the edge of the Everglades near the county line, where his wife raises orchids. He has an airboat, a four-wheeler, and various motorcycles. I know he likes to hunt, and he's got a big dog named Rex. From our talks I've learned he's never eaten Vietnamese or Indian food and he has no interest in it. Do you see what I mean about caricature?

I'm thinking that the source of most of Linc's awe might be in Rod's tools. The man has every boy-toy you would ever want, including every power tool known to exist. He could build a house from the ground up solely with the tools he pulls around in the silver trailer behind his pickup truck, which is always clean despite being used on construction jobs.

Rod is orderly, and I'm sure Lincoln loves that. He treats his tools with the same reverence Linc shows for his kitchen knives, and I have to say it's a pleasure watching him work. He will often stand back and survey a situation, and after several moments of silence he disappears into his trailer and returns with the correct tool, which is always clean and properly stowed in some leather tool belt or carrying case. He'll either drill or pound or saw or pry or bend with no faltering, no hesitation. He has such command over his tools. I have never seen him make a mistake, or if he did he certainly didn't show it.

Honestly, watching him work is like reading a haiku. No wasted movements. Very sure of himself. I have learned that there is something curiously sexy about the way a man's callused hand wipes shavings off a smooth board he has just penetrated with a power drill, and then he'll hold up that piece of wood and admire the hole he has made, and if it's a particularly beautiful piece of wood he'll stroke it and turn it in his hands, revering its beauty.

Rod is not only Spartan with movement but also with words. Having spent so many years living with a man who verbalizes his every thought, this has some appeal to me. But I would never say this to Lincoln.

So many women complain how uncommunicative their husbands are, but, frankly, the sound of silence is pretty appealing these days. I don't know how much longer I can absorb Linc's nightly reports on the construction at 363 Jacaranda Street. I don't allow my vice presidents at the hospital to share such copious amounts of minutiae, so why must I listen to him?

But I do . . . mainly because we are trailblazers in this gender-bender marriage thing. It's more common now to have a man at home than it used to be, but Linc is an uncommon man, and we've been doing it longer than anyone I know. And I've learned over the years, as a hospital executive, that when there is a wild variable in the equation you tend to have more patience with it—partly because you respect that wildness and partly because you're simply curious. You want to know how everything will fall out in the end.

9

Linc

I'm frying bacon in my cast-iron skillet on the gas grill when Violet comes outside. I internally grimace when I see her because I can already tell she hates the day. This is the way it's been lately, some days are good, some are bad, all determined by a mixture of variables beyond my control or understanding.

In the world's most unfair scenario ever, I am a man sharing a house with two estrogen-challenged females, one at the beginning of her fertility life cycle, the other nearing the end. As the son of a feminist and father of a girl, I have celebrated females most of my life. I love how they share their thoughts. I like the complex interconnectedness of their minds and their ability to see and feel things so deeply.

But lately I've had enough of Girlyland. I'm sick of it.

On Monday, I picked Violet up, and she was all dark and gloomy because she'd managed only two push-ups for the presidential physical fitness award. The next day she cried in class because she got an eighty-two on her math exam. The next day was deemed horrible because another girl in her class had worn the same top as she.

On Thursday I didn't even have to wait until after school. Violet got into the van after breakfast and said, "I just know today is going to be a horrible day."

"Why?" I asked her.

"Because of my shirt, and my shoes aren't right for these jeans."

"Then why don't you go and change your clothes?" I asked. "We still have time."

"You don't understand, Dad! I did! I did change clothes. . . . Arrgh! You just don't understand!"

"No, I don't, my darling. And I'm wondering, Violet . . . how many horrible days in one week can a teenage girl have? Are we going for seven? What's the world record here?"

All this emotional crap with the clothes—and the insecurities about the way she looks and what people say about her—I'm convinced this will drive me crazy and into an early grave. It just makes no sense. If you don't like your girlfriend, either duke it out with her or ignore her. If you don't like how your blue jeans fit then wear a damned skirt—at least you've got that option.

Which reminds me: *Get stock-option information to financial planner.*

Which reminds me: *Make bank deposit.*

Which reminds me of calcium deposits.

Which reminds me of my nighttime teeth grinding, caused by stress, and how it's eroding my gums.

Which reminds me: *Buy solvent to get glue out of Jo's brown knit top.*

Which reminds me: *Alert Rod to the black scuff marks on the new shower pan.*

On the patio, Violet's brown hair is piled atop her head with one of those plastic clips that looks like the mouth of a Venus flytrap. The air is especially humid today, and I know this will make her hair more frizzy, which she can't stand. Also, her face is dotted with that mysterious white gunk that she hopes will dry out her zits overnight. I have learned that there is a direct correlation between the number of those spots on her face and the overall quality of her mood. I want to tell her she looks like a celestial constellation this morning, but I have learned to keep my mouth shut.

"Dad?" she says. "I can't find my red cardigan." Her voice is heavy, sluggish, monotone, like Eeyore.

"I washed it on Friday," I answer.

She says nothing.

"I've washed it every Friday for a month, Violet," I continue. "Maybe it disintegrated into lint. It's outerwear. You don't have to wash outerwear every time you wear it because it doesn't come in contact with skin oils and sweat. And it's not good for it, anyway, I've told you that a thousand times."

Violet sighs. "Can I interpret that as a 'no'?" she asks. "Would that be correct?"

I hate it when she sounds like one of those unbelievable, precocious child actors in a laugh-track sitcom.

"That is correct," I say. "But watch your tone with me, young lady. I don't like it one bit."

She emits a puff of displeasure, turns to leave, and then, emboldened by a new accumulation of courage, whips around again to confront me.

"You know, Dad, you have unrealistic expectations of thirteen-year-old girls. We are generally unhappy and bitchy. Get used to it."

I catch myself grinding my teeth again and stop. It's been a problem of mine lately, so much so that my dentist has referred me to a periodontist because the extra pressure created by all this has caused my gums to recede at an alarming rate. He told me that if I can't stop the grinding I'll most likely have to undergo gum grafting. They would harvest—and that was the exact word he used: *harvest*—tissue from the roof of my mouth and stitch it to my gums to shore up what's left. Apparently, gum tissue does not regenerate. Once gone, it's gone forever, like so many other things.

"Violet!" I say, stopping her as she returns inside. "Come here."

"What?"

"Turn around."

"What?"

"Your butt. It's all white with Sheetrock dust."

I pat at her fanny to whisk away the white that looks like flour.

"I've said it a million times, honey: Don't sit anywhere, don't lean against anything," I say. "Man, I am so tired of all of us looking like Pigpen."

I hear Jo yell from the driveway: "Bye! Love you guys!"

It seems as if she has been leaving the house earlier and earlier and staying away later and later. She's actually hinted at a psychiatric intervention for me, not a mental ward but forced psychotherapy or something like Prozac. She says the reason Violet is getting so negative is because of me, and that renovating the house was my idea and I should suck it up and quit bitching about something I caused.

But you know what? I did not cause this. Rod and his subcontractors are all way behind schedule. The work ethic in Florida stinks. These guys don't show up when they're supposed to. It's like they're all on vacation. They must drive from job to job, hypnotized by Jimmy Buffett songs on their stereos: "Hey, guys, let's waste away in Margaritaville . . . just chill out and kick up those feet and screw the customers who are living like animals for weeks upon end because we're as professional as a dope-smoking burrito roller at Taco Bell."

If I catch Sean The Painter trying to use latex instead of enamel one more time on the woodwork I'm going to pour turpentine on the hood of his precious, new candy-apple-red Ford truck.

If Stan The Plumber orders one more wrong piece I'm going to pour Drano in his thermos.

I might kill someone before it's all over. It's become clear that gun-control laws were passed because of people like me.

So you think I'm a little negative these days?

Why don't you see how you feel after you've had to wash the dishes for two months in the bathtub?

I have to keep all our clean laundry in plastic bags because the construction dust will render them dirty overnight.

The AC conked out last week from sheer exhaustion, having to run while the doors are kept open for the workers.

Yesterday I found a hornet's nest on top of the motor of the ceiling fan in the bedroom.

Lighten up, Jo says. Treat yourself. Get a massage. Take a hot bath.

I'd love to . . . but the tub was ripped out of the floor three days ago and beneath it, on the dirt of the foundation, we discovered a thriving nest of possums.

While Stan The Plumber takes a cigarette break on the patio, I sort through our baskets of catalogs, looking for an older Restoration Hardware edition that had towel racks I want for the powder room.

I also have The Weather Channel on. The season's first tropical depression has already formed off the Leeward Islands, and they expect it to become a tropical storm within forty-eight hours. It will be named Arturo.

I hear a car door shut, and I look out the window to see a short man getting out of his green pickup truck. There's a magnetic sign on the door that says *Porpiglia Masonry. Specializing in Brick and Stone Work 345-3410.* I haven't seen him before. He must be here to build the new flagstone steps for the patio.

Instead of coming to the front door, though, he starts walking around the house, to the patio out back. I dart from room to room, following his progress through the windows, like turning pages in a picture book. I am careful when I pull back the cloudy-clear plastic tarps that hang over each window so that I don't draw attention to myself.

Hurricanes are not the only reason we're replacing our windows and doors; they leak like sieves. From inside, with the windows shut, you can practically hear someone dropping a pen on the brick of the patio. There is no such thing as private conversation anywhere on the property.

"How's it going?" asks the Italian.

"Not bad," Stan answers.

"Rod here?"

"Nope."

"Owner home?"

"Inside."

The Italian begins to offer his hand to Stan, who scrambles to move his cigarette from right hand to left so he can shake it.

"Tony Porpiglia," says the Italian.

"Stan Moore."

Without even looking at the hands, the two men clasp right hands in a shake I have never seen. Though they've never met, the union is oddly natural, familiar, as if they've done this hundreds of times before. It is not a traditional businessman's handshake. Nor is it one of those brothers-in-the-hood shakes, with curled fingers and bangs of the fist. It is something altogether different, some kind of off-kilter, open-fingered exchange.

Is it a blue-collar thing?

A native Florida-cracker thing?

No, that's not it—Tony's accent is pure Jersey. How do they know this when I do not?

They're too young to be Masons or in Rotary.

They're certainly not frat-boy material.

Why hasn't anyone—specifically any guy—ever shaken my hand like that? Maybe they've tried, but I didn't know how.

Is it something you learn in high-school sports? (I never got to play. Thanks, Mom.)

At a strip club? (Haven't been to one. Too much guilt to try. Thanks, Mom.)

Why haven't I noticed it before?

Have I spent too much time in Girlyland?

Women don't shake hands to greet, at least not as often as men do. They generally broadcast their friendliness and wariness in more subtle ways, with body language or their eyes, especially with each other. Maybe it's because they're sick of their personal space being invaded by stiff limbs. Conversely, men think nothing of thrusting their way into another's personal space.

I try to remember how many hands I've shaken in the past several weeks and months. Not many.

Is this handshake a creation of pop culture, born sometime in the past fifteen years while I've been in the Land of Estrogen?

Am I imagining all of this?

I go outside to introduce myself and talk with the new guy. When I get there, Stan drops his cigarette to the ground, snuffs it out with the toe of his work boot, and then, as he's been instructed to do by both Rod and myself countless times, picks up the butt and throws it into a large terra-cotta pot I use as a trash can.

"Are you the mason?" I ask.

He looks at me warily, sizing me up. "Yep."

"Rod's not here," I say, "but I can show you what needs to be done."

The man looks at his watch. "He said he'd be here at four," he says.

"I expect him any time."

Strike while the iron is hot, I think, and I offer him my hand.

"Linc Menner," I say, and as I hold it out I concentrate on keeping it in a neutral position, a blank canvas, fingers loose and spread, palm slightly turned upward at twenty degrees, just as I saw Stan do. I can do this, I can figure this out. If I can roll fresh spring rolls without breaking the delicate, wet rice paper I can certainly fall into and figure out a foreign handshake.

"Tony Porpiglia," he says, taking my hand. But he grips it as would Ward Cleaver or any random U.S. president and pumps as if we are sealing a deal on some TV commercial.

I want to ask why, but I say nothing.

I am sitting in the waiting room as I always do when Violet has a doctor's appointment. Moms who hover near the examination tables do their children no favor; it does nothing to foster independence. Even when Violet had five teeth removed in one visit—she lacks that enzyme or whatever it is that tells the baby teeth to fall out—I left her alone with the dentist. The nurses at the practice shunned me, they treated me with disdain from that day on. Yet they all have remarked on how mature she is for her age, even when she was five or six.

Hello? Can you see the connection here?

We're at Dr. Baumhover's today to get Violet's braces off. She's been living for this day for almost two years. Before we put the braces on in New York, Violet's mouth resembled Stonehenge, teeth jutting forward and sideways with no rhyme or reason. We even had to have an oral surgeon dig into the roof of her mouth and attach a wire to one tooth that simply did not want to come down.

I suddenly remember that I forgot to leave the door unlocked for Mike The Electrician, who is rewiring the ceiling lights in the living room.

"How much longer will it be?" I ask the woman at the front desk.

"It doesn't take long," she says. "They're probably polishing them off."

I zone out as I watch some boy playing on the PlayStation on the bank of TVs along the wall. It's some game with a mustachioed dwarf-carpenter frantically climbing ladders and jumping over rivers and oncoming barrels.

Which reminds me: *Clean out rain gutters.*

Which reminds me: *Get estimate on new fence.*

Which reminds me: *Take some dinner over to Mrs. Glickman, who's just gotten home from the hospital.*

Which reminds me: *Call Blue Cross about bogus rejection of Jo's mammogram charge.*

"Dad?"

It is Violet's voice, more hesitant than usual. I look up and see her walking toward me, dreamily, almost as if she were in a trance. Mary, the patient advocate, follows her, and she is watching me. Why is she watching me?

I take a breath to utter my command, that we've got to hurry and get home, that we have just fifteen more minutes before the electrician arrives because if he can't get in then we lose another day of progress in the home renovation from hell.

Then, she smiles.

Oh, my God, how stupid of me! How totally unprepared I am for this! How I never took the time to wonder what would happen on this day . . . how I would feel . . . how the balance and momentum of so many things would forever be altered because of this one seemingly small change in my daughter's life.

I begin to cry, and why? I feel this is the end of something and beginning of another . . . but of what? I'm not sure, but I do feel as if I am simultaneously mourning both the loss and creation of something precious. This is a woman's face—not my daughter's.

I hold out my arms and walk toward her. She comes to me, we hug tightly and then I push her away so I can see again. I am crying hard enough that one of the office girls has brought out some Kleenex, which she offers to me. I pluck four or five of them from the box.

"You look so beautiful," I say.

"Don't look so sad, Daddy. Why are you sad?"

"I'm not sad. Maybe I am. No. I don't know. . . . Oh, Violet. You're beautiful. Now the outside fits the inside."

I look up and notice that Mary, too, has teared up.

"I'm sorry," I say.

"Please," she replies. "This is why we do what we do."

Violet smiles all the way home. I can't stop looking at her. At one point a light turns green, and the asshole behind me has to honk because I can't peel my eyes away from my daughter who, freakishly, now looks so much like my wife of twenty years ago that it creates inside of me some odd stirrings, a slight sense of melancholy and . . . and . . . I'm not sure what else. There is a serenity to her I have not detected since before puberty. I am both curious and jealous of this transformation.

I reach for my cell phone to call and share my feelings with Jo, but I'm mad at her right now for being gone so much, and right now I just don't feel like sharing much of anything with her.

I could call my mom, but she'd want to talk too long.

I ruffle through the pages of my mental Rolodex. There's really no one else I could call, no one I can think of, anyway, and I slip my phone back into my pocket.

*Linc Menner's Handy Hints for
Caregiver Sanity*

Hint #16

No one likes to do laundry, especially the white load. To help keep the dirty whites to a minimum, simply wear the same pair of underwear for two to three days, but be sure to swipe your deodorant stick across the crotch a few times. Honestly, this works. You won't smell a thing because the odor-causing germs are killed, dead. And don't worry about getting a rash; deodorant, after all, was developed to be placed on the very tender, sensitive underarms.

10

Jessica

There's a lot about Violet's dad on Google. He used to be a landscaper for the stars in Hollywood. I'm not kidding. He did the Osbournes' house and Tom Cruise's . . . really fancy, humongous yards. There was this one music writer who had a hedge that looked like a big piano. Linc was standing beside it with his arms folded. He was thinner back then, but I like his current hairstyle better.

Most of what I found is from New York . . . Rochester. I'm guessing they moved there for her job. Her name pops up in a mess of stories about hospitals. She's some kind of hotshot executive, and I know she's got that same kind of job here in Naples. There was a picture of her, too, in the *Gulfshore Business Journal.* I have to say she's not unattractive. She's petite, like me, and we both have brunette hair . . . but if I were her I'd grow it out a little more to give myself a softer look. She looks real businesslike. Simple pearl earrings. Not a lot of makeup. She could pluck her eyebrows a little more.

All the interesting stuff comes from when they lived in Rochester. Linc started this kind of support group or play group for stay-at-home dads, and my favorite thing I found was this little box of quotes from him. He said that women's intuition was something you learned, not something you were born with. He said women's intuition was nothing but senses on steroids, and you get that way by having to be aware of your kids' needs. I thought that was real interesting.

He said guys pretend to be oblivious about things around the house because if they weren't they'd be expected to do more to help out. Ha! As if we didn't know that one already.

There was also this Q-and-A thing from some New York parenting magazine, and he gave his tips on raising a good child. I read this with interest because, as I've said, Violet is just about the smartest, politest kid I've ever met. She can get a little uppity at times—she's the one who always raises her hand with the right answer—but this is junior high after all, and someone almost always puts her in her place so I don't have to worry about it.

Anyway, he said that when a child asks for something without saying please or thank you then you need to make them repeat the sentence. The *whole* sentence, over again *with* the please or thank you. He says kids'll get tired of repeating entire sentences and they'll start using please and thank you without even thinking about it.

Oh, and now I know why Violet types faster than I do. Evidently Linc was worried about kids learning their way around computers at home, and that they'd learn some bad keyboarding skills. So you know what he did? Every time Violet wanted to go on the computer he made her do twenty minutes of some computer typing game. He had an egg timer right there on her desk. I swear that girl types seventy words a minute.

There was also an interview with him and some other stay-at-home dads in a parenting magazine. He said he gets tired of seeing parents trying to reason with toddlers. He said older parents are the worst. When a child is doing something wrong they try to negotiate to get him to stop, and what really needs to be done is for these parents to say, "Why? Because I said so, that's why," and grab his arm and carry him off to a corner somewhere, just like our grandmas used to do.

He had lots of good advice for parents—I mean, he thinks a lot about being a dad. There was this other interview . . . wait . . . let me go back online and find it . . . I don't want to butcher it all up . . . okay, here it is:

On anchovies and parenting: Oftentimes good parenting means we must withhold information. Don't tell them they're eating anchovies or they'll hate the food, even if they can't taste them. Don't tell them one reason you're seasoning the food with anchovies is so they unconsciously develop a taste for healthful fish entrées for later in life.

Don't tell them that the basket of books in the backseat has only nonfiction titles because you want to create in them an interest in the world around them.

So I called Momma and was telling her about him, and she got all preachy with me. You'd think I would have learned by now just to keep my mouth shut about these things. You'd think I wasn't twenty-five but sixteen and still living at home.

She said, "Jessica, don't you get sweet on this man. He's a married man."

"I'm not sweet on him," I said. "I'm just real interested in him."

And you know what she said? She said, "Well you have a real bad history of being interested in people you shouldn't be interested in."

11

Jo

TO: JVarnadore@CollierAcademy.org
FROM: LincolnM@AOL.com

I am writing in response to something Violet told me about your class, in which she is reading *To Kill a Mockingbird*. The novel by Harper Lee, I'm sure you know, treated the topic of race relations with an unflinching candor this country had never seen up until that time. I'm sure Ms. Lee wanted to give us a visceral, frightening picture of the racial hatred that existed in the pre-Civil Rights era. By having your students say "N" instead of nigger when they're reading passages out loud, not only do you rip the balls off the prose but you also are practicing revisionist history. Whites back then said nigger. NIGGER. It's an awful word, yes, but if we candy-coat the darker sides of history then we will make them seem more palatable and, thus, more acceptable, thus increasing the chance that humanity will make the same mistakes again.

Sincerely,
Linc Menner

TO: Headmaster@CollierAcademy.org
FROM: LincolnM@AOL.com

Mr. Burkert:

As you know, to get to the middle school we must first pass the pickup spot for the lower school. Herein lies the problem: the mothers of these children, driving cars so large they can't maneuver them. Have you seen any of them try to back up? It's frightening! It is not vandals who run over the dwarf junipers and periwinkle in the median; it's these moms on their damn cell phones, driving their Hummers and Escalades. (Actually, I think you should ban all cell-phone use in moving vehicles on the grounds. It would be much safer and emotionally beneficent to the children as well. If a parent is on the cell phone during pickup time, he or she misses out on critical connecting time with her child.)

But back to the pickup line. It irks me how these moms find it necessary to hold a parent-teacher conference right there in the active traffic lines, long after their kids have gotten into the car. This backs up traffic well onto U.S. 41, which is a hazard because that is a major highway, and any car stuck out there on 41, waiting in line, is going to get rear-ended. It's just a matter of time. This practice also wastes gas and consumes patience. If these mothers wish to talk to their children's teacher they should set up an appointment and do so at another time. I am fascinated and appalled at the drop-what-you're-doing-and-cater-to-me attitude among prep-school parents.

On another note, as long as the board of trustees insists on this year-round school calendar, I also ask that it revisit the dress code. These kids should be allowed to wear sandals during summer in the steamy subtropics.

And another note: I am being a good boy. I have not taken anyone's parking spot since we last corresponded.

Sincerely,
Linc Menner

I snoop by reading the e-mails in the out-basket, something I do because it helps me catch up on the goings-on of my family when I've been on the road.

Tacky? Perhaps. Necessary? Absolutely. That is when I find these e-mail atom bombs from Lincoln. It's no wonder he never gets asked to do anything at Violet's school. I wish we had some kind of software that filtered out these e-mails before they got sent, something that was triggered by the word "thus," a favorite word of his when he's trying to make a point.

In all fairness, I almost always agree with the points he makes in his arguments. Linc generally has a good clear sense of what is right and just, but the same exuberant expressiveness that makes both travel and conversation with him so fresh and wonderfully un-predictable doesn't always translate well into e-mail form. He comes off as imperious, almost frothing-madman scary. People un-familiar with him can't put his tirades in context. I, however, can tolerate his bursts of sarcasm and criticism because I have seen the other sides of Linc when he's excited about something . . . when a certain plant will shoot out its first blossoms, for example, or when he meets someone interesting in the grocery store and recounts it for me that night, bringing her to life as if she were a character in a movie.

We met through one of his infamous e-mails, when I was direc-tor of the ER at St. Elizabeth's/Riverside. Lincoln had come into the emergency room with one of his workers who'd sliced open his leg with a hedge trimmer. Despite the chaotic, bloody evening, Lin-coln still managed to take note of the untrimmed bougainvillea bush near the entrance and wrote to me, suggesting it was haz-ardous to have such a thorny plant near an entrance populated with people in wheelchairs. He even suggested aromatics to replace the bush, including lavender and chamomile, because the smells helped calm people's nerves. I immediately Google-imaged him and thought he was cute. When I met him in person I was immediately attracted to his energy and confidence. You could call it love at first sight, although Linc calls it "lust at first site."

At any rate, when you fall in love with a man as passionate as Linc Menner, things move with the pace of an immense meteor in freefall. Within a month, we moved in together. Within six months, we were married. If sometimes our marriage seems like a scary journey through a dark haunted house, I hang in there because I know we will burst forth into light once again.

Lincoln gets excited about things very easily. He's like a child in that respect, and he helps keep me from getting jaded. His eyes sparkle when he recalls something that amuses him. On the other hand, when he sees something he doesn't like—watch out.

Still, at the end of the day, it's all worth it; his highs make up for his lows. At least that's where I stand right now . . . though lately he's been testing my patience.

I used to have to wait until late at night to get onto the computer, but cable TV has changed all that. These two are doing their best to make up for all those lost years of cable.

For the next hour Linc has agreed to watch *Project Runway* if he can watch *Trading Spaces* afterward. They're in the guest bedroom. When he hooked up the cable Linc fashioned a TV room in there because it is the only room where the ceiling has already been finished. I am so, so tired of finding Sheetrock dust in my shoes and purse and waking up with it on my lips. I try not to get angry over this self-imposed torture Lincoln has brought upon us.

When we moved from Rochester to Naples, I tried to interest Linc in a condo with no remodeling or maintenance needs so he could start another landscape business like he had in California. Naples clientele are not unlike the fussy West L.A. crowd he had to woo, and with Violet now in eighth grade it's important they both get some of their own activities.

Instead, we moved into a tired old ranch-style home on Naples Bay. It's not even three thousand square feet. It has no pool. It's surrounded by immense, faux-Mediterranean mansions whose garages are almost as big as our entire home. The neighbors want it gone. Next to them, we look like Appalachia, and it would not surprise me if we came home one night from dinner and saw that it had mysteriously burned down. It should have been a teardown, but Lincoln, of course, wanted to restore the squatty house to its 1951 splendor. That would have been acceptable had he agreed to move us during the renovation into that cute rental cottage I found on the beach. But no, that would have been too easy.

I swear, sometimes I think he insists on taking the harder road just so he can have a sacrifice to bitch about.

I'm used to it, and I think I understand the source of this angst. He isn't bringing money into the household so he feels he must show me how hard he's working and how much he has to endure—to prove his worth. That's got to be it. Why else would someone subject themselves to so many avoidable tribulations?

But I worry about the impact on Violet. She's so negative these days, and I don't like the fact that most of her interaction is with Lincoln or people I don't know on the computer. I try to make up for it on the weekends, but she's now at that age when a day out with Mommy is no longer a treat.

I can't help but regret some of the choices I made earlier on in her life. I could have said no to some meetings, some trips on the road. I could have driven her to elementary school in the mornings, but did I? No. And why? Because Lincoln said he didn't want me to commit to the task because he needed someone he could count on, and that I had a track record of dropping these sort of promises.

I hate saying this, but he's largely right. I'm not as structured and disciplined as he is, and my work schedule has far more demands on it.

Frankly, I'm beat when I get home. It's always been easier on me if I let him take the parenting baton and run with it. If Violet was sick and coughing all night, I generally let him take care of her. Part of me knew he wanted to because he had nothing else to do in his life, no job or passions other than his daughter. Part of me let him because I knew I had to get up and go to work that next morning, and I needed my sleep.

But before I knew it, months had turned into years, and I became relatively invisible to my own child. When she's hurt she goes to her father for help, not me. Only this past year, with puberty coming on, has she started seeking me out.

How and why did I become so absent in my child's life? I suppose it happened because I wasn't confident as a mother. I wasn't here as much as he was. You've got to let people do what they're trained to do. I wouldn't let the head of maintenance be in charge of recruiting nurses now, would I?

I've always had good intentions as a parent. Things just didn't work out quite the way I planned. I remember a few years back when I promised to start grilling dinner every Sunday night to give him a break in the kitchen. I did it one time and stopped. Partly because I forgot. Partly because Lincoln is so insecure about his contributions to this family that he goes out of his way being Super Mom and makes everyone who shows even the slightest interest in something domestic feel incompetent.

When I try to scramble an egg he actually smirks and says something like, "That's the wrong spatula, the wrong pan, and you didn't beat the eggs well enough."

I'll do something as simple as toasting a bagel and he says, "You're not going to leave that residue of cream cheese on that knife, are you?" And I'll say, "Yes, Lincoln, that's what a dishwasher is for." And he'll say something way too involved and unnecessary like, "Well, I'll have to run the dishwasher on extra hot—because cream cheese is worse than egg yolk—and that hotter temperature will degrade the Tupperware that's being washed at the same time."

And, yes, I'm sure there would have been days when I mistakenly scheduled a meeting that conflicted with the drive to school. God forbid!

But so what if I missed a day?

So what if I want to lie down and talk with Violet for ten minutes after I get home from work, even if it's after her bedtime?

He can be such a domestic bully. And I let this slip because I feel guilty. It was he who gave up his career to stay home. I realize he chose to give it up, but that doesn't help me feel much better.

Rod and I stand beside his truck, the blueprints rolled out before us on the hood. The construction job clearly lies in Lincoln's sphere of influence, but I have decided to take matters into my own hands because his moods have soured even more. The sooner that man is back in his full kitchen the sooner we all can be happy.

"Why can't we put the carpenter full time on the kitchen?" I ask.

"I want him to finish that ceiling first," Rod says. "It's messy. I know you're tired of all that dust. I want to get a cleaner environment for you."

"And I appreciate that, Rod, but that kitchen . . . as I'm sure you're well aware of by now . . . it's the heart of Linç's life and this house."

I hear a car approaching from down the street and am surprised when I look up and see Lincoln's white van. I had tried to time this visit while Linc and Violet were shopping. I knew he would be mad if I interfered.

He pulls up to us and rolls down his window. Violet is in the passenger seat, listening to her iPod. She waves and mouths, "Hi, Mom."

"What are you doing home?" he asks.

"I stopped by for some papers," I say. "I forgot some papers."

He cocks his head and squints his eyes; it's obvious he knows I'm lying.

"Why are you looking at the blueprints?" he asks.

"We're getting ready to move into the kitchen," Rod says. "I was showing her what comes next."

I'm surprised and warmed at how Rod covers for me. Lincoln would never have done the same.

"Are the cabinets in yet?" Linc asks.

"Yep. Got 'em in today."

"Cool. Are the countertops finished?"

"Yep. In fact, I don't see why we can't get you back into that kitchen in ten days or so."

"Oh, man, you don't know how happy this makes me," Linc says.

He looks again at me.

"Can I go in and get your papers for you?"

"Already got them," I say. "Got 'em. They're in the car. I got my papers already."

Linc gives me a long look then rolls away, up the driveway. Unfortunately, Rod takes this time to give me a wink, and the second he does this I intuitively look at Linc's rearview mirror and am horrified to see that he is watching.

12

Linc

It's a four-day break for Collier Academy students, some strange combo of a weekend sandwiched between a teacher's workday and Rosh Hashanah, which Violet first called "mashed banana" when she was three, and the name has stuck with us all these years.

I used to enjoy these days off from school. I would blindfold Violet and have her point to a spot on the map of western New York, and we would get into the car and go to whichever town fate had chosen for us that day.

In Seneca Falls, one time, we visited a psychic in her haunted Italianate mansion. She served us orange Fanta in a bottle and told us about the near-drowning accident that gave her her powers.

On a different adventure in downtown Jamestown we followed a homeless man for two hours, watching him rifle through trashcans for food—sliced brown-gray beef from Arby's; tomato and lettuce and sub roll from Quiznos; some sort of breaded Italian entrée in marinara sauce from behind an Italian mom-and-pop restaurant—and we were amazed at how he deftly constructed a sandwich out of all this, which he carried with him to a favored bench in a park several blocks away and ate while watching the ducks in a pond.

The morning was a gold mine, as parenting goes. The two of us talked about natural resources and wastefulness and the simple pleasures in life, which grow even more important the harder life gets.

But no such simple pleasures today. Oh, no! With her braces now off and high-speed Internet access to things like my-space.com, Violet has turned into a social animal overnight. It almost seems as if a new girl has moved in with us, and Violet herself has gone away.

She asked me if I wouldn't mind driving her and her friends to the Urban Outfitters in Tampa, which, she said, is the closest one to Naples. You're wrong, I told her. The closest Urban Outfitters is in south Miami, about an hour closer.

"No, Dad, you're wrong."

"No, Violet, I am not."

Her friends are sitting in the backseat with her, and I catch them exchanging glances that scream, "Damn! What do we do now? We're lying and he knows, so now what can we say to get what we want?" Kids are as transparent as taut Saran Wrap. How brain-dead some parents must be to not see these things.

"Okay, what gives?" I say. "And no bull, Violet."

She gives a painful, pleading look to her friends, and they all shrug their shoulders. I watch all this in the rearview mirror. What I love about kids who are not old enough to drive is that they don't understand the omnipresence and scope of the rearview mirror, and, thus, think they're invisible to the driver if he is facing forward. I will miss this little secret after Violet turns sixteen.

"Okay, Dad. . . . Stephanie and her friends are at the Urban Outfitters in Miami."

"Stephanie?" I ask. "As in boyfriend-stealer-and-stalker Stephanie?"

Again, I watch for reaction in the mirror. The girls are obviously shocked that I know the stories of their nemesis.

"As in *bitch* Stephanie," one of them says.

"That was unnecessary, Brianna," I say. "Totally unnecessary."

"Sorry, Mr. Menner."

After the trip to Urban Outfitters they want to hit the big mall next to the airport, and I oblige. As native southern Californians, accustomed to the hippest, grandest malls in the world (Fashion Island, South Coast Plaza, etc.), we always search out the coolest malls any place we visit or live. I had researched this mall online.

We go inside and gather at a central spot beside a fountain ringed with benches.

"Okay, now, somewhere in here is a new store we need to see," I say. "You guys are the right age now. It's called Nau, and there's only three in the country: LA and Seattle and here. Let's go look at the mall map."

I turn to walk away and see in the corner of my eye that they remain standing there, looking at Violet quizzically. After a few moments, Violet comes over to me, takes my hand and walks me to a spot away from her friends, near the fountain, whose sound scrambles our words so they can't hear what we say.

"Dad," she says. "I know you and I always shop together, but these girls . . . they're not used to that."

"Don't they know I'm the one who finds all the cool clothes?"

"No, Dad, they don't. I can't tell them that."

"I'm the trendsetter for that snooty little school. They all copy you, Violet. And I'm the one who pulls you into these stores. I was the one who first found Gadzooks—remember? You'd walked past it a thousand times. I was the one who told you to buy that cool rubber belt with the bottle caps on it. Then they all went out and bought one."

"But they don't know that," she says, "and I don't want them to."

"Well what do you want me to do?"

She looks pained for a moment, then says, "Would you mind just hanging out on one of those benches?"

"You're relegating me to The Man Bench?"

I must look hurt and confused (I certainly feel hurt and confused) because she grabs both my hands as if we were lovers soon to go our own ways and gently squeezes them as she looks me in the eye.

"Dad. Please. I'm sorry. This social thing is new for me. Please. I'm very self-conscious about things. Please."

Later, we head home, back to Naples, and I am wishing that more than one of them had brought their iPods because their voices are loud and getting louder. I don't know what it is about female voices from the age of puberty on up, but when there are more than two of them and they get excitable they really do start to sound like a tin shed of turkeys whose occupants have been startled by the blast of a shotgun, and as they noisily flap around I am crouching in the corner, desperately scraping mud from the ground to pack into my ears.

At first I try to engage the girls in conversation, but I soon learn the other girls seem absolutely incapable of either talking with an adult or expressing any thought deeper than a puddle. So I let them go on and on with their empty gaggling, and it gets louder and louder and louder, and soon I wish it were me who had the iPod.

I open the sunroof in hopes that some of the noise will escape like smoke.

To comfort myself, I paint a picture of what this ride would be like if it were just me and Violet. She would talk on and on about the seemingly mundane but critical details of her life, scraps that a caregiver pieces together to create the quilt that is this child's life: Who is (and, more important, isn't) sitting at her table at lunch; the classmate who evidently went down on some boy in the movie theater; the most recent eccentric outburst from Pakistani-Tourette's boy who wears the orange sneakers; how the student council had to change the "Happy Christmakwanzikah" sign because both a Jewish and a Christian mom thought it denigrated their faith. Violet would deliver all this with entertaining commentary and astute observations of human behavior.

But now . . . they're saying nothing! It is empty conversation. How much is there to verbalize about makeup that really matters? How long can four girls discuss the details of other girls' clothing? Evidently, the answer is, "Longer Than Thirty-Six Minutes," because that is how long they've been at this, and I hear no end in sight.

There are five people in this van, yet I am all by myself. And I am wondering who stole my daughter from me. Was it puberty or American culture? Or the, like, popular girls of, like, Collier Academy . . . like?

What has happened to my antisocial, intellectual Violet? Why has she all of a sudden started wearing too much makeup and taking a straight-iron to her hair to look like all the other girls at Collier Academy? Why has she stopped reading and started typing out instant messages hour after hour after hour?

Which reminds me: *Set new rule of only one hour of non-homework computer time every night.*

Which reminds me: *Rent* The Stepford Wives. *Perhaps she will see the inanity and futility in struggling to look like everyone else.*

Which reminds me of the bat mitzvah Violet went to last year, dressed very much like Holly Golightly—she'd just read Breakfast at Tiffany's—and at the next bat mitzvah two weeks later there were four girls all dressed in black skirts and white tops and white pearls with their hair pulled up in a chignon.

I just want to grab Violet by the arms and shake her and say, "They'll follow you, honey! They think you're cool. Lead them into the light! Give them a taste of substance and meaning and they'll convert!"

By the time we reach Fort Myers, still about half an hour from the silence of home, I notice I have been grinding my teeth so hard that my jaw has begun to ache, and it hurts to open my mouth. Honestly, I have been trying to listen and take interest in their conversation, but they lost me again somewhere after Burt's Bees lip shine.

"Dad," Violet says from the back, where she chose to sit to be closer to her friends, which I can understand. "Can we stop at Aubrey's house and watch a movie?"

"After we call and ask her mother," I answer.

"Oh, it's okay with her," Aubrey says.

"No," I say. "I need to hear it from her. Can you get her on your cell for me?"

Aubrey dials her mother on her cell and hands me the phone. It's a Razr, of course. The sophistication of the gadgets of prep-school kids continues to astound me—there are simply no limits. Several of Violet's classmates had Palm Pilots in the fourth grade.

I clear the deal with Aubrey's mother and make plans to pick up Violet at ten o'clock. The girls climb out of the van with all their shopping bags, and Violet walks over to my open window and leans in and kisses me on the cheek.

"Thanks, Dad," she says. "I love you."

"See?" I whisper to myself, looking at the girls, all of whom have left without saying thank you, I might add. "You haven't ruined her completely."

I am reveling in the silence on my way home when I notice for the first time on Rattlesnake-Hammock Road a small barbershop sharing a building with a 7-Eleven. I've been this way hundreds of times and have never seen it. Why this time, I'm not sure.

I turn into the parking lot. It is just before six P.M. and the lights are still on at Hoyt's Barber Shop. I open the door. A little bell tinkles on the handle, announcing my arrival.

There are four men inside, no one under seventy, and not one of them looks up to see who's come in. Two play checkers at a small table in the corner. Another is getting his hair cut by a man I assume is Mr. Hoyt. There is a big American flag tacked onto one of the wood-paneled walls. On the counter near Mr. Hoyt, next to the clear-glass container filled with turquoise-blue disinfectant where he keeps his combs, I see a framed, small sign leaning against the mirror that says, *Don't argue with your wife, just dicker!*

But what I notice most is the absolute, sweet silence, save the faint Big Band sound from a transistor radio.

There is a bank of chrome-and-red-vinyl chairs along the wall to my left and in front of that, an old wooden coffee table filled with magazines like *Guns and Ammo* and *American Cop* and *Playboy*.

I recognize one of the copies of the latter from my adolescence, before my mother discovered my stash in a pillow case inside the zippered grass bag of the lawnmower. I figured it was a safe spot since it was I who always cut the grass, but I'd forgotten to move them one time when I went to Sacramento for a Model U.N. competition one weekend, and Mom decided to mow the yard as a surprise. I was grounded for three months . . . three months for just being a teenage boy who had to beat off at least once a day or burst from an accumulation of semen. You'd have thought she'd found mutilated babies. Indeed, she told me later that she would have preferred finding drugs over porn because they weren't as destructive to women. I'd have killed for the Internet back then.

So here I am, years later, and I pick up that issue from 1976, the one with the cover of the Playmate of the Year, a brunette, lying seductively on her side atop a huge piece of emerald-colored silk, the folds strategically covering the parts that you would see inside.

Wow! Looking through this jerks me back to a time so many years ago. I soon realize I still know the order of these pages, these images. After the center-spread should come that feature they had every year about the sexual highlights in mainstream movies . . . and, yep, there it is. And where's that cartoon of the woman who's just had sex with the puppeteer? Maybe it was a different one. No! Right here it is. You're good, Lincoln!

"You need a cut or a shave?"

It's the barber talking. I have been digging this silence almost as much as the porn trip down memory lane. In ten minutes, I've heard only three sentences collectively uttered from the men: "Can't do that." "You want your ears trimmed?" "Sorry."

I run my hand through my hair, then rub my cheek.

"I don't know. Shave, I guess."

"That's gonna be eight ninety-five," he says.

"Okay."

"I'm almost done here with Bert."

"Sounds good. I'm just going to enjoy your free reading materials here."

A few minutes pass, and Bert gets up, pulls his leather billfold from his back pocket and slowly plucks out seven dollars. He sets them on the counter by the sink. "Keep the change, Ben," he says.

"Thank you, Bert," Ben says. He then looks at me. "You want a shave or you wanna look at girly pictures all day?"

He turns to get something as I sit in the chair, wondering what it is about this old man that intimidates me so. Why do I feel like such an outsider here? Is it because this womb of manhood I've walked into is unabashedly, unequivocally his, and I'm a little worried that I'm going to break one of his rules, like boys in a clubhouse up in a tree?

And then I realize it is his silence. I think of Rod and his silence, and of my Grandpa Dave and his silence, and how all three of them, even this stooped old man with his hairy nostrils and veined hands who probably drives a Buick sedan, radiate remarkable strength . . . and all due to an absence of words. Maybe that's why Jo doesn't listen to me. Like a desperate, impoverished government that prints too much money at one time, my own words have become devalued because there are too many of them.

With a flourish, Bert snaps open what looks like a freshly laundered, oversized tea towel, and he ties two corners of this around my neck. He then steps on a lever somewhere down below, and I sink backward until I'm lying at a ninety-degree angle.

He walks over to a stainless-steel container on the countertop that I'm certain is one of those old warming trays from a cafeteria. He lifts the silver lid. Steam rises and fogs the man's glasses as he takes out two more white towels, these ones wet and very hot, which he lays across my neck and on my face, from my nose down. It stings for a few seconds, then feels luxuriant.

After a few minutes, he removes the towels, and only then do I realize I had just fallen asleep. My face feels tingly, new, vulnerable. He then starts to pat warm shaving cream onto my beard. It's mentholated, and I hungrily inhale.

"You want it all?" Ben says.

I open my eyes to see him standing over me with an open, gleaming straight-edge razor.

"I'm sorry?" I say.

"You want to keep a mustache? Part of a beard? What?"

"I never thought of it," I said.

"Well you'd best be thinking."

While I've frequently gone unshaven for several days at a time, I have never sported planned facial hair. It's just something I've never considered.

"What do you think?" I ask him, but he says nothing, just stares at me, waiting for an answer.

"I mean, do what you think looks good," I say.

He stares at me for the longest time (again, no words!), then finally shrugs and goes to work. As I hear the scraping of my whiskers I feel very uneasy because no one has ever shaved me before. I have a raised mole on the right side of my chin that I've cut open periodically over the years, and I worry that he'll slice the whole thing off, but it proves to be no obstacle at all. His hands confidently pull and push at my chin and cheeks and temples as he maneuvers his way around my face and neck. At one point I mumble to see a mirror, but he pretends not to hear me.

After about fifteen minutes he brings out a fresh hot towel and wipes the remnants of cream from my neck and ears and face. He then picks up a clear bottle with liquid the color of lime Kool-Aid, rubs a bit into his hands, then pats it, almost slapping me, onto my neck and lower face. It smells much like the mentholated cream and, for a few seconds, burns like lemon juice on a cut.

He brings me back up to a sitting position and twirls my chair around so I can see in the mirror on the wall behind us. It is Linc Menner with a mustache, melting down into a goatee.

"Hey, man, I like it!" I say.

The old man nods his head. "Don't look too bad," he says. "You've never had a professional shave before?"

"Never."

"Oh, there's nothin' like a good professional shave."

And then, the party's over. I no longer like what I'm seeing in the mirror. Ah, I know exactly the problem here. You know how when you get new carpeting or wallpaper or fresh paint in a room, and all of a sudden the furniture that you swore would look just fine with the changes instead looks tired and out of place? I had this square-like patch of fur on my face, very angular and strong in line, and my longish curly hair looked like a dirty mop.

"We've got to do something about my hair," I say.

"What did you have in mind?" he asks.

I shrug my shoulders. "You picked out the beard. Why don't you pick out the cut?"

He stood there, quiet, for nearly a minute, studying me in the mirror.

"How attached are you to that hair?" he finally asks.

"Not. I'd just as soon someone invent a pill that stops hair growth. I hate to shave."

"I think a flattop would look real good."

I run my hand over the top of my scalp. "Flattop?" I ask.

"Flattop means business."

Flattop? Flattop! I'm thinking military guys. Cops. Grace Jones. Dolph Lundgren. Bruce Willis, back when he had real hair. As I'm nodding, he turns the chair around and ties an apron around my neck and goes to work, and I continue to search my database for others: Kurt Russell . . . Kurt Warner, the Rams' quarterback (Not that I care or have ever seen him play, but, hey, he is from LA.) . . . Arnold Schwarzenegger . . . Wesley Snipes. . . . Yeah, all these guys could kick my ass, and if I can detect a theme here it would be Guys Who Don't Think Too Much . . . so why would I want to look like them? . . . And, then, I suddenly get very excited—"Sit still," Ben cautions. "These clippers'll cut your nose off."—because I have finally thought of my Halloween costume for this year. I always dress up to hand out candy for trick-or-treaters, and I make things interesting and challenging by self-imposing one rule: I always have to dress as an inanimate object.

Last year, having just moved to Florida, I blued my face and cut a hole in the middle of a blue sheet and wore it like a poncho, and I safety-pinned onto this little objects from Violet's toy-junk drawers. I attached plastic ponies and cars and trees and pieces of fence and houses and dolls, all of them hanging on me like ornaments on a Christmas tree. I was disappointed, though. Only two mothers correctly recognized me as a hurricane.

Had trouble with that one, dear Nordstrom-dazed mothers of Naples? You'll never get this next one. I'm going to tie the backs of two of Violet's old playhouse chairs to my waist so that they flank me like bookends, and I will dye my new flattop kelly green.

I will be Mesa Verde.

Mesa, of course, is table in Spanish.

TO: Rod

FROM: Linc

RE: Updates and changes on project

Hey, welcome back from your hunting trip. Thanks very much for getting workers out here while you were gone. So . . . where do I begin?

Look over the cabinet trim in the master bath. (Molding around top, etc.) It's not as tight as it should be. Looks very sloppy. What do you think? Lester's guy is less than meticulous. One of the outlets he cut is crooked by an entire centimeter. He messed up the sink while the caulk was wet and it had to be reset. He didn't even bother to come and tell me or the plumber.

I don't like the electrical fixture we picked for the master bath. I've got a replacement fixture that will fit the spot and I'd like to put a dimmer switch on the wall, same style as the dimmers in the rest of the house. (Uniformity is a MUST!) I think they come from Seminole Lighting on Evanston Avenue.

We need to replace that nasty-looking plastic vent cover on the ceiling of powder room ASAP. These little details are IMPORTANT. It doesn't make sense to overlook such minor-but-important details when we're giving the entire home a makeover, an entirely new identity.

HUMAN RESOURCE ISSUES: I still don't believe Bud The Dry-waller when he tells me he's not smoking in the house. Even if he isn't, that man's tobacco wake is strong enough to knock you down. I've left a bottle of Febreze at the back door. Please tell him to spray himself before coming in from his frequent smoking breaks.

Charlie needs to be called and told to put the sealer on all the grout before we start using the bathrooms. Please tell him to stop parking on the grass.

Thanks, Rod.
Linc

13

Jo

After nearly thirteen weeks of having no kitchen, it is finally finished, and we are celebrating with a dinner. I even had to secretly pay Rod to make an extra trip to Miami to pick up the tile for the backsplash. Otherwise, it was going to sit on the docks at U.S. customs for another week before getting shipped over to the west coast. I am amazed how a home-remodeling project can be held up just by one missing piece, but it makes sense if you think about it, especially in a kitchen. Everything is connected. Nothing is free and clear. The cabinets run into the sink, the sink into the counter, the counter into the oven and walls, and on and on.

On my way home from work I stop at Total Wine and buy a bottle of Linc's favorite white Bordeaux. I call from the car as I pass the Publix where Lincoln shops.

"Is there anything you need from the grocery store?" I ask him.

"No," he replies. "Got it all. Where are you?"

"Ten minutes away."

"See you then."

"What are we having?"

"A surprise."

He hasn't had an oven all this time, so I'm guessing it will be something savory that must be roasted. I am thinking of all the creations he bakes in his great-grandmother's Dutch oven. Will it be the Portuguese snapper? Paella? His enchiladas smothered in green chili? The Mexican pot roast with yucca? Maybe roast lamb?

I come inside, turn to drop my purse in the basket by the door and see that some contractor—it looks like the carpenter—has decided to use it as a trash can. It looks like wood soup, with chunks of cut pine and sawdust and dried gobs of caulk and empty paper boxes. Evidently Linc has not seen this yet or there would be a note on it, written in red Sharpie marker. I will say nothing, at least not until after dinner. I want tonight to be a celebration. Tonight is the night my husband becomes happy again. Tonight, Linc Menner regains some control in his life. Though we still have much of the ceiling-raising work to do, and the windows and doors have not been replaced, and Violet's bathroom still has no walls to speak of, I feel that, with this completed kitchen, we have crested the highest mountain and are on our way back down. Maybe I won't have to kill my husband after all. Or he, me.

I go into the bedroom to change, lifting the black tarp from the dresser, careful not to let the white Sheetrock dust get on my cardigan. I open the drawer and find the cotton shirt I want in a Ziploc bag. I am so tired of living like this. There are so many obstacles, so many hurdles.

When I emerge, Violet is at the table and Linc is bringing a large silver pot with handles to the table. I don't recognize it.

"What is that?" I ask.

"Pressure cooker," he says.

I look at Violet, quizzically, then again at my husband.

"Pressure cooker? When did we get a pressure cooker?"

"Today. I saw it on the Food Network. I got it at Macy's."

"What's in it, Dad?" Violet asks. She sits up in her chair, leaning toward the center of the table to get a good look at the contents in the pot.

"Something you've never had. Sauerkraut, kielbasa, and pota-toes."

"Sauerkraut?" she asks, wrinkling her nose.

Linc frowns at her and sets it down on the table, then goes to the refrigerator. He pulls out the mustard and a half-gallon of milk.

Violet and I look at each other, again our brows furrowed in cu-riosity. We say nothing, though we think and wonder plenty. In Linc Menner's world, kitchen shortcuts once ranked right up there on the evil scale with MSG and Cheez Whiz and bottled salad dressing. This is a man who bought carrots with the green tops af-fixed even though he would cut them off and throw them away. One year, Lincoln got a Crock-Pot from his mother for Christmas, and he used it to boil and clean the rocks and gravel from the aquar-ium. He has regifted electric knives, electric can openers, and elec-tric knife sharpeners.

I look down at the paper plates set before us. "I thought the dish-washer was hooked up," I say.

"It is," he answers.

"Why the paper plates?"

"Because I had some left over from outside, and it's easier than washing dishes. I wish you'd realize my time is as valuable as yours. I've been very busy."

It is a hard meal to eat, mainly because the food is so horrible and plain, but also because Violet and I are, figuratively, biting our tongues. Of course we know not to ask him about the pressure cooker because he'll probably blow.

Toward the end of the meal, Linc excuses himself to go to the bathroom. Violet leans into the table and conspiratorially whispers, "Mom, what gives? I mean, I was expecting the best meal in the world tonight."

I finish chewing my kielbasa, which has been cooked into some-thing akin to rubber.

"Was he busy?" I finally ask. "Running errands for one of the men? Did something happen today?"

"No," she answers. "He was online."

"Doing what?"

"Looking at pickup trucks. Mom . . . should we be worried?"

Linc Menner's Handy Hints for
Caregiver Sanity

Hint #49

If you don't already have a pressure cooker, then
go buy one. They're nothing less than the Arnold
Schwarzenegger of Crock-Pots! You toss in all
the ingredients, screw on the cover, then go
about your business. In an hour or less, you have
dinner! Here's one of my family's favorites:

    1 quart water
    4 pound corned beef brisket
3-4 Idaho potatoes
    1 head cabbage, in quarters

Put water in pressure cooker. Add meat and
brine from package, along with any included
spices. Put whole potatoes on top. Cook at high
pressure for one hour. Remove cooker from heat
and let pressure lessen, naturally. Remove meat
and potatoes but keep liquid in cooker. Add cabbage to cooker and liquid. Cook at high pressure
for three minutes. Release pressure quickly.
Slice meat across grain and serve with cabbage
and potatoes. Spicy brown mustard goes great
with this, as does a good, dark beer.

14

Linc

Violet has gone to a friend's house to do homework, and all I want to do is sleep. I was up too late last night—Jo is in Orlando—watching home-makeover shows. I swear there are thirty different ones, all variations of the same thing, but I haven't grown weary of them. I love watching the metamorphosis from tacky to trendy. I'm wondering if the same model would work on a show about landscaping.

It's hard to relax with subcontractors banging around in the corners of your house, but I lie down on the sofa, hidden by an ersatz wall created by the new shower pans, still in their boxes, which lean against it.

Rod comes in the back door, yelling for Stan The Plumber, who has been here all morning, rattling and pounding about in the guest bathroom. I hear them talking but pay no attention until I hear the word "he," and my ears prick up.

"That's not what he ordered, and you know it," Rod says.

I wonder what in hell they're talking about. I fight the urge to get up. They don't know I'm home. I parked my van at a neighbor's so a truck could back up into the driveway earlier that morning to deliver a pallet of tile.

"He won't even know the difference," Stan says.

"The hell he won't," Rod replies. "He's one picky mother-fucker."

I've never heard Rod cuss. It surprises me.

"They look the same," Stan says. "They're both Groehe."

Ah, the faucets. He's ordered the wrong faucets. No surprise there because I know he's oblivious to detail. My first clue was when he hung the bracket for the handheld showerhead upside down. It's true that that average person would not notice because both ends are identical, but if you look closely the word *Groehe*, in that very small but very cool modern German font, is upside down. I made him take it down and set things right.

I'm almost ready to get up and go see them when I hear the voices grow louder and realize they're walking down the hallway, toward the living room and me. I bring my legs up and curl my knees into my gut so that I can't be seen.

"He's an asshole," Stan says. "What's his deal anyway? What's he do?"

"Stays home. Takes care of his daughter."

I can practically hear Stan sneer.

"Hey," Rod says, "I haven't seen you complain about his brownies."

"What kind of man would stay home like that?" Stan asks.

Evidently Rod shrugs his shoulders because I hear no reply. Good boy, Rod.

"What's his wife do?"

"Big job at the hospital."

"Must make some bucks to live here on the water like this. I'd like to sit home all day on my ass. That's why he's so damn chatty."

"Where are you going?" Rod asks.

"Take a piss."

"Not inside you're not."

"They're not here."

"I don't care, Stan. That's what the johnny's outside for."

"Those things are hot and smelly."

"I don't much care. You don't use your clients' bathrooms. . . . Are those the shower pans?"

Lying on my back, I hear Rod's boots on the floor, coming closer, and I stop breathing when I see his hand grab the top of the box just two feet away from my face. I can hear my heart beating to a bursting point in my chest.

"Did you look at these yet?" he asks.

"Yeah."

"Are they right? I don't want the same thing happening here that happened at the Feldmans'."

"They're the right ones. See—that one's been opened."

"I just don't want any mistakes that are going to cost me more time. These poor people—look how they've been living. For three months now."

"Why didn't they move out? Get some condo down at the beach. They could afford it."

"I tried to tell him."

"Yeah, I'll bet that one went over real well. He's as sassy as my wife. . . . You think he's, you know . . ."

"What?"

"You know—queer."

"He's married, Stan."

"You seen his wife?"

"Yeah."

"She hot?"

I'm not sure what he says because the next sentence out of Stan's mouth is, "Bet she wears a strap-on."

"You've got no class, Stan," Rod says.

They start walking toward the hallway. "You're a great plumber, but you've got no class, buddy. Now go order those new Groehes, would you?"

They leave the house, and I hear their muffled dialogue through the windows as they walk to their trucks.

Believe it or not, in my thirteen years at home no one has ever uttered emasculating comments to my face. (Behind my back? That's another story.)

I don't mind what the stupid plumber thinks of me, but I do care about Rod's opinion because I like him, I want his respect. And as I play back in my mind their conversation of minutes ago I find nothing to worry about, other than the fact that he might think me stupid for keeping my family in this disaster zone of a house.

There was that comment about Jo being hot. Did Rod nod or shake his head when Stan asked him? Which answer would have provoked the comment of the strap-on dildo?

I go into the bathroom to look at the faucets. Though they're not the ones I asked for, they look very similar. These flare out five or ten degrees at the neck, and the ones I chose did not. I'm impressed that Rod could see the difference.

Then I wonder if it matters at all. I do act like such a damn woman sometimes. I obsess over visual details way too much. What is that? Have I always been like that? Or have all these years of being chief-nester made me that way? I wish I would have kept a journal so I'd know how this sweet-and-sour job from heaven-hell has changed me.

I recall a commercial I saw last night on television. Was it an ad for Home Depot? Verizon? I'm not sure. What I do remember is how the man was portrayed. He was at home, cooking with an apron on, when his wife called from some home-improvement megastore, where she'd gone to buy a ceiling fan. She took a picture of the fans on display with her cell phone and sent it to her husband. He looked at it on his own phone, broke into a smile and said, "That one in the middle is perfect!"

That one in the middle is perfect?

Perfect?

On one hand I'm relieved. I am no longer alone in the middle-class American male's transformation into eunuch. The anatomy may be intact, but our syntax has softened, our interests and packaging have changed. Our culture has been wussifying the male for some time now. He's gone from clipping his nasal hairs to waxing his back. We as a gender are in no-man's-land, figuratively and literally.

I wonder if this whole new trend of redneck-chic—you know what I mean, those fads of cowboy hats and boots and pickup trucks and country music and Larry the Cable Guy—is because both men and women long for the days of true gender differences.

And ain't I the hypocrite for saying so?

That one in the middle is *perfect*.

Who am I kidding? I'd probably use the word "fabulous."

I know the difference between teal and aqua.

I have strong opinions on symmetry and asymmetry.

I can spot a table lamp from the Design Within Reach catalog.

And, for the record, he was right: The ceiling fan in the middle *was* definitely the coolest.

It was . . . *perfect*.

15

Jo

We have fallen into the nightly TV trap. It has proven to be seductive. After all these years of Linc refusing to have cable in the house, it feels strange, almost illicit, but I'm surprised at how calming, almost numbing, television-watching can be, a wonderful way to unwind at the end of the day. Even better, it engages my husband so he doesn't spend the entire night obsessing about our chaotic, ripped-up home.

We watch a lot of Nickelodeon's TV Land and Turner Classic Movies after Violet has gone to bed. And, of course, The Weather Channel, which, allegedly, is the reason why we got cable in the first place. It's on nearly every night when I get home. Lincoln has always liked The Weather Channel. He's been a fan since its inception. We are all well versed, thank you very much, on how its quality has eroded over the years.

Our resident critic-at-large has complained of The Weather Channel's evolution from the original, techy, unpolished production into something like *Entertainment Tonight,* with slick, packaged hour-long dramatizations like *Storm Stories* and surgically altered blond newscasters with names like Jennifer and Brittany. He says Weather Channel anchors shouldn't have silicone breasts or glossy lips that divert your attention from a hurricane's cone of uncertainty, and that it's hard to trust a meteorologist with a perfect dimple in his silk necktie.

What really irks him, though, is how they all try to be actors these days, feigning remorse and concern over the victims of Mother Nature when they are supposed to just give us the dips and rises of the jet stream and a heads-up on airport delays. He hates how the meteorologists now use the words "we" and "here" when reporting the weather in any locale, even if they're not broadcasting from that spot. Lincoln says it's outright lying, and he's likely to send them an e-mail about it.

Tonight we watch a special on tornadoes, hosted by his hero, meteorologist Mike Sartore.

Sartore is the one who follows the hurricanes and plants himself on the vulnerable spot where landfall is predicted. He is bald, intense, and chiseled, and when chasing storms on the road he is always packaged in a tight-fitting T-shirt.

"I don't know why he wears those glasses and a suit when he's in the studio," Linc says. "It looks like he's playing dress-up. I'll bet those glasses are fake."

"I don't know," I say. "He's still sexy."

We are sitting on the couch when I say this. Lincoln rears back and gives me a puzzled look.

"Sexy?" he says.

"Yes. But I'm not the only woman who thinks so."

"What's sexy about him?"

"Oh . . . his intensity, I guess."

"Bullshit."

"It's not bullshit," I reply. "I find intensity sexy, Lincoln. It's why I think you're sexy."

"What is it, really—his muscles?"

I shrug. The last thing I need to do these days is make my husband, who is large but soft, increasingly self-conscious about his body.

"I don't know," I say.

"He's got a nice frame. Admit it, Jo."

"I guess so. Yes."

"So you do like his muscles."

"A little. Sure."

"Aha!"

"Chill, Lincoln!"

"That's what you like about Rod, too, isn't it?"

I grab the remote from his hand and press the mute button.

"Now you're getting ridiculous," I say.

"I'm not blind, Jo. I see how you look at him. What was that wink about the other day on the driveway, huh?"

"Rod winks a lot, Lincoln, in case you haven't noticed."

"He doesn't wink at me."

"You know what, mister? It's not me who has the crush on Rod. It's you."

"Ha, ha. Very funny."

"You run to meet him at the door like a dog. You're infatuated with him."

"I'm doing everything I can to get this house back to normal. And if that means helping Rod, then I'm going to help Rod."

I turn off the TV and take a moment for my anger to settle and the air to clear. I wonder if we would even be having this stupid argument if we'd been making love more often, and Lincoln felt better about himself.

Our sex life is average, better in quality than quantity. Since Violet was born we have probably averaged two or three sessions a month, and that includes some dry, one-month spans. If that sounds alarmingly low, consider the logistics here: my out-of-town travel and late hours; Linc's constant flow of negativity from being left alone too much; and my anger from having to listen to him complain all the time.

I worried for a long time that Linc simply lost his attraction for me after Violet was born. I had read in a men's magazine how some men's opinions of their wives' vaginas change forever after watching their children squeeze out of them, and I wondered if this was true with Lincoln.

I said earlier that one constant, extra hurdle in our nontraditional marriage comes from the fact that we have no silent sufferer in our household. We also have no sexual aggressor in our family. Let's face it—it's usually the man who is the pursuer in that arena. And if the man doesn't feel like a man he's certainly not going to act like one.

But, no, I'm almost certain now that our problem is more of an occupational hazard. How can Lincoln feel like a man when he's fulfilling duties that have historically been associated with women? Every day I go to work and leave him at home I'm basically saying, "I am the man. You are the woman."

Maybe our sex life would be better if I felt more like a woman— I could seduce him if I wanted to, right?—but I seem to have dropped my femininity during my climb up the corporate ladder. I'm not sure when it happened.

Just as Linc has to act like a woman to get things done in his culture, I must act like a man. I can seek other opinions and collaborate, but at the end of the day I must decide quickly and mobilize the troops. I must be an authoritarian. It's far from being seductive, I know. I have forgotten how to be seductive. A seductive Jo Menner would seem insincere and unconvincing.

I come home, spent, secretly wishing someone was waiting for me with a backrub and a stiff drink. I simply cannot be the docile woman at home. I have been trained to fight. If I let colleagues bully me as Linc tries to do I'd still be a #2 in the accounting department.

On the road, it's me and the boys. I can't share my feelings or solicit the feelings of others who might be sitting beside me in business-class. Oh, we do talk about our gadgets, though, the pros and cons of a BlackBerry and the sound-eliminator headphones so popular now on transcontinental flights. But we can't look each other in the eyes for more than a millisecond, searching for some sort of connection as women so often do. We can show pictures of our children, but can we talk about their bed-wetting problem or emotional insecurities? Are you kidding?

Look at the successful women in our culture and tell me with a straight face you might bump into them at Victoria's Secret: Condi Rice. Hillary Clinton. Carly Fiorina. Margaret Thatcher. Oh, yes, can't you just see them lying in their beds at home in a fire-red negligee with a come-hither look? You get my point. We are all products of the subcultures in which we must thrive.

Same goes for Lincoln. I would never point this out, but over the years he has built an affinity for shopping and even gossiping. The ragged edge he once had in the tone of his voice has been sanded down into something less intimidating to female ears. His body language is not nearly as aggressive as it used to be. He no longer walks into a room as if he owns it. I'm certain he has done all this unconsciously to help him better fit into the circles of moms.

It hasn't worked, though. Lincoln is still an outsider. He's a Man Without A Gender.

16

Jessica

There are lots of things I don't like about Naples. For one, it costs too much to live here. The teachers in this town are like ski instructors trying to live in some expensive mountain town like Vail or someplace.

I have two jobs—I work at the Victoria's Secret at Coastland Center on Tuesday and Thursday nights—and like most of us I have to live way, way out, even past Golden Gate, almost in the Everglades, and I still pay almost $900 in rent. I mean the money in this town is crazy. The Costco in Naples sells Picasso paintings—real ones for, like, $50,000. It's crazy.

But with all that money comes something I love: Gulf Gun. It's the fanciest gun range I've ever had the pleasure of shooting in.

A lot of times the guys who work at gun shops are kind of gross, lots of facial hair with military tattoos and tacky T-shirts tucked into their blue jeans even if they have a belly, but whoever's the boss at Gulf Gun sure is doing a good job because I swear the boys behind that counter look just like J. Crew models. They always wear crisp, button-down white shirts with *Gulf Gun* embroidered on the chest. It's pretty obvious they want to create a real female-friendly environment here. They put a little packet of disposable wet wipes in your gun basket so you can wipe the gunpowder off your hands when you're done. They even sold pink ribbons during breast-cancer awareness month. I've seen two Collier Academy moms here, but only one of them talks to me. The other one pretends she doesn't recognize me, but you can always tell when people recognize you. They've got that third eye on their forehead that's looking you up and down even while their real eyes are pretending they don't see you.

I've always shot guns. There was no boy in my family so my daddy took me hunting all the time, and there's not a rifle I can't shoot.

But what I'm interested in now are combat handguns, and I've been working my way through the collection here at Gulf Gun. I'm partial to forty-fives. My favorite so far is the full-size Glock G37, although I did like the Hawg 9 because it was a little easier on the paw.

It's already 5:30, and the range shuts down at six, but Benjamin—he's one of the salesmen here, or clerks or whatever you call him—e-mailed me at school and said he had something he thought I'd like to try, so here I am.

They all greet me when I walk inside. "Hey, Miss Varnadore. . . . Hello, Miss Varnadore."

"When are y'all gonna start calling me Jessica?" I ask.

"Jessica," Benjamin says.

"Jessica," Tommy says.

"So what do you got for me, boys?" I ask.

"Something totally cool," Benjamin says. He squats down to pick up something from the floor behind the counter and stands up with a black plastic case. He sets it on the counter in front of me, opens it, and reaches in for the gun.

"Awesome," he says. "It's a Springfield XD Service forty-five GAP."

"XD?"

"Extreme duty. But it's light."

"How light?"

"Little over four pounds."

I take it from him and pop out the magazine. "What's this barrel? Four inches?"

"Yes, ma'am. Nine-round magazine. It's a real up-and-comer with police forces. It's getting some awesome reviews."

I weigh it in my hand. He's right about it being light. I'm already worrying about the kick.

"What do you think I should use?"

"Ma'am?"

"Ammo, Benjamin."

"Uhm . . . maybe Remington Silvertip?"

"Okay. Why don't you give me a hundred rounds then."

The only other person in the shooting gallery is an old man with a white crew cut, most likely retired military, and thank God he's not still out there protecting our country because he's resting his hands and gun on some kind of board covered in carpet. It just about takes a blind man to miss a target if he's resting his gun on something like that. The challenge of marksmanship is to have control over your muscles and coordination. Anyone could get a bull's-eye if they rested their barrel on some stupid block.

I clip my paper target onto the line, flip the switch, and send it on down to the very end of the range, as far as it'll go. When he sees how far I'm gonna shoot, the man next to me starts looking at me out of the corner of his eye.

I look down at the target. It's different this time. I almost always pick the bull's-eye, but for some reason today I picked up the outline of the man with the red circle where his heart's supposed to go. This might be related to what happened to me today at school.

During third period, Mr. Burkert called me to his office. Apparently one of my smart-ass students ratted on me for not knowing what a dangling participle was. I told him, yeah, I did learn about participles but that I'd just forgotten that little detail, and he told me it was embarrassing for students to know something that their teachers don't, and then he had the gall to give me a copy of some stupid grammar book called *Elements of Style*. And he put a letter in my personnel file. I just wanted to tell him that he could take his English classes and shove 'em somewhere dark and smelly. I did remind him that I don't want to be teaching English anyway, that I'm supposed to be teaching social studies, that's what my degree's in. I asked him again why I couldn't just coach volleyball like they hired me to do, but he said it wasn't a full-time position, and that I also had to teach, no matter how great of a coach I am.

I'm sorry, but, like, there's not enough money at Collier Academy? Please! If they want to win back that state title I can win back their stinking state title, but don't get me all upset by making me teach something I don't want to teach!

So . . . this one is for you, Mr. Burkert. And so is this . . . and this . . . and . . . this! I think you've probably stopped breathing by now. But what the heck, mister, here's another!

I like this trigger, it's soft, but this kick's gonna knock me on my hind end.

I reload my magazine and call back my target, and I replace it with another and send it on its way. And then I'm thinking about Coach Klaussen. Today in the teachers' lounge, for about the twenty-six-thousandth time, he pushed up against me when I was getting a Coca-Cola out of the vending machine. Oh, yeah, he's proud of what he's got up front there in those gym shorts, but that is no excuse for sharing it with me and Miss Eidem. That man has no manners whatsoever.

Nice gripping area. I like how this . . . fits! . . . in! . . . my! . . . hand! . . . Lord, I wish this magazine held more than nine shots! Days like this I should ask for an automatic. Daddy always said automatics were for poor shots, people who needed more than one try.

I call back the target. I've just about totally shredded this poor guy's chest. The man next to me, he's stopped shooting. He says something, but I can't hear him. I slip my ear protectors down off my head and rest them on my neck.

"I'm sorry?" I say.

"I said 'you must be one of Charlie's Angels.' "

"No, sir," I say. "I shoot better than Charlie's Angels. Did you ever see those girls kill anyone?"

I sweep up my shells and dump them in the basket on the floor and then go back outside to the counter.

"You rock, girl," Benjamin says, nodding at the bank of monitors on the wall. He takes my targets and unravels them on top of the counter. The other two boys come over and look at them.

"We've gotta show these to Larry," says the third boy whose name I don't know. He's probably new—today was no better than any others, but he hasn't watched me before. Larry's the owner of Gulf Gun and the Arby's next door and Lord knows what else. His son's a third-grader at Collier Academy. His wife drives a green Hummer. She's been ugly to me more than once.

"How'd you learn to shoot like that, ma'am?" he asks.

"Helps to be mad at your boyfriend," I say.

"I sure wouldn't want to tick you off if I was your boyfriend," Tommy says.

"Smart boy," I say.

I'm thinking to myself what Linc would look like with this gun in his hands. I think he'd be a good marksman because he's got that real focused look to him, like he's got his mind on a target and he won't stop until he gets it. I think that's probably something we have in common.

When I get back to my car I reach down for my phone that's charging on the floor. My screensaver's a picture of him. I took it from the window in the chorus room one day after school last week. He's outside the van, helping Violet load up her science-fair project. He's got blue jeans on and a pair of black work boots. I think they're new, I've never seen them. They look real good on him.

I'm finally going to call him. I mean I've got a good excuse now, with that e-mail he sent me about *To Kill a Mockingbird*. It was an ugly note, but I'm not mad because I agree with him. It wasn't me who decided the kids couldn't say nigger—it was Ms. Hutchinson. I forwarded it on to her so she could know how some of the parents agreed with me that I thought it was just plain stupid to change the word like that. I want him to know it wasn't me.

I've called and hung up four times now. Violet answered twice, and her momma answered one time. When I finally got him on the line I just froze up. I'd never heard his voice before. It's exactly what I thought it would sound like. Kind of a mix between Dennis Quaid and my second fiancé, Robert.

17

Jo

The phone rings one evening just when Linc is cleaning the kitchen and I am whittling away at my health-care trade journals on the couch.

"Can you get that?" he asks. "My hands are all wet."

It is Linc's gym friend, Dot.

Dot is an old woman, I think nearly ninety, whom Lincoln has gotten to know at the Wellness Center, where they walk the treadmills together. She's a former PE teacher, almost six feet tall, with very short white hair and a no-nonsense way of speaking.

"Is Linc all right?" she asks.

"He's fine, Dot," I answer. "Why?"

"I haven't seen him all week."

"I know he's gone to the gym. I've seen his tennies by the back door. Let me get him."

I listen to Linc's conversation from the couch. When he finally hangs up, I say, "You quit the Wellness Center?"

"Yeah."

"Why?"

"Just wanted a change."

"So you joined another gym?"

"Universal Gym."

"The muscle gym by the Vietnamese restaurant?"

"Yep."

"Really!"

"I needed a change," he repeats.

"Why?"

He instinctively picks up a damp kitchen rag and begins to wipe off the counter, which is already clean.

"I don't know. I guess I was just tired of flapping my gums with all the old farts. I need to get more serious about my workouts."

"But you love Dot."

"And I invited her out to dinner next week. I do love her. I think she's awesome."

I should have guessed this. I recently saw Linc snatching glimpses of himself in the reflection of the patio door, watching him flex his triceps and frown as he leaned on a broom.

"Are you lifting weights?" I ask.

"Yeah."

"I thought so."

"You can tell?"

"A little. I guess."

The comment seems to melt his frigidness, and he quickly grows animated. "I haven't been doing it for long, just a week. I know it's silly. It's just something I've been wanting to do."

"There's no need to apologize, Linc. There's no law against lifting weights. But don't they have weights at the Wellness Center? We get the hospital-employee discount there."

"There's no weight-lifting culture there," he says. "The free weights just gather dust."

"So that means there are no lines and waiting."

"Please, Jo, don't make me feel guilty about this. I know it costs more, but it's something I really want to get into. And I need to be around other guys who lift. Otherwise it's dangerous."

Actually, it isn't the cost that bothers me. It's the sharp curve he

threw me by choosing that particular gym. My Mr. Fussy. My resident Felix Unger who washes reds separate from the other dark
clothes has joined a gym known only for its muscle-heads and dirty
floors. It simply does not compute.

"If that's what you want," I say.

18

Linc

The buzz at the barbershop is all about Arturo. He is the earliest-forming tropical storm in history, already a Category One hurricane. Last night it passed over the city of Roseau on the island of Dominica. (Ben Hoyt, my barber, pronounces it Doe-MIN-ih-cuh. He also pronounces Miami, "Mie-AM-uh," a sign that he is a true Florida cracker, which means he's an honest-to-God native.)

For every hurricane, the National Weather Service draws on their map something called the cone of probability. It's a big, flan-colored area the shape of a piece of pie with the hurricane's eye being at the point, and the storm will move from this spot to somewhere in that cone. The more unpredictable the storm, the bigger they draw the cone. Ben says they do this to cover their ass because they've been wrong about landfall so many times in the past. And, indeed, the cone now seems to be a huge joke. Right now—and I'm watching it on the TV with the other guys in Hoyt's—it stretches from Myrtle Beach, North Carolina, all the way down to the southern tip of Cuba.

"I call it the cone of stupidity," Ben says.

I'm in the chair now, getting my hair cut. I have been coming here once a week, lingering for as long as my schedule allows.

None of the guys seem to care much at all about the storm, but I'm not so sure. Naples lies at about the center of this cone. Doesn't this mean there's a greater chance of landfall here than any point farther north or south? I know that wouldn't make much sense, mathematically, but I'm a visual person, and it just feels right, aesthetically, that it would come here.

The erratic, unpredictable nature of these things drives me crazy. Of course there are hundreds of different paths it could take. The hurricane could enter somewhere around Miami and slog its way through the Everglades, and by the time it got here it would be worn down and not as dangerous—at least that's what Rod has told me—but I'm not so certain about this, either. Florida is a skinny state, and they say hurricanes feed on warm water, and I ask you this: What exactly are the Everglades? Hello? Earth to Mars! The Glades may look like grasslands but it's all *warm water*!

Or, like Charley in 2004, it could sweep under the entire Florida peninsula, veer north like Katrina did, and then swerve back eastward, as if it had forgotten to flatten a particular city it had had on its agenda of destruction. This, of course, would mean a direct hit.

"Ain't coming here," Ben says.

"How do you know?" I reply.

He just shakes his head and combs through my flattop, then stoops so he can scan across it to make sure he hasn't missed any wayward hairs.

"Now Donna, that was some hurricane. Nineteen sixty."

"Winds were two hunnerd and twenty miles an hour," says Bob Ritchfield, a regular at the barbershop. He is here every time I come, every time, no matter what time of day. He's now playing dominoes with Lou Stoltz, who lost one of his legs in World War II. He gets around in one of those scooters that you see fat people riding in the supermarket, only this guy really needs it.

"No, that was Darcy. You're thinking about Darcy," says Lou.

"No, sir, that was Donna," Ben says.

Respecting the owner on his own turf—or simply not caring enough to carry on this argument—Lou keeps his mouth shut and makes another move.

"Donna . . . she changed her mind more than any woman I've ever known," Ben says. "She went this way and that way before she slammed right into us."

I, too, keep my mouth shut. I have read four books on hurricanes since New Year's. It was indeed Donna, but her winds did not blow past two hundred. She came ashore just south of here, near Marco Island, and brought with her a thirteen-foot storm surge, leaving twelve people dead and causing more than $350 million in damage—and that's counting it in 1960 dollars.

There are five categories of hurricanes. A Category One blows up to 95 miles per hour. Some trees will lose limbs. Kiss that gazing ball in your garden good-bye.

A Category Two blasts up to 110. This is when power lines start snapping and swimming-pool cages start to shed their screens. Trees get stripped of leaves. Businesses' signs get blown out. The older, more brittle asphalt shingles get torn from roofs like pages from a word-a-day calendar.

In a Category Three, with winds up to 130, you'd better be thinking of leaving town for the day. Mobile homes and anything made of aluminum, which is about half of the construction down here, begins to shred, and the pieces fly through the air like a pair of wayward nunchucks, knocking out windows and slicing through power lines. Lots of storm surge, lots of flooding.

A Category Four is anything with sustained winds stronger than 145. Flooding is so bad that cars and other big things start to float and collide with houses or anything else in their path. Entire trees fall over, ripped up from their roots. The towering live oaks down here aren't as mighty as they appear. Because the aquifers are so close to the surface, there are no deep taproots that act as an anchor, so these giant trees have root systems that spread out instead of down. I've seen photographs of big oaks and jacarandas and banyans that simply fell over, pulling their entire root structure, which looks like an immense, shallow plate of spaghetti noodles, out of the ground with them.

"How bad is a Cat Five?" I ask the men. "Have any of you ever seen one? I mean, it's total devastation, right? Katrina was only a four."

They all shake their heads and remain quiet. Finally, Lou says, "Andrew was a five, and Homestead Air Base ain't there no more."

Ben reaches for the remote and turns down the volume. I know I'm pushing the rules as far as talking is concerned, but I want to know something. The conversation in this place reminds me of an old toilet. Each sentence is a flushing, and then there's nothing more to spew forth until the tank fills up again.

"What will you guys do to get ready for a hurricane?" I ask.

"Stop by the liquor store," says Bob, holding his stare on the table of dominoes. "All I need for a hurricane is my friend, Jack."

"What about you, Ben?" I ask.

"I sold my house when my wife died," he answers. "I live in a condo on the fourth floor. Not much I need to do. No roof. Flooding's no problem for me."

"Well, I live on the water," I say. "I'm not taking any chances."

Two or three minutes pass when none of the men say anything. Finally, Ben asks, "You got storm shutters?"

"No," I say.

"You need storm shutters. Aluminum ones."

"We're getting those hurricane-impact windows, but they're not in yet."

"I saw those on TV," Lou says. "They shot a two-by-four at 'em, and it bounced right off."

Ben detaches the strip of paper from my neck and takes off the white cloth that is peppered with my hair. (What are these things called, anyway? Aprons? Drop cloths?) "You want a shave?" he asks me. "You're looking pretty scruffy."

"Hey," Lou interrupts. "Turn that back up, Ben. Look at that— it's a Category Two now."

"When did that happen?" I ask.

"Just now, I guess."

On the screen is Don Maley, gesticulating in front of a map of the cloudy Atlantic. I like Don Maley. He's the last nerdy guy left on The Weather Channel, the only one I can think of who hasn't been all dolled up like a model. I trust him. I know he's in it for his love of weather, not vanity. He's balding in a huge way, and he wears shirts and ties that look like they come from Sears. And he proceeds to tell us that the internal pressure of the hurricane's eye is dropping faster—and this is a bad thing; dropping means more strength—than any hurricane on record.

It's also picking up in forward speed, about 14 miles per hour, which means it could reach the Florida peninsula within the next four days.

I think of all my potted plants, of the kayaks, of the pile upon pile of construction materials on my driveway, of the Porta-Potty. Lord, what would a Cat Three or Four do to a Porta-Potty?

I need batteries and candles and a house phone that doesn't require electricity as do all of our cordless telephones. (I haven't yet read this on a hurricane-prep list! I'll be sure to send in the suggestion when this is all over.)

Which reminds me: *I need plywood to cover all the doors and windows.*

Which reminds me: *No air-conditioning . . . no electricity for days . . . extra propane needed for the grill.*

Which reminds me: *Need to take photographs of everything in the house in case an insurance agent grills me about items destroyed by flood or wind.*

"No shave," I say. "I've got to get home."

"Rod, come here and read this."

I've commandeered the computer from Violet, who slunk away, silent and grateful, when I said she could go in and do her homework in front of the TV.

I have pulled up the description of a Cat Five hurricane on the National Weather Service Web site. It is nothing short of a local apocalypse. I suddenly realize why the universally recognized, oscillating red symbol for the hurricane looks exactly like the blade in a Cuisinart.

> . . . Winds greater than 155 mph. Storm surge generally greater than 18 ft above normal. Complete roof failure on many residences and industrial buildings. Some complete building failures with small utility buildings blown over or away. All shrubs, trees, and signs blown down. Complete destruction of mobile homes. Severe and extensive window and door damage. Low-lying escape routes are cut by rising water 3–5 hours before arrival of the center of the hurricane. Major damage to lower floors of all structures located less than 15 ft above sea level and within 500 yards of the shoreline. Massive evacuation of residential areas on low ground within 5-10 miles (8-16 km) of the shoreline may be required.

"It's not a Cat Five," Rod says. "You're worrying too much. It's way too early."

I then pull up the page that shows the five computer models the weather service uses to help formulate its official prediction. It is a map of the Atlantic basin with the hurricane and five different-colored lines, each a computer-generated prediction of the path, emanating from it. It's true—at this point they seem to disagree like eccentric, argumentative sisters. One yellow line zigzags northward, toward Jacksonville. Another pretty much makes a beeline toward Cuba. One of them, a green line, actually lingers south of the Bahamas, completing two circles, as if twirling about on the playground.

"Too soon, man," Rod says.

"But look what they all do," I say. "They all agree that sometime in the next day or two they're going to curve northward, and if it waits to curve northward after it passes Miami then we could get a direct hit."

Rod calmly shakes his head. "That thing could go to Venezuela, Linc."

He walks off, down the hallway. I watch him. I wish I could be that calm, I really do. It's very cool . . . but not possible. I am genetically programmed to be uptight. I have German genes on both sides. Angst, after all, is a German word. Incidentally, my last name, Menner, comes from the German word for *men*. How's that for irony?

"Violet!" I yell down the hall, toward the guest-bedroom-turned-TV-sanctuary.

"Yes, Dad?"

"I need your help."

Pause.

"Right now?" she asks.

"Right now," I say.

She comes into the family room. "Yes?"

"Get your shoes on, darlin'. We've got some heavy lifting to do."

"What are we doing?"

"See all that on the patio . . . and on the driveway?"

"Yes."

"It all needs to move in here."

"Oh, Dad, no."

"Oh, Dad, yes. Look at it as payback for that time when you pooped your panties when you were three and tried to hide it all over your bedroom. Okay?"

"Thank you, Dad. I have tried to forget that one."

"Lord, so have I."

"What about Rod? Shouldn't he be doing this?"

"He just left. He doesn't think it's necessary."

Violet cocks her head in a quizzical look.

"It needs to be done." I say. "This could be catastrophic." I give a sweep of my arm toward the clutter on the patio. "Imagine all these things as airborne missiles."

"Missiles? Please, Dad. Don't be so melodramatic."

"Look it up in the dictionary, young lady. I'm being literal here."

We first spread out every tarp and tablecloth and beach towel and sheet that we own, onto the wooden floor. I then prop open both sets of French doors, one of which leads to the waterfront patio and another to the driveway.

First, the construction materials. I carry the bigger items, the boxed toilets and sinks and the bigger boxes of ceramic tile. We have no dolly so I enlist the help of Violet's skateboard. Seeing how well this works, I go inside and rummage through the attic until I find Violet's old Barbie Winnebago, which, thankfully, wasn't made of plastic but steel, and it has a nice flat roof.

"Dad!" she exclaims when she sees it. "You kept it!"

"Don't be so surprised," I say. "I keep all your toys. I don't have the right to give these things away—they're yours."

After the big items are inside, we start on the assorted wood scraps and a pile of 2-by-4s. There are buckets and boxes of nails and screws, shingles and usable scraps of Sheetrock. We bring in braces and levels and coiled extension cords and, ironically, boxes of hurricane straps, which are metal brackets that Florida contractors have had to use when cojoining two boards in any framework ever since the early 1990s, after Andrew blew through.

We work for an hour and then, exhausted, stop for a big glass of water. We sit on the grass in the shade of the oak tree, though it is far from comfortable outside. The rainy season is upon us in Naples, and I have never encountered such atmospheric wetness outside of a steam room. At this time of year when you walk outside from an air-conditioned environment your glasses immediately fog over.

From the patio, we carry in all the tables and chairs, the chaise lounges and the glider. Like any good native Westerner, I have a huge selection of mature (Read: BIG) succulents in heavy terra-cotta pots. I swear some of them weigh up to two hundred pounds. If it weren't for the skateboard and Winnebago we would have had to leave them outside to perish.

I have a weakness for yard art, pieces I've bought all over the United States and Latin America, including sculptures of a demonic mermaid and Buddha and Mikhail Gorbachev, of a dinosaur lying in his egg and a basketball-size head of Charlie Brown who, with his look of "Oh, Good Grief" on his face, appears to be buried in the ground from the neck down. It's my favorite piece.

I have a collection of immense Vietnamese pots of different, funky shapes, some turquoise, some red, others orange and chartreuse. All together, scattered about the patio, some of them pushed onto their sides, they have the appearance of a giant's colorful necklace that has broken apart.

Do I fill them with water and leave them here? How possible is it for something that weighs a few hundred pounds to become airborne and come crashing through a window?

But what if something were to come up over the seawall and hit them? No, they, too, must be brought inside.

And then there is my collection of bromeliads and orchids, sitting on the bows and in the elbows and hanging on the limbs of the three guava trees. I must have fifty or sixty. I put Violet on a step-ladder, and she goes to work.

"Dad, that smell!"

"It's cow manure," I say. "On the orchids."

"Yuck!" Instantly, she slows down, unconsciously extending her pinkies as she unhooks each wooden orchid basket from its limb.

I drag my two kayaks inside and then begin on the fifty or so pot-ted tropical plants, the Mosquito Magnet and its three extra propane tanks, and the extension ladder. (Have I mentioned we have no garage or storage shed?)

Every time I look up I see something new, as if it has just sprouted from the ground. Oh . . . the bamboo wind chimes and the spots for uplighting the canary palms, which aren't anchored but rather just set in pots on the ground.

"I feel like I'm taking down Christmas decorations," Violet says. "This is just like *The Grinch Who Stole Christmas*. We're taking everything, even the roast beast."

But I do not feel like the Grinch. What I feel like is a very frantic Noah rushing the plants and animals of the entire world into the ark in the final hours before the rains arrive.

When Violet and I finish we come inside and shut the doors. We have been outside for so long, exposed to the breeze and waves sloshing against the seawall, that the silence seems to weigh heavily on our ears. My face suddenly feels hot because there is no breeze, and our cheeks and necks and foreheads are flushed from more than two hours of frenzied work.

We turn around and see there is no place to walk. We have left no paths. There is no room for a path.

"Ah, over there," I say. "The kayaks. Follow me."

I push aside plants and patio furniture, squeezing between big pots, turning my feet with toes outward as if I'm walking a tightrope, and we eventually make it across the room.

Each of us lay down on an overturned watercraft. I feel as if I have just finished a full day of downhill skiing. The fatigue is still so fresh that nothing yet hurts, but already my lower back is starting to feel stiff.

Both of us have closed our eyes. The lights are off. The sun dipped below the horizon sometime in the last twenty minutes, and a golden-orange glow comes in through the patio windows. All that chlorophyll, all that soil, all those mossy, moist saucers, all the accumulated algae-infused rainwater in the crevices and depressions of things both manmade and natural . . . all these things give off a dank, earthy smell not unlike rainforests we have visited in Central America.

I look over at my daughter. With her hands resting on her chest, she reminds me of Sleeping Beauty in the glass coffin. She's a good kid. She didn't complain but once, just that peep about the manure.

I hear her restful, rhythmic breathing and know she has fallen asleep. I know the sound, the cadence of this breath better than my own, and it has not changed since she was weeks old and laying in my arms.

I'm wondering what I can throw together for dinner, but before an entrée materializes I, too, find myself falling backward, and inward, into blackness, as I hear the bewildered rustling of lizards in the foliage around us.

Linc Menner's Handy Hints for Caregiver Sanity

Hint #68B

I don't make the beds in our house anymore, and you shouldn't, either. If guests drop by and notice the unmade beds, simply say this: "Oh, no, I never make my beds anymore! You've got to let air kill all the bacteria that drops from the body and gathers on the sheets, and covering everything up lets the bacteria breed. It's very unsanitary. I read it in some medical journal."

19

Violet

Okay, so here's a situation you do not want to be in as a thirteen-year-old: Pulling your old, rusty wagon down the street and filling it with stinky, dripping coconuts that have fallen from the trees when you're expecting your new boyfriend to drop by any minute.

I am going as fast as I can. I can't even imagine how stupid I look pulling this thing. If he sees me doing this I just might as well tie this wagon to my ankles and jump into the bay. God, just when I'm starting to become normal like other kids my dad wants to sabotage it all.

I tried to beg my way out of it. I even asked if I could do it after dinner. But begging has never worked with my dad. In fact, begging and whining only makes him madder and more determined to have his way.

My dad is obsessed with everything in this neighborhood that can become a missile—that's the word he's been using and I am sick of it—during a hurricane. Today it's coconuts. I'm supposed to scour the neighborhood, collect and toss them all into the bay so they don't become cannonballs. If I had a younger sister or if there were other kids in this Neighborhood of People Older Than Planet Earth this job would be theirs, but, oh, no, it is Violet and Violet alone who must save all of Jacaranda Street from the horrible Arturo. Yes, this is what I am doing today for after-school, extracurricular enrichment. Oh, joy!

My dad has become a weather wacko, which is way beyond a weather nerd. I'm not sure where the storm is now, I couldn't really care less, but he is monitoring it like crazy. The "favorites" list on our computer is all weather-related now, he has deleted everything else. I'm chased off the computer thirty times a day, I swear, so he can check the coordinates of the storm and whether it's changed direction.

Category isn't even a question anymore. I guess old Arturo is breaking all records. He's now a strong "Cat Four" as my dad says in his hurricane-speak.

Two days ago he walked the neighborhood and listed everything in everyone's yard that could become a missile, even Mrs. Chapin's big cherub fountain. I'm sorry, but even a healthy tornado couldn't pick that thing up and chuck it through the air. It must weight five hundred pounds.

And then, yesterday, he went door-to-door to tell each person what it was in their yard that had to be either brought inside or gotten rid of. Of course most people are ignoring him. I mean, wouldn't you?

The most annoying thing he's done was to make me put together a memory box. He came into my room a few nights ago when I was reading a Gossip Girls book on my papasan chair.

"You need to collect your most important things, Violet, and put' them in this box," he said.

"Dad, what do you mean?"

"We very soon might be refugees," he said. "We can take with us what we can fit in the car . . . like the Joads in *The Grapes of Wrath*. We each get one box for sentimental purpose."

Of course he would bring up that book! It had a profound impact on me, as did books about the Holocaust, because they are stories of people being ripped away from their material possessions. I don't have lots of lovely things. Most of my friends, if I let them into my room, which I will never, ever do, would think my prized possessions are junk.

When you have a dad who plays and interacts with you all the time, there's just no need for playdates. When I did play with someone I always found them boring. They were not as funny as my dad, and definitely not as interesting. The only thing Dad would not do is play Barbies with me. I guess that's asking too much, even for a dad who's a mom.

What he did was play great make-believe. We each would pick out a little plastic animal and spend hours building houses for them out of books and scraps of material and things we'd pull from my junk drawers.

The brainstorming we used to do! When we decided that our pets needed a particular household item, the two of us would pick our way through the drawers and closets of the whole house, scavenging until we found what we needed. There was one rule: Nothing could be used in its true form. No doll beds for beds, for example. And Dad would forbid me to use my favorite plastic, pink-floral plates rimmed in gold from my Barbie bakery unless they were used as, say, cobblestones in a yard.

I remember making a Weber grill out of half a lime with three toothpicks pushed into its rind for legs. We used rose petals as steaks.

When you spend most of your free time for the first eleven or so years of your life either reading or playing make-believe, you collect a lot of things. My bedroom has six bookcases, and only one of them is used for books. Every other inch is occupied by a collection of tchotchkes (a word I have picked up from my Jewish friends at school). Each item has played an important role in taking me someplace special that only I have seen. I have visited many of these places more than once.

So when Dad comes in and hands me a Chiquita banana box and says that that's all I can take with me to the end of the world I start to panic.

"Only the things that are very, very important to you," he says.

"What do you mean, 'important?' " I ask.

"I mean, Violet, the things you will need to bridge you back to your childhood when you are ninety years old with a failing memory. Take only the most symbolic of items, only the most representative from each phase of your childhood. Then come on down and get the camera and take photographs of everything else."

"Dad! You're scaring me."

"That is not my intention. My intention is to be prepared."

"Well you're scaring me."

"Landfall in under . . ." He looks at his watch. ". . . thirty-seven hours."

"Is it really coming here?"

"Anywhere from Port Charlotte to Everglades City. He's wobbling like crazy right now. Very unpredictable."

I can't remember ever seeing my father react to something so strongly. Yes, he obsesses about things all the time, but he's never given the impression that he's smaller and weaker than the forces he's battling. I'm wondering if at least part of this behavior comes from the repressed Boy Scout in him. Grandma Carol wouldn't let him join when he was a boy. She says they discriminated against homosexuals, and she didn't want to be a part of that culture.

My dad needs something new in his life. I think he's bored out of his mind. He's always been project-oriented, and I used to be his project. That's really no longer true. He's got me on cruise control these days.

He leaves me alone in my room so I can sort through my life's possessions, and the thought of having to pick favorites makes me sick to my stomach. I pick up a painted plastic fairy who is bent over a small pond, looking at her reflection. She has been my sister, my mother, and a friend who has taken me into the deepest, most secret center of a rainforest. We have also been to the moon and to Paris several times.

There is the piece of fool's gold I got at Wall Drug in South Dakota. I know it's totally worthless, but it's been a sought-after treasure in countless adventures. It can also sing at times, giving away its whereabouts.

There is the porcelain mermaid who sat on the bottom of our aquarium during our fish phase. She's always the villainess, probably because she has a scary face, with blood-colored lips and beady, black eyes that were painted on in a lopsided manner. I love her for her loyalty, and I could never leave her behind.

There is my snow globe of Mickey Mouse dressed as the sorcerer's apprentice and . . . oh, I think this might be my favorite . . . or is it?

Then I walk into my closet. I have so many stuffed animals they are smooshed into the top shelves like raisins in a box. Mom has nagged at me to give some of them to Goodwill, but over the years I have slept with every single one of them, and I still rotate them all so each one gets a chance to sit out on my bed.

I look at my two shoeboxes full of paper dolls I've collected over the years. Dad would help me find paper dolls to match characters we'd seen in movies.

And my dress-up trunk! How could I forget my dress-up trunk? I have the best dress-up trunk of any girl I know. Over the years my dad has filled this thing with cool stuff from vintage clothing stores. I mean, I have everything from kimonos to hippy beads to old tuxedos and sequined party dresses . . . even a pair of ruby slippers. (Okay, they're actually covered in red glitter.)

How am I to decide what, of all these wonderful things, will stay behind and perish? There's just no way. This is an unfair thing to ask of anyone.

I walk to the door of my bedroom and yell as loudly as I can, "There is no way I'm going to fit everything in that one box, Dad! . . . No! Way!"

It is silent. All the workmen have left for the day.

"Dad!" I scream again. "Daaaaad!"

"I heard you, Violet," he says, calmly, from the kitchen.

I storm out of my room, down the hall, and into the kitchen.

"I can't do it, Dad. Can't we put some of it in the rental storage place?"

"You'd be more comfortable with your precious things in a building made of tin?"

"Okay, then, there's got to be some solution."

"There is. It's called editing your life. Now go do it or I'll do it for you. You're damned lucky I'm giving you a box to yourself. Your mother and I are sharing one."

"Dad . . ."

"You haven't even tried, Violet. I won't talk to you again until you've spent two hours winnowing through all that shit."

"It is not . . . shit!" I yell back, surprised at how foreign the word sounds when it finally stumbles out of my mouth. I don't think I've ever said it in front of him. And he doesn't even flinch. He just keeps on chopping that zucchini or whatever it is.

"I mean, what's wrong with you anyway, Dad? What's going on with you?"

"There's a hurricane bearing down on us, Violet."

"Really! I had no idea."

He suddenly cuts himself with the knife.

"Fuck!"

"Fuck!" I repeat.

"What did you say?"

"Just repeating the man who is supposed to be my role model,"
I answer. He never used to cuss like this. Mom says he's depressed
and that I should be patient as we weather this remodeling and the
hurricanes, but I'm sick and tired of him. Sick and tired.

Dad sets down his knife, walks over to his kitchen junk drawer,
and pulls out a bandage, which he unwraps and puts on his large,
middle finger. He then walks over to his new desk and fumbles
through another drawer until he pulls out a red Sharpie. There is a
calendar on the bulletin board over this desk, and he draws a huge
X through the entire month of June, then turns the page and does it
with July as well. He replaces the cap on the Sharpie, takes down
the calendar, and hands it to me.

"I never thought I would have to do this," he says.

"Do what?"

"Ground you."

"What!"

"You may do nothing social for the next two months. X marks
the spot."

"Dad! . . . Why?"

"One month for the 'fuck.' Two weeks for the 'shit.' And two
weeks for the overall nasty tone."

"What! You said 'shit' before I did!"

"Just listen to you! You're horrible. You're spoiled rotten. What is
this 'what' stuff? Is that the way your new boyfriend talks?"

"Two months!?"

"With no instant-messaging privileges, either."

"You're kidding me."

"I am not."

"You're a hypocrite, Dad."

"Would you prefer three months? Do I have an offer for three
months? . . . Anyone?" he says, pretending to look at a crowd

of people beyond me. "Do I have an offer for three? . . . Going once. . . . Going twice."

"You're psycho! You're out of control."

"Yes!" He slams his hand on the butcher block hard enough that I feel a vibration through the floor. "Three months to the spoiled prep-school girl with the potty mouth."

20

Jo

We all remember the nightmarish scenes and stories from hospitals in New Orleans after Katrina, all those elderly patients who were left behind, some of them even murdered with lethal intravenous cocktails because doctors couldn't stand to watch them die a slow, awful death of abandonment. Katrina was to the health-care industry what Enron was to Wall Street, a wake-up call that spawned a mother lode of new legislation and protocol and overall paranoia that, if I'm not careful here, will breed sheer hysteria.

Even though we have no idea where Arturo will hit, we must assume the very worst, and that is why I have spent this entire day involved in emergency planning. And someone from Collier County Emergency Preparedness has just told me and my group of directors, via speakerphone, that although this county has more than 300,000 residents we have emergency shelters that can hold a whopping—drumroll, please—48,000 people!

I am so disgusted! This would never happen in California or New York. There would be some law forbidding it, something that would force developers to build emergency shelters for the subdivisions of new residents that fill their pockets. It's nothing short of criminal. By definition, it is manslaughter.

Suddenly, my assistant, Marcie, pops her head inside the door. She holds up a handwritten sign: *mother-in-law on phone.*

In my eighteen years of being a member of this family, Carol Menner has never called me at work. Linc forbade it long ago, and perhaps it is best—she's a talker, like her son. And I am busy, especially today. I am in charge of ParkeHealth Incorporated's six hospitals in the southeastern United States. All of them, unfortunately, sit in the hurricane belt.

I hold up my hand to the long table of people before me— "Excuse me."—and I get up and walk over to Marcie at the door.

"You do mean Carol Menner, right?" I whisper.

"Yes."

"Did she say what it was about? Is it an emergency?"

"She wouldn't say. But she did say it was about Linc."

"Has Lincoln called?"

"No."

I look back at my directors.

"I need to take this one," I say. "Is everyone clear on what happens next? . . . Bill, I need that information on the buses before you leave tonight. Carlos . . . call Phil Landry in corporate I.S. He used to be with the Navy. He might have some good advice on acquiring aircraft. . . . Any other questions? Okay . . . And, please, people, I can't stress to you enough the importance of having those Black-Berrys and radio phones with you at all times."

I return to my office and see that Carol has hung up. I look at my watch—it's eleven o'clock in Bakersfield—look her number up on my BlackBerry, and call her.

Of course it is she who answers the phone. Don is rarely home. The man has built the largest Lincoln-Mercury dealership in California, and he does it by practically living there. Sometimes I wonder if his success is fueled by wanting some distance from home life. Hmmm . . . probably something universal here. I, too, find myself avoiding home lately. I work later than I really need to and have started to shower most days at the gym. Being home right now is like camping at a construction site. And guarding that site is a very ill-tempered dog who growls and seems ready to snap at any time. Add a sulky teenager addicted to the Internet and you get a perfect picture.

I miss our beautiful things, the Persian rugs, the art, the light reflecting on crystal stemware. I am so weary of using my bed as a chair, sofa, clothesline, and a temporary storage spot for anything that might have been moved for the workers earlier that day.

I miss Linc's warmth and laughter. He used to greet me with rich details of his and Violet's day. Now it's a litany of misdeeds of the contractors, stated in a way that makes me feel responsible for them, although I know I am not.

"Carol . . . It's Jo."

"Oh, Jo, I know I shouldn't call you at work. I'm so sorry, I'm just so sorry. That's why I hung up."

"It's no problem," I say. "What can I help you with?"

"You know I've never called you at work? Never in almost twenty years?"

"It's fine, Carol. Really. Are you okay?"

"I didn't want to call at home because I don't want Lincoln to know I'm calling. It's about him: Lincoln. Is everything all right?"

"I think so. What do you mean?"

"He hasn't returned one of my calls for weeks."

"Carol, the house looks like Iraq. I don't think he calls anyone back these days."

"But it's more than that," she says.

"What?"

She pauses. "Did you read Violet's essay about him?"

Questions like this put me on the defensive, though I know Carol didn't ask it to purposely expose my ineptness as an involved mother as some of Linc's stay-at-home mom peers have done. Sometimes I think Betty Friedan and all the feminists lied to us, making us think we could have it all if we worked hard enough. All I know is that every step I take to get closer to the boardroom actually takes me farther away from my little girl, who has grown into a princess who wants no part of a big job like her mom's.

"No, Carol," I answer. "I haven't seen Violet's essay. Is it something I should read?"

"You know she e-mails me most everything that she writes for English class."

"I didn't know that, no," I say and then wonder why Violet doesn't send me a copy as well. Am I supposed to ask for these things?

"Well, she just wrote an essay about her father, the most influential person in her life. . . . What are these changes in Lincoln, Jo?"

"What do you mean?"

"Well, the new hairstyle, for one thing."

"Oh, the crew cut."

"Yes."

"It actually looks really good, Carol."

"What about the boots? And there was something about muscle magazines? Violet says he's acting like Arnold Schwarzenegger."

I had not seen the magazines; he must be hiding them. In fact, Lincoln has been unusually quiet about his new life at the muscle gym. This is a stark contrast from his days at the Wellness Center, which provided him daily anecdotes to share about his elderly friends on the treadmills.

Lincoln has always been very strange about his works in progress. As a landscaper he covered each finished section with blue tarps and waited until he was finished to unveil it all at once for the owner. Carol once told me about how Linc, as a child, would not let anyone see him learn anything new until he had mastered it. Once, he locked himself in his room and didn't emerge for thirty-six hours until he taught himself how to shuffle a deck of cards.

He's likely doing the same thing with his weight training. He wears big, baggy shirts a lot of the time now. Last week when I hugged him he seemed firmer on top, around his back and shoulders. I teased him, asking for a muscle show. He said, "There will be no wine before its time."

"You know what she called the essay?" Carol says. " 'The Metamorphosis.' "

"The Metamorphosis," I repeat.

"Yes. That's what alarms me."

"Can you e-mail me a copy of that?"

"Oh, you haven't read it?"

"No. I already said that, Carol. I haven't read it. Can you send it to me, please?"

"Why don't you ask Violet for a copy?"

"I don't want to alert her to a marriage under stress."

"Oh, my God, so things aren't going well," she says. The intonation barely swings upward at the end of the sentence. It is more a declaration than question.

"Things are fine, Carol. They're just really, really stressful now. This home renovation has been hell. And now we've got the hurricanes to worry about, and he's fretting about them in the way you'd imagine."

"Obsessive."

"Of course."

"It's because he has no control over them."

"I know," I reply. "That said, he has not been himself lately. He's . . . quiet."

"Quiet?"

"I will say 'pensive.' "

"Pensive? . . . Lincoln?"

"Yes."

What I don't tell her is that he seems very secretive these days, too. I didn't mind the muscle-gym switch. What I mind is that I learned about it by overhearing one of his phone conversations with a friend.

Lincoln has never hidden anything from me.

Why now?

And what else?

21

Jessica

Miss Nancy—the eighth-grade aide—is a real sweetheart. She reminds me a lot of my Aunt Johnetta. Not in the body, but in the face. My Aunt Johnetta weighs about three hundred pounds. Miss Nancy's as thin as a pencil.

She does just about everything I ask her to, even things she's not supposed to do because she's just an aide. She'll post the grades online for me, which is something I just hate doing. I've even got her to grade some essays. She's got different handwriting, but no one has seemed to care much, so I just let her grade away! I think she likes doing all this because she really wants to be a full-blown teacher instead of an aide.

"Miss Nancy," I call to her, outside the door of my room. She sits at a desk in the hallway, up against the wall. "Can I ask you a big favor? . . . Would you be a sweetheart and watch the class for me while I go outside and talk with a parent in the pickup line?"

I get my purse and stop by the bathroom to freshen up. When I take it back to the room Miss Nancy gives me a strange look, and I'm wondering if it's because she's noticed I just put on lipstick. I wear Fire Rose for days like this. There's no mistaking you've got lipstick on when it's Fire Rose. Mr. Burkert, the headmaster, told me once I shouldn't wear this lipstick at work, but he's already gone for the day.

I head outside. He's farther back in the line these days. He doesn't come as early as he used to. So I have to walk past twenty or so cars of moms who are all talking on their phones.

I'm real nervous. I'm feeling jumpy and breathless. I've never talked to him in person, just through e-mails.

He's reading some magazine. I totally love that new haircut of his—and his beard, too.

I almost lose my nerve and walk right on by, but I catch his eye when I get closer, and he doesn't stop lookin' so I take a deep breath and walk right up to the passenger window. He rolls it down right away, even before I can say anything. It's pretty clear he wants to talk to me.

"You're Violet's daddy, aren't you?" I say.

"That's correct," he says.

"Well, hey," I say, and I stick my arm through the open window. "I'm Jessica Varnadore, Violet's English teacher?"

"The famous Ms. Varnadore!" he says.

"Oh, no, please call me Jessica. I'm way too young to be a Ms. Varnadore. And I don't really like that whole Ms. thing anyway. I think girls should just be girls. Miss or Mrs. . . . . But Jessica to you."

"Okay . . . Jessica. What can I do for you today? Is there a problem with Violet?"

"You must be kiddin' me. She's the sharpest tack in the class."

"Okay . . . what then?"

"I just wanted to say something about that e-mail you sent me. I've been wanting to say something for a while now, but I've been so busy. I just wanted to say I agreed with you about using that word in class."

"Nigger?"

"It's Ms. Hutchinson—she won't let me use it. I mean is that the silliest thing you've ever heard?"

"No," he says. "I've heard sillier things about her."

"Well, don't get me started there. I don't want to sound unprofessional."

"No apologies needed," he says. "I just thought it was important to weigh in on that. . . . Hey, listen, while you're here, I want to ask you something. Do they plan on having school Wednesday?"

"I think so. Why?"

"Arturo," he says. "Landfall's Wednesday night."

"Oh . . . the hurricane?"

"Yes, the hurricane," he says, and he laughs at me in that way that boys laugh at girls when they're surprised they don't know something.

"You really think it's gonna be bad?" I ask.

"Could be catastrophic. . . . Aren't you ready for it? You've got to be prepared, girl."

I pretend my elbows are tired from leaning on the windowsill of the door, and I lift them and spread them a little farther apart. Oh, he notices all right. He looks right at my chest and then catches himself and looks back up in my eyes. I'm hoping the edge of my scalloped pink bra is showing when I'm leaning over like this. Thank you, Victoria's Secret, for these womanly weapons!

"How do you mean?" I ask.

"Missiles," he says. "Have you picked up everything outside that can get thrown through a window?"

"Well," I say. "I do have a big ol' potted plant on my balcony. I mean real big. It could sink the *Titanic*. It was my daddy's plant, God rest his soul. . . . But there's no way I'm gonna get that thing inside by myself."

"You should ask a neighbor for help," he says.

"Well, one neighbor's an old man and the other two are lesbians who won't talk to me. They're teachers at Naples Vo-Tech."

"Surely there's got to be someone," he says.

"In case you haven't looked, sir, there's not a whole lot of big strong men like you around here. Collier County's a pretty lonely place for a woman who doesn't have gray hair."

The school bell rings. Any second now kids will start pouring out of that building like angry hornets.

"Well . . . where do you live?" he asks.

"Out in Golden Gate Estates."

"Whoo. Edge of the universe. . . . Tell you what. I can come out and help you with that tree."

"Oh, no, I couldn't ask you to do that."

"No, really. It'll be my pleasure. I don't do anything much in the school. I'll consider it my volunteer work. How's that?"

"You really would do that for me?" I say.

"Absolutely. Can I stop by tonight? Tell me where you live."

"You sure you got time?"

"I'll make time."

I give him directions to my apartment. And then I go in and gather my things real quick because I've got to get to Home Depot and buy myself the biggest plant I can find . . . and somehow lug that thing out onto my balcony.

Jessica Varnadore, you are b.r.i.l.l.y.u.n.t.!

22

Linc

The Weather Channel has been in storm-alert mode for the past sixteen hours. Things are serious enough now that they've replaced the pretty faces with my heroes, Dr. Don Maley and Mike Sartore. Right now, Sartore is at the foot of Naples pier, less than a mile from my house.

Of course, Arturo could wobble this way or that—that's the official word meteorologists use to describe a tangential change in direction: wobble—but at current trajectory it appears we are ground zero. It's been a very unstable storm, and it seems it can't make up its mind whether it wants to be killer hurricane or simple pain in the ass. During its path through the Atlantic and into the Gulf it has swelled up to a Cat Five, back down to a Cat Three, then back up to a Cat Four.

I am furious with myself for having listened to Artie Nimitz, one of my neighbors, about the plywood for the windows. He talked me out of it, said these old jalousie windows were stronger than normal ones because each pane is so small, so the surface-area tension isn't as great, which means they won't bow and explode into shards from pressure created by the wind.

If our new windows and doors were installed I'd have nothing to worry about. They're made of impact-resistant glass, some space-age-like material so strong firefighters have trouble pounding their way through them with an ax. Little good they'll do me with Arturo, though. At this very moment they are on a truck, en route to Florida from the factory in Indiana.

I should have put up the damned plywood! Idiot! I asked about it at the hardware store, but they said I needed a hammer drill to penetrate the old, hard stucco of this house, and then I realized I had no way to transport all that wood for thirty-six windows, and I just talked myself out of it. Idiot!

And now I'm realizing how irresponsible I was because I've since learned the dynamics of how a hurricane destroys a home. It begins with a single missile penetrating a window. Once that happens you're screwed. Air instantly fills the house, and within seconds there's enough of it to push the roof off the walls.

I suddenly hear a loud scraping sound outside on the concrete of the driveway. It's a sound I don't know, and I hop up from the couch and look out the window.

It's Rod. He has pushed the Porta-Potty up against two big clumps of areca palms, and he's tying it to the trees with a long line of green rope.

I run to my bedroom and pull on my boots and join him outside.

"I've never seen a palm tree get blown over in a storm," he says, finishing the knot. "If my house goes, I'm tying me and my wife to one of these. . . . Sorry you had to cart all that crap inside by yourself. I should have been here to help you."

"I had help," I say.

"I'm here to make it up to you."

He points to his truck, its bed filled with big sheets of plywood, stacked on their sides like giant soda crackers.

"Oh, man," I say. "You're a vision. I could kiss you."

"You got some work gloves?" he asks.

I shake my head. Even though I'd owned a landscaping business, I was the architect and boss. I pitched in and got my hands
dirty at times, but, truth be told, I rarely worked with the planting
crews. Honestly, I just don't like getting my hands or feet dirty—I
never have. I don't mind fresh mud, but when dirt dries on me . . .
yikes, I hate that! I just don't like that gritty feel, it gives me the
heebie-jeebies, like chalk screeching on a blackboard. (Maybe
there's a connection there; chalk, like fine sand, is gritty.)

Mom has told stories of me as a child and how I would try to
clean my dusty bare feet by licking my palm and using it as a cloth.
Honestly, this is one reason I don't mind housework. It's wet work,
for the most part, Windex and soaps and ammonia, lots of rinsing
things clean.

Rod walks to his truck and unlocks the shiny steel bin flanking
the rear of the cab. This kind of storage unit on pickups has always
reminded me of saddlebags on a horse.

He opens it, then pulls out a pair of creased, dirty, brown leather
gloves. He throws them at me, overhanded, as one would throw a
baseball. They separate midair, but I catch them both.

"This stuff'll eat your hands alive," he says, and he shuts and re-
locks the bin. "You'll need those." I hold the gloves up to my nose.
They smell of dirt and sweat and pine resin and rawhide.

"You're not wearing any?" I ask.

He smiles and holds up his callused hands. "Don't need 'em."

We carry the first five sheets of plywood out back, to the patio on
the water.

"You sure picked this place clean," he says.

"Thank you."

Over the next several minutes we develop a system. Rod is the
man with the power tool, I'm the guy who holds the plywood. After
we lift the board into place, I hold it there while he drills all the
holes, then changes bits and power-drills in all the blue Tapcon

screws. It goes remarkably fast. We average a window every four minutes.

"That thing's incredible," I say. "My drill didn't even move in this stuff. It was like drilling into rock."

"That's what it is," he says. "Concrete is pulverized lime-stone."

"Yeah, but yours sinks right in . . . like the house is sponge cake."

"Did you already try this?" he asks.

"I just dabbled. I didn't know what the hell I was doing so I quit."

"Did you use a masonry bit?"

"Yeah. I got one at the Ace Hardware."

"With a hammer drill?"

"Aren't all drills hammer drills?"

He looks at me quizzically, as if I'm pulling his leg.

"Man, I don't know this stuff, Rod. You're speaking a foreign language to me. A cheese soufflé, hell yes, I can do that, but not this."

"There is no way you can penetrate this old concrete stucco with a regular drill. A hammer drill has dual action. It rotates, but it's also got a pounding action. That's why it's got a rougher sound. . . . Here," he says, and hands me the drill. "We're almost done. You do the last few windows."

"Oh, no, I can't do that."

"Yeah, you can. It's easy."

"No, that thing intimidates me. I don't mind being the board bitch, I really don't."

Again, I've surprised him. If I can do anything, it's make Rod smile, and I don't think it is a common action for him. It's not that he's a scowler, he's just not a smiler. A smile looks unnatural on him, forced and labored, as if someone had brushed his cheeks with egg whites and they'd dried and stiffened when he was in a neutral, nonsmile position.

But right now he is smiling. Big. I don't believe I've ever seen his back molars before. It appears he's missing the last one on the upper right side.

"Board bitch?" he says.

"Kind of like a shower bitch," I explain.

"Shower bitch?"

"The woman at the wedding or baby shower who gets stuck writing down all the presents and who they're from."

"That's one I haven't heard. . . . Here," he says, handing me the drill. "You might want to use two hands at first. Keep a very steady right angle."

I hold the drill in my hand. It's the same model used by almost all the subcontractors, a yellow-and-black DeWalt whose streamlined size belies its power. It really doesn't look much bigger than some of the morphed-out electric toothbrushes you see these days. I'm surprised at how light it is. I move it around, lifting it high and from side to side as if playing with a toy airplane, pleased at the freedom I'm allowed by having no cord. I squeeze the trigger a few times to get a feel for it. I'll be damned if I'm going to use two hands—mine are bigger than his. Still, I'm not sure what to expect, recalling very well the unsuccessful attempt with my regular power drill the day before, which broke the paint-surface of the stucco and then stopped short, despite my leaning into it with most of my body weight.

I am expecting a fight. I am secretly damming up all my upper-body strength and getting ready to open the floodgates so it all can come rushing into my right arm. I take a deep breath, touch the tip of the drill bit to the *x* that Rod has marked on the wall—I'm shaking just a little right now—and with every ounce of concentrated energy I can muster I push into the wall and pull the trigger, wincing at the ratchety noise and vibration that travels up my arms and into my shoulder, tickling my breastbone.

Less than two seconds later, Rod yells, "Whoa, man! Stop! You're in."

"I'm in?"

"Open your eyes. Look. You're at the hilt. Now pull out. No . . . squeeze the trigger to pull out. Otherwise you'll bust that bit off. . . . Come on . . . We've got two more windows, and then we've got my house to do."

I make another hole, and another and another. I no longer wince at the sound and vibration but find myself hungrily absorbing it. Why does this feel so good? All of a sudden I understand Tim on *Home Improvement*, which I've been watching lately, and his mantra of, "Yeaahhhh, more powerrrrr!"

It's more than phallic symbolism, although you can't ignore the similarities. I am getting the chance to ruin something (in fact, I am destroying this once-perfect stucco) just as all little boys like to do . . . only I'm doing it with the purpose of completing a bona fide task. If you look at it, construction is made up of little acts of satisfying violence, piecemeal destruction for the sake of an overall, larger project. Manipulation of one's environment.

Hey . . . MAN-ipulation! I'm sure there's some linguistic relationship there.

After driving for nearly half an hour, we finally turn off of County Road 858 and onto an unpaved, private, dirt road that winds through undeveloped, subtropical pine forest, thick with scrub palmetto, untrimmed sabal palms, and towering, ancient live oaks that form a dark canopy. It is hairy and wild, so unlike the tamed, Disney-like landscape of Naples. I roll down my window and stick out my arm. The temperature must be fifteen degrees cooler in this shady spot.

I thought of telling Rod about Jessica when we passed the turnoff to her house, but there really wasn't much to say. I moved the tree for her, onto some newspaper in her living room. I guess I wanted to share the encounter with him because of the Daisy Duke outfit she wore when I was there. Short-short cutoff jeans and a shirt tied at the waist and unbuttoned far enough to tease. No bra, either. She's got bigger boobs than Jo has. And strong-looking legs, almost beefy. You can tell she used to play college volleyball.

After moving the plant, I also reset her jammed garbage disposal for her and moved a dresser in the bedroom. She was so grateful and sweet. I don't know why Violet doesn't like Jessica. She's got a great spirit. Great smile, too.

After a curve here and there Rod and I finally enter a sunny clearing, and when I see Rod's house I instantly realize that hanging the plywood—that's the verb contractors use for installing plywood and Sheetrock: hanging—here will be a much more formidable task. The home is on pilings, the windows a good twenty feet off the ground. I'm just hoping to God we don't have to get on the roof.

We drive down a gravel path and stop in the driveway. Rod gets out of the truck and walks into the yard. He puts his hands on his hips and cocks his head, frowning in contemplation as he studies the house.

Saying nothing, he disappears into a room underneath the house and comes out with two extension ladders, one in each hand as if they're nothing more than moderately heavy suitcases.

He sets these on the grass and disappears inside again, this time coming back with a handful of shiny, silver hooks that still have the adhesive price tags attached to them.

"Get that drill," he tells me. "I want you to put on the biggest bit and drill a hole in the middle of each sheet of plywood, up closer to the top edge, though. Understand?"

"Board bitch to drill stud in one hour," I say. "Man, that's progress."

He leaves again and comes back with a long coil of rope and another cordless drill. He loops the rope around his neck, picks up one of the ladders and leans it against the house. He climbs to the top and drills a hole over one of the windows. Into this he screws one of the hooks.

I'm good at visualizing, it's why I was a great landscape designer, but visualizing as an artist is altogether different from visualizing as an engineer. I've learned this from watching Rod. An artist visualizes in a way in which function follows form. The engineer-type visualizes the other way around: performance first, beauty second. I think this is the main sticking point between architects and contractors, and the very source of tension between the two of them during construction of a project. The architect knows what he wants the house to look like. It's up to the contractor to manipulate the rules of the physical world to make that come true, and quite often it's physically challenging, or impossible, to do.

It's more than that, though. Guys like Rod have brains that just see things in a different way. Something I view as whole and intact they instantly see as a thousand different pieces, aware of the relationships between them all and what would happen if one were to fall out of the equation. I'm just in awe of that.

He yells at me to bring him the first piece of plywood. I oblige, soon wishing I still had the pair of gloves on. As I feel a sliver of wood push into my forefinger I decide to grin and bear it and say nothing.

"Loop the end of that rope through the hole in the plywood," he says. "Make a good knot."

"Aha!" it finally dawns on me. "A little pulley action."

"Yep."

Using the hook as a pulley he pulls the rope, lifting the board.

When it is hovering before the window he yells, "There's an apron in that toolbox on the floor just inside my shop. Fill it with Tapcons and put it on. Then grab that drill and get your ass up here."

I go into Rod's shop and pull the string on the fluorescent light on the ceiling, revealing a big workroom the size of half his house. People do this in Florida. If you live in a flood plain—and a good chunk of us do down here—you must build your house on pilings as Rod has done. By law you're not supposed to have any "living space" beneath it, but in this Land of No Basements it's just too tempting to leave it be. As Rod has done, most people use half the space to park their cars out of the sun, and they build some sort of storeroom on the other.

I am not surprised to find Rod's workshop Spartan, fastidiously organized with a clean floor. A regulation fire extinguisher hangs on one stud, a first-aid kit below that. There's even one of those emergency eye-wash centers you use in case of chemicals gone awry.

All the lumber is neatly sorted by size in a corner of the room, the longer, skinnier pieces set end-down, like uncooked fettuccini in a glass, in empty plastic buckets that once held spackling compound. The only sign of disarray lies on the main workbench, a disassembled small engine of some kind. For some reason it looks more hobby than work-related to me. Is it its diminutive size or the fact that he leaves it here, unfinished, as my family once left big jigsaw puzzles on a card table in the living room?

In another corner is an exposed toilet on a plywood pedestal, hooked up to the drainpipe that obviously comes down from a bathroom or kitchen somewhere above. The toilet-paper roll is a sawed-off piece of metal pipe suspended by a piece of wire that runs through it. I walk over and look through the pile of magazines piled neatly at the toilet's side. There is no porn but plenty of back issues of *Custom Builder* and *Popular Mechanics* . . . also one copy of *People,* which surprises me. It's a rack copy, there's no subscription label on the cover. I wonder if he or his wife bought it. And then I wonder why they never had children, and if the reason his wife is so obsessed with orchids is because she's infertile and incapable of building life within her own body. It would make sense for a nurturer from a childless couple to immerse herself in the task of propagating rare orchids that so many others can't reproduce.

I see Rod's tool belt—he must have more than one—on a counter against the wall. I walk over and pick it up. It's heavier than I thought it would be. The hammer and other larger tools dangle from it like charms on a giant's bracelet.

I put it around my waist and buckle it in front, and look around for a reflection of myself. I finally find one in a pane of glass leaning against a piling, and I pose in front of it, hooking my thumbs in the belt as I've seen Rod do at my house.

All of a sudden I feel a slight burn in my chest and heart, and I realize I've been taking shallow, insufficient breaths to minimize my presence, just as I did when Violet and I used to play hide-and-seek and she'd open the closet door and I'd be hiding behind the long coats in front of her, just inches away.

Which reminds me: *I wonder if I did Violet any favors by not letting her win at games like that. I know that moms always fake losing for their kids, but doesn't that create a false sense of superiority? How are kids to improve and become the strongest, most competitive adults when you've created in them a false sense of accomplishment and ability?*

Which reminds me: *Ask Violet about the false eyelashes I found in her jeans pocket last week.*

Which reminds me: *Teach Violet how to do laundry so I don't have to.*

Which reminds me: *Test-drive Toyota Tundra pickup.*

Rod yells from outside. "Get a move on it!"

I scurry to take the belt off and replace it with the canvas apron filled with screws, and I return outside.

"Sorry," I say. "I saw the toilet and realized I had to pee."

As directed, I erect the second ladder a few feet from his and slowly ascend. I'm glad I have my boots on. The heels snugly fit against the rungs as they would in stirrups.

We slowly work our way around the house, ascending and descending ladders, pulling sheets of plywood up with the rope. Rod drills and screws his half of the board and then hands the drill over to me for my half. This works very well until the last window.

Up to this point I had been using the ladder on the right, but for some reason Rod climbs the right one this time and I am forced to use the left, which soon proves to be a problem. I've been working out, yes, and I'm stronger than I've ever been, but I'm still left-handed. I'm also very tired by this point, and when I start an anemic attempt to make my new set of holes with my lesser hand Rod immediately senses my problem.

"Get the ones closest to you," he says. "I can stretch and get the others."

It is on the last screw, the farthest from his comfortable center of gravity, when Rod gets into trouble. With the drill bit embedded in the wall he steps on the orange extension cord, pulling the drill's plug free and cutting off the power. The longer orange lifeline drops to the ground, banging against the rungs of the ladder on the way down, and Rod can't pull the drill from the wall because he has no juice to turn and loosen the bit.

He wiggles it a little and curses. Wiggles again, but very carefully, so as not to break off the bit.

And, then, something seems to snap in him. He's obviously surprised and pissed that he can't retract this drill, and he goes at it again, this time not giving in, and within fifteen seconds he resembles an angry, clenched fist. The muscles in his shoulder, especially the medial and anterior delts, swell and ripple under the strain. His face has turned crimson, his eyes squinted in overexertion. The veins in his neck, now coursing with blood, push and twitch at skin level.

But I don't really grasp the strength behind all this until the bit suddenly pops free, and when this happens Rod's arm flies back with such a force that the tool is catapulted from his hand. I turn to watch it soar through the air, over my shoulder, but this lasts just a second because I soon see from the corner of my other eye that Rod has also kicked away the ladder—it is falling away from him—and as he is going down he instinctively reaches up toward me. I grab for an arm, miss, then fortuitously snatch his belt.

He dangles for a second or two, suspended in my frantic clutch, as his ladder crashes to the ground like a fallen pine tree. After a few more seconds, he gets his bearings and grabs and straddles the underside of my ladder. And then, as if he were on the monkey bars on a playground, he descends the ladder, rung by rung, until it is safe to drop to his feet.

Rod bends over and rests his palms on his knees, breathing heavily. After several moments he finally looks up at me.

"You okay?" he yells.

I have so much adrenaline running through my body that I feel as if I've been electrified. I am light-headed. My scalp and fingers, once tingling, have begun to itch because the blood that just seconds ago was pounding at the terminus of my extremities has again retreated. My heart pounds so loudly it seems to resonate on my palate.

I try to answer him, but I can't. My windpipe is raspy and cold and drained of all moisture. I taste blood in my mouth.

"Linc!" he yells again, and I'm a little embarrassed because it is he who should be emotionally incapacitated right now, not me. I wave at him with a *yeah, yeah, yeah, I'm fine just shut up I can't talk right now.*

I finally climb back down, and Rod is there. He puts his arm around my shoulders. "Man! Holy shit! I owe you one."

I look at him, surprised. "No, you don't. You fell because I couldn't drill my own holes."

"I fell because I wasn't being smart," he replies. "I should have gone back down and moved the ladder."

Suddenly I smell something, a sweet yet salty odor that every caregiver knows all too well.

"Oh, maaaaaan," I moan.

"What?"

I look down at my wet crotch. I expect Rod to laugh, but he's very cool about it.

"That's completely understandable," he says. "Happened to me one time in a motorcycle wreck."

God—I've peed my pants!

"No big deal," Rod says. "Get over it. . . . Come on. You can't walk around like that."

He takes me to the stairway on the east side of the house, and I soon learn of a secret room he has made beneath the stairs by making walls of lattice laced with healthy Confederate jasmine. He pushes on a cedar half-door, on spring hinges, like the ones on saloons in the movies, and I step inside. It is an outdoor shower and, next to it, an old, white claw-foot tub, also with plumbing. For a floor he has laid randomly sized and shaped pieces of sandstone, letting natural grasses and weeds fill in the cracks. There's also a small white sink and an old-looking round mirror hanging on the lattice wall over that. On the sink's deck is a shaving brush and an honest-to-God straight-edge razor just like the one Mr. Hoyt uses on me at the barbershop.

"This is too cool," I say.

"There's nothing like showering outside."

"Your wife likes that?"

He shakes his head. "The bathroom upstairs is hers. This is mine. It's a his and hers thing. . . . That towel on the rack's clean, the yellow one. Use that. I'll get you some clothes."

"You sure you don't mind?"

"Don't be a jerk, Linc. You saved my neck."

As I turn on the water and step into the stream I notice Rod walking up the stairs and into the house. The cool water feels good—there's no such thing as bracing, cold water from a tap in the subtropics—and I don't even turn on the hot.

I must have been washing my hair when he came back down because when I turn off the water there is a pair of fresh blue jeans, some white Jockey briefs, and a blue T-shirt sitting on the wooden stool beside the swinging door. I've always worn boxer shorts, haven't worn briefs since before puberty, and I soon discover that I prefer the briefs. I like how they cradle my package instead of having everything hang all loose. I can see how these also would be good in hot weather, absorbing sweat, and I vow to get to the mall ASAP and buy ten pair.

I find Rod in his shop. He has retrieved the drill and is cleaning it up with a white rag. He looks up when I come in.

"Jeans are tight, but they'll get me home," I say. "Thanks for sharing."

"Can't go yet," he says.

Rod stands up from the workbench and walks over to another cupboard. He pulls out a nearly full bottle of Jack Daniels.

"I don't do much of this," he says, "but I sure need some today."

We sit down on two folding chairs, and he pulls the cork-top from the bottle and hands it to me. I hesitate, wondering if I should wait for a glass, but when he doesn't move I realize I'm supposed to take a draw from the bottle itself.

I've never acquired a taste for straight booze—wine's always been my thing—but I take a swig. The fiery liquid burns my throat for a moment but within seconds is warming my stomach. It leaves a sweet flavor on my tongue. I can taste that this brown liquor was born from corn mash.

I hand the bottle back to Rod. He takes a drink and rests the bottle on his thigh, his fingers wrapped around the thick square base of the bottle.

"Where's your wife?" I ask. "I'm sorry, I can't remember her name. Nancy?"

Rod takes another drink and hands the bottle back to me.

"Kristi," he answers. "She left yesterday. Packed up her orchids and headed to her folks' in North Carolina to get out of the storm."

"Jo's camped out at the hospital," I say.

And then I remember Violet, at home. I didn't tell her where I was going. I reach for my cell and discover I left it at home. "Can I use your phone?" I ask.

Rod unclips his cell phone holster from his jeans and tosses it to me. I look at my watch, it's nearly five o'clock. I call Violet and tell her there's some leftover dinner from the night before. I realize, however, that she'll probably opt for a few bowls of Captain Crunch with Crunchberries. She has made no secret of hating my pressure-cooker meals lately. Jo, too, seems to have more business dinners these days.

I've got to find something to make cooking easier. It just takes too much time, and time is something I don't have. I don't like to cook anymore. It's a pain in the ass. I need a timesaver because I'm spending so much time on the house . . . on these subcontractors' butts. Hence, the meals these days are kind of piecemeal and predictable.

Last week, Sean The Painter made the mistake of divulging to me in casual conversation the location of another job he was working, on Cajuput Road up in Bonita Springs. When he didn't show up for three successive days I Mapquested the street, hopped in the van, and drove the forty-some minutes to hunt him down. You should have seen how shocked he was to see me leaning against his van in that driveway.

And then last week, I stopped Mike The Electrician from leaving the house by parking the Man Van behind him. When he asked me to move it I asked him why he was leaving. When he said he needed a part, I promptly offered to drive to Graybar Electric myself and get it for him. As I pulled away, I saw him pull out his cell phone and talk to someone with a look of disappointment on his face . . . obviously a friend who would have to go fishing without him on that fine day. These are the kinds of things that are taking so much of my time.

We pass the bottle back and forth, like pirates drinking rum. It's pretty obvious the incident on the ladder has rattled us both. Before "the Jack," as Rod calls it, my muscle strains and scrapes had started making themselves known, as something roasting in the oven begins giving off an aroma once it hits a certain temperature. But, thankfully, as the adrenaline that masked our injuries begins to ebb, the bourbon moves in to numb them again.

We're sitting on the workbench, and I find myself leaning my head back, against the wall, closing my eyes as the two of us talk.

Over the past few days we've both been hovering over the National Hurricane Center's Web site, checking the updates at 5 A.M., 11 A.M., 2 P.M., and again at 5 P.M., and we now share our opinions on the different meteorologists and how their reports vary in tone. They always sign their dispatches with the word "meteorologist," in place of their first names, so all we know is their surnames.

"I like Steyman," Rod says. "He's right to the point."

"Rodriguez is my favorite," I say. "He's got that musical quality to his writing. I wonder if it's because English is his second language."

"That other guy. Starts with a P. He's too scientific. Too hard to understand."

We talk about other things. I want to know his opinion on trucks, and I ask him questions about the private lives of the subcontractors. (I knew my intuition was right about Ted The Stucco Guy: Apparently he's been in and out of rehab these past few years.)

He asks me about high-sun groundcover options for the north side of his house, and then this leads to a fascinating discussion of the wild hogs that frequently emerge from the scrub forest around his house and dig through his yard, looking for grubs. If he catches them in the act Rod says he oftentimes will hop onto his four-wheeler and chase them back into the forest, shooting a gun in the air to scare them.

"Sons-a-bitches," he says. "They're destructive as hell. Sometimes I'm tempted to shoot 'em, but I don't want to have to clean 'em."

"Can you eat them?" I ask.

He shakes his head.

"Way too gamy. Some people might, but no way. Not me."

I take a smaller drink so I do not hasten the ending to this very wonderful moment.

"Man, Rod, your world is so different from mine."

He cocks his head in curiosity, which is most likely a feigned reaction. After four months of construction, the man knows us and our lifestyle, our habits and patterns probably better than God himself. But I will humor him. He's a curious guy; I think he truly wants to know my take on this.

"You know . . . guns and boy toys and this whole Man Kingdom underneath the house. Rod, I have never driven a motorcycle, I've never even ridden on one. I've never held a gun. I've never worked a circular saw or band saw or whatever the hell that scary thing is called that cuts through plywood."

I take another drink and give a deep sigh.

"Do you know what I did today? This morning I had to go to three different grocery stores to find suntan-colored L'eggs sandal-foot pantyhose. Do you even know what that is? Let me enlighten you. Sandal-foot pantyhose don't have the reinforced toe in them—you know, that darker patch on the toes—so they look better when your feet are exposed. Pretty fascinating stuff, huh? That's my life, Bud."

He starts to smile but catches himself and stops, probably thinking he'll offend me.

"That doesn't make much sense," he finally says.

"What?"

"Well, if you look at the foot, especially with high heels . . . all that weight is put on the ball of the foot near the toes. You'd need reinforcement there. I mean, the other variable'd be the toenails themselves. They'd easily cut through nylon that isn't reinforced. Why would they have pantyhose that's designed to fail? That just doesn't make sense."

My eyes closed, I'm nodding my head in agreement: No, it doesn't make sense. So, so much of it doesn't make sense anymore, and it used to. I have dwelled in GirlyLand for nearly fourteen years now, and I have adjusted to the subtle, secret language. I know when my wife or daughter feels fat during menstruation by the way she unconsciously drapes her forearm over her stomach as if she's injured herself. I know that a woman's yes doesn't necessarily mean yes, that indeed a yes might even be a no, transmitted by the way she looks away, obliquely, when she says it, or the manner in which she lets her hair fall into her face. I know that when

Dawn The Dry Cleaner asks me if I want the clothes on Wednesday or Thursday that it's my duty to choose the latter because I'm expected as a caregiver to do anything I can do to make a girl's life easier. Most men would say they needed them on Wednesday, even if they didn't. I am very tempted at times, let me tell you.

I have learned how my daughter's day can be ruined or salvaged by a combination of internal and external forces: what someone said to her the day before . . . a new, never-tried-but-successful combination of a particular purse and shoes and skirt . . . the melancholy created by walking past the stump of an old oak tree that's been felled to widen a road.

"Let me ask you something," I say. "Do you ever do the laundry?"

He shakes his head.

"Cook?" I ask.

"Grill," he says.

"Ah, of course. . . . You ever buy a wedding gift for someone?"

He shakes his head again.

"Buy a throw pillow? . . . (shake) . . . braid a girl's hair? . . . (shake) . . . Take dinner to a sick neighbor?"

He shakes his head again, this time smiling as if he's been caught in a benign lie. "Kristi does all that. I do my thing, she does hers. I take care of the cars, she takes care of the house."

"I wish it was that simple for me," I say. "You can't pigeonhole yourself like that when you're the caregiver."

Rod motions for me to hand him the bottle and takes another drink. I find his constant, blank poker-face reaction both calming and maddening. It is maddening not knowing what he is thinking, but the absence of a reaction sends the message that all is fine, no matter what you've done or said, and that whatever emotion has grabbed and strangled you soon will lose its grip and drop away and leave you alone.

"I really thought all this would work out just fine, Jo working and me at home. But I'll tell you what, man, it's confusing as hell sometimes. . . . I don't even stand up to pee anymore, Rod. I'm the only one who splatters in the house, and if I sit then I won't have to clean the toilets as often. Is that messed up, or what?"

Instantly unhappy that I shared that last comment, I can't look him in the eye. I scrutinize and pick at a dried spot of superglue on my shirt that's been there for two years or so, when I dripped while fixing the porcelain head of the baby in Violet's dollhouse. We sit there, silent, as we do in the barbershop, for two or three minutes before Rod finally speaks.

"Do you need to get home?" he asks.

"Yeah, probably," I answer. "I need some water, though. Let me get a drink out of the hose."

"Nah, I've got a better idea."

Rod hops down from the bench. "You've never shot a gun?" he asks.

"No."

"You want to?"

"Excuse me?"

"You want to shoot?"

"Yeah, I . . . I guess."

"Well come on then."

Rod swats at the dust on his butt.

"You want a rifle or a handgun?"

"What do you think I should use?"

He purses his lips in thought for a moment. "How about a thirty-eight?"

"And that's a pistol, right?"

"Last time I checked it was."

He retrieves the gun and a box of bullets from a locked oak

cabinet in the shop. We then hop into an old, blue, open-air Jeep.

"My swamp buggy," he says.

I sit there for a moment, waiting for us to make a fun, jerking start, and then Rod says, "Put on your seatbelt."

I note they are much newer than the Jeep, a nonmatching maroon that has not yet been faded by the sun.

We soon are bouncing through the shaded woodlands. There is no path, but Rod seems to know his way as he winds around palmetto brush and stands of cypress trees and low-lying lakelets of mucky water. There are no doors in this Jeep, and if it weren't for the seatbelt I would have probably bounced out by now. I feel light and free, as if we are breaking the rules with no fear of getting caught. College . . . it feels like college . . . one of those spontaneous, untethered outings fueled by alcohol and testosterone.

Grasping the roll bar, I shout a loud howl into the forest—"Whoooooaaaaaahhhhhhh!"—until I'm dizzy from lack of oxygen.

We reach a clearing and stop the Jeep.

"Is this your land?" I ask.

"Very edge of it," he answers. "Everything up to that stake over there."

The clearing is long and thin, and at the end is a man-made embankment of earth as tall as me. In front of this are three wooden pilings peppered with staples that trap small scraps of paper.

From the glove compartment—and isn't a renaming of that handy cubbyhole long overdue?—Rod pulls out a staple gun and a rolled-up target. We walk the twenty or so yards to the pilings, and he unrolls and staples the paper target to the middle pole. It's a simple design of circles that shrink as they move toward the center, alternating black and white. It reminds me very much of the geometric drawings I taped on the rungs of Violet's crib for visual stimulation. I did these things a lot when she was so young, though everyone made fun of me. Another trick was dumping into her bathtub a bucket of small foam letters so that Violet bathed each night in what looked like alphabet soup. Laugh all you want, but that girl knew her alphabet by the time she was two, both the appearance and sound of every letter . . . also diphthongs.

We walk back to the Jeep. Rod reaches beneath the seat and pulls out two sets of noise-suppression earphones. He tosses one to me.

He then deftly loads the chamber—I'm not sure what else to call it—of the gun with seven bullets, and, with a snap of his wrist, clicks it back into place, frowning in concentration the whole time.

He brings the earphones up from where they rest on his neck and puts them on. I quickly do the same.

Rod then spreads his legs shoulder-width, grips the gun with two hands and fires off three shots. The explosions startle me, and I jump back.

"Damn!" he curses. "Still shaky from that fall."

He rolls his neck a few times to stretch out the muscles, then shoots off the final four rounds. When I open my eyes I see that he has pierced the inner three circles of the target.

"Okay . . . now you."

"I don't know, man," I say. "I really don't need to do it. I get a kick out of watching you. Very cool. Really, that's enough for me. Go ahead."

"No, Linc, you're gonna shoot this thing. There's nothing to be afraid of."

"What about the kick?" I ask. "Doesn't it hurt?"

"There's no kick with a thirty-eight. Come on."

My breath is shallow, my heart racing as he grabs my hand,

turns it upright, and sets the gun in my palm. I'm surprised at how heavy it is, about the weight of my lava-stone pestle in my kitchen at home.

I load the barrel as Rod showed me, my hands slightly shaking, afraid the bullets will explode in my hands if I touch them a certain way. You need to know something here: I wasn't even allowed to own a slingshot or popgun as a child. My mom was determined to make me a pacifist. Talking, not fighting, she said, would usher the human race into the Age of Aquarius.

"Now take the proper position," Rod says.

I have trouble wrapping my fingers around the gun in the proper way—Rod moves in and manually puts them into place—and I can't help but wonder if I'm having trouble making the connection because this object seems to be from another world. Indeed, I have only seen guns in make-believe scenarios, on TV and in the movies. They are as surreal to me as Farrah Fawcett's lips or a sorcerer's magic wand.

I smell gunpowder for the first time, and it drives home the reality that what I have in my hand is a deadly weapon. If I wanted to, I could stick the barrel in my mouth and kill myself right now. Bang! Just like that. Or I could take this gun, point it at Rod and kill him, beginning a domino effect of human suffering that would start with his wife and parents, then ripple outward to friends, acquaintances, community. I feel both frightened and empowered by the life-changing potential of this thing I hold.

Squinting and still shaky, I fire the first shot. The bullet misses the target and buries itself in the dirt wall behind it, emitting an unceremonious light-brown puff. But the sensation surprises me. It does not feel like a simple "bang" or "pop." It is a complex and universal sensorial experience, leaving an electrical tingling in the fingers, the wrist and collarbone, the gut and gonads and nipples, down to the toes and along the walls of the inner ears. It is akin to standing beside an immense, thunderous waterfall, the power penetrating my body not only through sound but also vibration and smell and touch. Okay, the Jack Daniels is probably responsible for some of this euphoria, but still . . .

I fire a few more rounds and manage to rip a hole in the bottom corner of the target.

"Rod! I hit it! Look!"

Twelves round later, I get a bull's-eye.

"I had a feeling you'd be good at this," Rod says.

"I love this!"

I'm jittery with excitement and do a little jig. Rod looks down at my feet and laughs.

Linc Menner's Handy Hints for Caregiver Sanity

Hint #374

Talk your wife and daughters into showering at the gym on hair-wash day. This may require some careful monitoring of their hair-washing schedule, but it cuts down on all the long hair that dirties up the bathroom and also helps keep the shower and bathtub drains running faster.

23

Jessica

Violet's not doing real good in English. Oh, it's still B work, and sometimes As, but what I'm having trouble with now is keeping her attention.

There's a boy two seats behind her—Robert Fugate—that's got it real bad for her, and she flirts with him just as much. They pass notes all the time. And I'm just really interested in this change because all year long she's been a serious student with icy stares that could have just about killed a boy.

She's wearing makeup now, and the other day she wore a jean skirt that for sure broke the Collier Academy rule for length. You know . . . the arm test? If you think a skirt's too short you have the girl hang her hands down her side, and if the skirt hits above their fingertips it's too short. Of course most of them shrug their shoulders up when you ask them to do this, and that's good for a couple of inches. And of course we don't call them on this most of the time because it's not worth putting up with the screaming mom who has to interrupt her shopping at Waterside Shops to bring in a pair of pants.

Violet's still a real nice girl, she doesn't get sassy and all high-and-mighty like some of the others. These prep-school kids, they've got this sense of entitlement, like they were royalty or something. You can tell they're never told "no" at home, and that their mommas and daddies all think they're better than the rest of us. I'll tell you what—it's not good when a student drives a nicer car than his teacher does. That parking lot is filled with brand-spanking-new BMWs and Audis. Violet's not like that. Linc's done a good job raising that girl. I'm not even sure she has an iPod yet. Maybe she does, but I don't think so.

She's turned into such a social butterfly it's starting to affect her schoolwork. Mr. Workman—her math teacher?—he told me he's fixing to drop her down to a C in his class. That's when we have to send home a special report to the parents . . . when they drop below a B.

Anyway, none of this made sense to me until Violet brought in her essay. I gave it an A. I just loved the secrets it shared.

The Metamorphosis

My father is definitely the most influential person in my life because I am around him so often. My dad, unlike most, is a stay-at-home parent while my mom is the one who works outside the house. Dad does the laundry, cleans, cooks, waters plants, and makes lunches. He takes me shopping, gives the cat her medicine, and sews the buttons back on clothes. He is your typical "housewife," and always has been. In a way, he is like both a mother and a father to me because he has the qualities of both. I have always had two sets of parents: a mom who is also a dad and a dad who is also a mom. However, now it seems as if I am losing one of the parents who has helped me grow for so long.

Dad used to always take pride in his job as caregiver. He would micromanage everything, down to the last detail. He would scrub the floors on his hands and knees with a wet rag until they gleamed because a mop didn't do a good enough job. He would prepare new meals every night from an assortment of foreign cookbooks, and brag to my mom about how he had helped me find a pair of black dress shoes that fit. Now, however, something is different. It seems like my dad is trying to act more like a man.

The first time I noticed this was when the construction crew began working on our house. Every time Dad needed to talk to Rod, the head of construction, he would deepen his voice and put on some sort of swagger, like a cowboy in an old western. I think he looks up to Rod because he is so macho. He bought a pair of black work boots identical to Rod's, and never wears his clogs anymore. He now goes to the gym five times a week to lift weights, and he has subscribed to Muscle and Fitness Magazine when he used to be content with the Stairmaster with his retired friends at the Wellness Center. Sadly, he doesn't even like to cook anymore. He throws a bunch of random pieces of food into the pressure cooker and calls that a meal.

Despite the mushy, tasteless meals, Dad's new bout of manliness has its perks. I am now allowed to buy sugared cereal. We also just recently got cable, which Dad used to complain about incessantly. I thought that he would only let me watch The Discovery Channel or Animal Planet, but I put on MTV Spring Break while he was sitting with me and he didn't care. I rarely have a chance to watch TV though. Dad is always on the couch, watching Spike TV, the manliest channel on the planet. He has abandoned The Food Network. I recently caught him watching a show with a blond bimbo in an American flag bikini teaching how to shoot a machine gun.

One thing about Dad's new image that unnerves me is that he seems to be ashamed of me. We used to have heated debates and discussions when he drove me to school in the minivan, but *now we sit in silence except for the occasional "What did you do at school today?" It seems like he treats me like a leper or at least like someone he wants to distance himself from. However, this doesn't bother me too much. I need to be more independent and like hanging out with friends more often. I guess it's normal that we go our separate ways.*

Despite the recent changes in him, my father continues to be the most influential person in my life, and always will be. His new characteristics help me develop in new ways. We both affect each other and that, in my opinion, is what makes someone the most important person in your life.

Part II

24

Jo

Arturo wobbled like a drunken sailor trying to find his way
back to port. He was headed right for us and then wobbled
once, twice, three times toward the north before continuing his
eastward path. It was good news for us here in Naples but horrific
news for the poor people of Manatee County.

Arturo slammed into the peninsula as a Category Four. It will
take months for normal life to resume up there. The wind peeled
off nearly the entire roof of Bay Pointe Hospital. We immediately
sent up a maintenance van filled with bottled water and four men
with chain saws to help clean up tree debris at employees' homes.

Linc's reaction to the near miss was intriguing to say the least. In
the days that followed he hung around the house and seemed to
pout all day, as if the men of the village had all gone off to war and
he'd been told he was too young and had to stay home with the
women and children.

I went out of my way to praise him for his preparedness. I
stressed that it had not been all in vain. I even shared with him a
clipping from the newspaper about the errant, airborne coconut
that crashed through a Sarasota taxi driver's windshield and killed
him. I pointed out that if Arturo hadn't wobbled the way he did we
would have been safer than anyone for miles around because he'd

dutifully denuded the landscape of all potential missiles. (Lincoln even took the hubcaps off the van, thinking they might pop off and go sailing down the street.)

In some ways, I wish Arturo would have smacked us head-on, as planned. Lord knows my job would have been hell, but we might have been able to abandon this awful torn-up house and leave it for the bulldozers as we should have done Day One. I stepped on a nail three nights ago in the hall and had to stop by the ER for a tetanus the next morning. Of course I didn't tell Linc because he would have lectured me about not wearing hard-soled shoes 24-7 in the house, as we've been instructed to do, oh, at least six thousand times.

Sorry. I'm just so weary of all this. Every woman must endure such stages now and then when her husband slips away, if not physically then certainly emotionally, as he wanders about in a fog, searching for something of which he has no idea.

But this particular phase of Lincoln's, this wobble, if you will, is testing me—me and Violet, actually—as we've never been tested.

For years (thirteen for Violet and nearly nineteen for me) Lincoln has been nothing less than omniscient. He has monitored both Violet's and my needs with a sixth sense, filling them even before we ourselves recognize them. In all our years together, I can't remember ever running out of tampons, pantyhose, or cotton balls. Maybe once, but no more than that.

One time, about five years ago, Lincoln wondered if I was deficient in iron, sensed by a slight change in my skin color and energy level. He'd ask me what I ate on the road and then fashioned meals that made up the nutritional deficit while I was at home.

Imagine having a stay-at-home parent watching you that closely, being that tuned in to your needs and performance for your entire life. And then, suddenly, he drops you to the ground and walks away. This appears to be what Lincoln has done these past several weeks, and it should come as no surprise that Violet would react the way she has.

I discovered Violet's late-night adventures about a week ago when I came home and noticed the muddy handprint on the edge of her window, outside, on the wall of the house. My first instinct was that it belonged to either Linc or Rod from when they put up the plywood. But when I left the next morning I looked at it again and decided it was not big enough to match either man's imprint.

That night, I decided to forgo the retirement party of the head of radiology to get home early enough to confront Violet before bedtime. I wondered what Lincoln would do in this case, how he would bluff and entrap her.

I knocked on her door.

"Violet? Can I come in?"

"Mom? What are you doing here? Dad doesn't tuck me in anymore."

"This won't take long."

I sat on her papasan chair, picked up and started leafing through a copy of *Teen Vogue*, trying to look casual.

"I want to know where you went three nights ago, young lady," I said.

She gave me a look of fake curiosity.

"Out the window?" I continued.

If you think husbands are transparent, try children. She immediately dropped eye contact and began scratching at a phantom itch on her right arm, then another on the left thigh, as if lying to one's parents created some sort of bothersome rash.

"What do you mean?" she said.

"Please, Violet. I watched you leave," I lied.

Regaining some footing, she folded her arms across her chest.

"Then who was I with?" she asked.

"I don't know the silhouettes of every human form in Collier Academy," I said. "Where did you go?"

She looked at me, through me, actually, for a long time, until her eyes started welling with tears. Her proud stance, the shoulders held back and chin up high, instantly melted. She was growing heavy with shame.

"To the beach," she said.

"On the night before a Category Four hurricane? Violet! What on earth were you doing? Surfing?"

She nodded.

"What in hell were you thinking?"

She caught her breath, then wiped a sniffle with the back of her hand.

"God, Mom, it's the only time we have surf on this lame coast . . . during a hurricane."

"That's no excuse for sneaking out of the house. And you don't surf!"

"I didn't get in the water, Mom. Honest."

"I don't care! My God, what would your father say?"

Her eyes grew round and large. "You're not going to tell him," she said. The tone of the sentence rounded upward, slightly, and I couldn't tell if it was a question or challenge.

"And why shouldn't I?"

"Mom, he's crazy right now, that's why."

Okay, I'm no doctor, but he clearly needs one. She's right. So I make a mental note to call the doctor the next morning.

Vernon Spitzer is as close as you can get to a boutique doctor without falling off the insurance rolls. He takes patients only with referrals, and even those referrals have their referrals checked before he agrees to sign them on.

He's a clinician par excellence but has grown weary of the physiology of the human body and has moved on to the brain . . . psychiatry, specifically, only without the full degree. I know that may sound alarming, but he's very bright. His acute listening skills, advice, and meds have helped me through mild depression and a potential divorce.

I have kept him abreast of Lincoln's wobble, and Vernon had suggested that I get Linc in here the next time he had anything even resembling a treatable physical ailment. I used Linc's recent pains in his rib cage as the excuse to schedule the visit. Linc thinks he hurt them when he saved Rod from falling off the ladder, a story so unbelievable I didn't buy it until Rod backed him up.

I spoke to Vernon in advance of Linc's visit, then arranged things so I could meet up with Linc directly after his appointment.

I am sitting here in the waiting room, internally cringing as I await his exit. He'll want to bite my head off.

And here he is. Okay . . . he seems calm. Doesn't look too mad.

"Are you okay?" I ask.

Old Lincoln would have said something like, "Am I okay? You're kidding, right?! My wife has outright lied to me, staged a clandestine psychiatric intervention because she thinks I'm clinically depressed, possibly schizophrenic, and I'm supposed to do what? Jump for joy as if I've won the lottery? Please! Do you really think I'm okay?"

Instead, he says, simply, "No broken ribs. . . . You ready to go?"

I am stunned and not sure how to respond here. Did Vernon not touch upon the behavioral issues? He had to—Lincoln was in there for more than an hour. I scrutinize his face, trying to get an accurate read on the state of things within, not unlike the hurricane plane flying into the eye of the storm to gather data on the storm.

"So you're okay?" I ask again.

"Yes, Jo," he says, "I'm okay."

"Does Vernon want to see me?"

"Why would he want to see you?"

"I . . . I . . . just to say . . . 'hi.' "

I'm stammering here! This is not what I expected to happen. I was prepared for nuclear fallout. I thought Lincoln would come storming into the waiting room, flames shooting from his nose and ears, drag me back inside there with him and demand that the three of us all duke it out.

But no reaction! Nothing.

Yell, Lincoln!

Scream!

Complain!

Bitch!

Say *something*!

"Did he give you a prescription?" I finally ask.

"Yeah."

"Should we stop and fill it on the way home?"

"I'll do it at the grocery store tomorrow."

"I have time. We can do it now."

"Shouldn't you get back to work? I can drop you off."

Because I knew he'd be suspicious, I had feigned car failure that morning, leaving my car at work, and I'd told Linc I needed his van because I had to drive up to Fort Myers for a meeting and that I could sneak away from the hospital long enough to drive him to his doctor's appointment.

"No, that's fine," I say. "Let's go home. Early dinner? Want to do Korean takeout?"

"What about your car?" he asks.

"I had the guys from maintenance pick it up. I'm sure it's back at the hospital by now. It was picked up. The maintenance people."

It is retiree rush-hour in Naples, which means it's about 3:30, and not only are the school buses out but the old folks are cruising U.S. 41, trolling in their luxury sedans for the early-bird specials. I'm glad I'm driving. Lincoln usually has no patience in situations like this, where thousands of people and their questionable driving habits eat away at his control.

Then again, maybe a good blowup is what we need right now.

"Do you want to drive?" I ask.

"No, that's okay."

Speak, Goddamnit!

Say something!

Anything!

But right now Lincoln is uncharacteristically calm. I steal glances at him whenever we come to a stoplight or have to slow down.

He looks good these days, really trimmed down. He has started wearing short-sleeve shirts again, in fact has bought a new bunch of knit polo shirts that hug his muscled arms.

Lincoln seems amazed by his physical metamorphosis. I sometimes catch him looking down at his arms or chest or, when he's wearing shorts, his thighs. He pokes and presses on the muscles as if he's trying to determine whether they are real, just as I've seen Violet scrutinize, then touch her expanding bustline.

I have watched Linc these past months with both fascination and apprehension. His vanity has never been so obvious. I've seen him change workout clothes several times before deciding what to wear to the gym. He's started an amazing collection of cowboy boots and work boots and never wears flip-flops or his clogs anymore.

He's constantly going off to help Rod on other jobs. It's as though he's taken a vacation from caring for Violet and me.

For the first time in our marriage he no longer talks to me. Oh, he's talking all right, but he's not sharing in that very-verbal way I have grown accustomed to. I can't help but draw a parallel to our friends, Nadine and Mike.

A passionate Jewish couple, they often disagreed and openly

argued. We always worried about their relationship but speculated that this fiery passion also found its way into their bedroom, re-nourishing the marital connection.

And then, one day we noticed they had stopped arguing. When-ever we saw them in restaurants or at black-tie galas they were polite to each other, speaking in the unemotional tones one uses when speaking to voice-recognition software.

It did not take long for me to realize the reason why: At some point, they'd simply given up on each other. They didn't care enough to fight anymore. And indeed I was right; within a year, they were separated.

We all build walls around ourselves in times of unhappiness, to protect ourselves and to heal. And let's face it—every marriage has bad days, bad months, even bad years.

Linc's past barriers were always made of barbed wire because he likes an audience. Even when emotionally estranged he is con-stantly vocalizing and analyzing his inner moods.

But this wall is tall and opaque. I can't see across or through it. I am mystified . . . no, flummoxed.

I wonder if he's even noticed that I have canceled almost all my business travel. I'm home most evenings by six o'clock these days. I'm falling behind in my work, perhaps irreversibly, but feel an ur-gency to save our marriage and family.

Okay, I might be overreacting a little here, but I feel the need to get more involved in the day-to-day workings of this family right now. Or something's going to happen. Either to Violet or to my marriage.

I turn onto Airport-Pulling Road, as he asked.

"Down there," he says, pointing. "On the right. By Lipson Fab-rics."

We've been here before, the two of us, to pick out fabric for the living room couch. I take this as a good sign, this rekindled interest in one of his favorite pastimes: decorating.

So imagine my shock when I park the car, watch him get out, and instead of turning right he turns left and walks into . . . Gulf Gun!

I am more than mystified. I'm slightly frightened. But considering the fact that I just performed an intervention of sorts on my husband I realize I can't follow him inside at this moment. I have to leave him at least a portion of his dignity. Chasing him into the store would show complete distrust.

I explore answers. He could have a new friend who works here, someone I don't know. Or he could be using the bathroom. He could be buying a gift for someone, maybe one of the subcontractors he's become friendly with. Maybe he's collecting auction items for a fund-raiser at school?

I suddenly feel the need to connect with Violet, so I text-message her, a little I-Love-You to greet her when she turns her phone on after school. I've just recently started doing this, thinking it'll send a message that at least one of us is watching her.

I look at my watch. Five minutes have passed. I am just about to burst out of the car and go inside when Lincoln comes out of the store, holding a camouflage-print cardboard box under his arm. He steps into the car and sets the box at his feet.

"Let's go," he says.

"You can't go into a gun store and come out with a box and just say 'Okay, let's go,' " I say. "What's going on?"

"I bought a gun."

"A gun?"

"A thirty-eight."

"A gun!"

"Yes."

"What do you know about guns?"

"Rod taught me."

"Rod taught you."

"Yes. We need a gun in the house."

"We live in Naples, Lincoln. The only crime here is insulting someone's pedigreed dog."

"The next time the power's out because of a hurricane we'll be safe from looters. I'll shoot 'em."

"You'll shoot them."

"Why do you keep repeating me?"

"Because I'm increasingly shocked at the words that are coming out of your mouth. And I must repeat them to make sure I've understood you correctly, and that I am not hallucinating."

I bang the palms of my hands on the steering wheel.

"What is going on with you, Lincoln?"

"Nothing. Why?"

"Tell me you're not my husband. Tell me the real Linc Menner has been snatched away by aliens."

"Nothing's going on."

I have never felt this disconnected from Lincoln—ever. How long has it been since we made love? Three months? Four? Our kisses these days are rote, brief little pecks that mean nothing. He is mad at me, I am mad at him.

Lincoln has always experienced those odd funks common with so many creative people. His mother gets the same way. She turns inward, isolating herself, drinking a little too much wine in the evenings. I've never met any two people more expressive than my husband and mother-in-law. It would be hard to keep up that energetic expressiveness; perhaps they're simply turning themselves off and are recharging for the next go-around.

When I first noticed these funks of Lincoln's I worried that he was having an affair and avoiding me out of guilt. I even kept dropping in at the house, unannounced, pretending I'd forgotten something. But I soon learned that this was just a cycle of his, and that the best thing I could do is sit back and leave him alone and step back into his world when the charging light changed from red to green.

But this . . . this is different. I honestly was expecting Vernon to diagnose him as mildly schizophrenic, or, at the least, severely depressed.

"Why don't you talk to me anymore?" I ask.

"Of course we talk. We're talking now."

"No, Lincoln, you don't share your thoughts anymore. You can't be Mr. Full Disclosure for eighteen years and then suddenly just shut up cold turkey. You just can't do that."

He thinks for a moment, chewing on his lip, then says, "I think we're too tied together. It's not right. Not natural."

"I don't understand. What are you saying?"

"None of the guys at the house talk to their wives like you and I talk. I mean, Rod and his wife, they do their own thing. They don't argue over paint colors or fabric swatches like we do."

"Is that what this is all about? The color of the master bathroom? Listen, if you feel that strongly about it then we'll go with the green. That's fine with me."

"No."

"No, what?"

"It's more than that."

"Then tell me. Lincoln, please. Tell me what's going on in your head."

I reach over and gently touch his forehead, as if checking for a fever. He winces and rears back, away from my hand, and I feel a quick burning sensation in my chest. He sits there, soaking in a contemplative frown for a long moment.

"I don't know," he finally says.

Nor do I.

Arturo was scary, but as I drive us back home I can't shake the feeling that the real storm I need to watch is brewing right now in my own house.

Linc Menner's Handy Hints for Caregiver Sanity

Hint #111

Next time you're grilling chicken, go ahead and grill twenty breasts and twenty thighs, then freeze them, en masse, and break them off as you need them. This way, your meat is always cooked and ready, and all you have to do is boil pasta, steam a veggie, and toss it all with some olive oil, salt, and grated hard cheese. And there it is: dinner in less than fifteen minutes!

25

Linc

"I need a truck," I say to Violet as we inch our way through the sluggish traffic of U.S. 41.

"Dad, you don't need a truck," she says.

"Yeah, I do."

"Why?"

"Lots of reasons."

"So give me one."

"Okay, Miss Smartyboots. Last week, Stan The Plumber's pickup was filled with pipe for another job, and we had to fit the Corian walls for the shower in the van. We couldn't even get the door shut. It would have been easier if I'd had a truck. It was a safety issue, Violet. Safety comes first. Always."

"But the renovation's going to end, and you won't need a truck anymore."

"Yeah," I say, "but I can always use a truck."

"Well, I'd feel stupid riding around in a truck."

"They're cool, Violet. Look at that one," I say, pointing to a silver Ford F150. "Now that's a truck."

"No, I like that one," she says, pointing to the white Chevy Silverado behind it.

"That's a chick truck," I say.

"Dad! Please!"

"There are two kinds of trucks. Chick trucks and man trucks. That's a chick truck."

"Why?"

"Because it's got a backseat. Real trucks don't have backseats. Real pickup trucks are for transporting things. Most of the trucks out there today are chick trucks. That one? Chick truck. There's another and another. They're all chick trucks. Ninety percent of the ones out on the road today are chick trucks.

". . . Look at that one . . . The designers steal the space from the bed of the pickup truck to make room for those stupid seats. Look. Can you see that? You couldn't fit a kiddie wagon in the bed of that truck, let alone two Talbots shopping bags. Women drive those trucks. Or men who wear gold jewelry. Real men don't drive those trucks."

She giggles. I haven't heard her giggle around me for the longest time. It gives me a warm feeling in my stomach, prompting me to talk more.

"And the other thing? See that pickup over there? And that one? . . . And that one? You see what they all have in common?"

"What? Wheels."

"Funny, honey."

"No, what?"

"See how the beds are black? They've all got plastic liners in the beds. I hate bed liners. You might as well call them panty liners."

"Dad, they keep the pickups nice, so they don't get scratched. Right?"

"Pickups are working automobiles, like mules. They should be filled with scratches. Driving a pickup truck with a bed liner is like eating barbecue with a bib on. Men who drive trucks with liners are pussies."

Violet looks at a blue Dodge Ram stopped in the lane to the right of us. It's a king cab, but not with a full second seat. It's one of the shortened versions with jump seats you can pull down when you're not storing stuff back there.

I used to like Rams until I saw a posting on truckblog.com. Someone pointed out how the new Ram logo looks just like an encyclopedic illustration of a woman's sexual anatomy, the top of the horns being the ovaries, the mouth being the vagina. They really do look similar.

"What about that one?" she says, pointing to the Ram.

"Better," I answer. "But it's still a chick truck."

"He doesn't look much like a chick to me, Dad. He looks like he could kick your butt. And he's giving us a really nasty stare right now."

"He'd be cowering if I were in my black, full-bed, F250," I say.

Which reminds me: *TiVo the World's Strongest Man competition on ESPN.*

Which reminds me: *Mention crack in new stucco wall to Rod.*

Which reminds me: *How old are you when you start getting varicose veins?*

26

Jo

Lincoln is an odd combination of his gregarious car-dealer dad and creatively frustrated homemaker mother who once ran away from home. Don, my father-in-law, had asked her to drive her Lincoln to the dealership because he'd sold it, but instead she drove down the highway and didn't return for nearly a year, leaving a trail of e-mails sent to us from libraries across the United States. She never called, just e-mailed, and she only e-mailed us. In the end, she sank her car into a lake somewhere in Kansas, then came back home.

She's a little flaky in that artist's way, but I owe her a lot. If it weren't for her fiery feminism, I'm sure her son never would have considered staying home with Violet. Sometime in the seventies Carol had Lincoln memorize the lyrics to Helen Reddy's *I Am Woman*. She forbade him to drink Hawaiian Punch because Donnie and Marie Osmond were the spokespeople for the drink, and as Mormons they gave 10 percent of their earnings to the church, which was spending loads of cash to defeat the proposed Equal Rights Amendment.

Best as I can tell, most rites of manhood were nearly nonexistent in young Linc Menner's world. No contact sports. No motorcycles. No guns. No G.I. Joes. She clearly set out to make sure her son did not grow up to be an insensitive jock, but I think she might have gone overboard.

Though sex together seems a distant memory at this point, Lincoln has always been obsessed with the intensity and frequency of my orgasms in an unnatural way. Luckily, we have no problems in that area, but when he detects that the intensity isn't what it usually is—and he always does—he'll obsess about it, asking me very detailed questions about my specific reactions to every movement of his, which still embarrasses me to discuss.

It's unnatural, I realize, and a little pathetic. It makes sex more like a blue-ribbon science-fair project. You get the results you want, but there is no unstructured, wild passion to it. You minimize the chances of failure through methodical, systematic execution. I have tried to explain to Linc that sometimes a woman simply wants to be used as an instrument of pleasure. A woman also likes to be reminded of a man's strength. This is a relatively new realization of mine, one that I will not share with my husband. He has grown far too paranoid to process the concept properly.

Still, I'm grateful for what Carol created. I can pursue my own professional dreams, unfettered. Few men are fully comfortable staying home with the kids as their wife goes off to work.

Little did I know he would make a career out of it.

Little did I know he would pour so much of his heart and soul into it.

The energy this man has spent on parenting in the past thirteen years! How many people could sustain that kind of intensity for such a long time?

He finally burned out. I guess I shouldn't be surprised.

27

Violet

Sometimes Dad forgets to sign off when he's on the computer, and I get to read his e-mail. Yesterday after school I found a hilarious letter someone had sent him, the address one of those weird combos of letters and numbers ending with *@aol.com* that can be dreamed up only by grown-ups who think they're being creative and witty. I call it Boomer Humor. It's really lame.

The subject line was *girlyman test.*

1. If you are over thirty and you have a washboard stomach, you are a girlyman. It means you haven't sucked back enough beer with the boys and have spent the rest of your free time doing sit-ups, aerobics, and doing the Oprah diet.
2. If you have a cat, you are a Flaaaaming girlyman. A cat is like a dog, but gay—it grooms itself constantly but never scratches itself, has a delicate touch except when it uses its nails, and whines to be fed. And just think about how you call a dog . . . "Killer, come here! I said get your ass over here, Killer!" Now think about how you call a cat . . . "Bun-bun, come to Daddy, snookums!" Jeeezus, you're fit to be framed, you're so gay.
3. If you refuse to take a dump in a public bathroom or piss in a parking lot, you crave a deep homosexual relationship. A man's world is his bathroom; he urinates wherever he pleases.

4. If you drink decaf coffee with skim milk, you probably like to wear silky things to bed. Coffee is to be hard, strong, black, and full aroma. A manly man will never be heard ordering a "Decaf Café Latte with Skim" and he will never, ever know what artificial sweetener tastes like. If you've had NutraSweet in your mouth, you're beyond repair.

5. The only thing a real man knows about the kitchen in his home is how to fix the garbage disposal and where in the fridge to find the steak sauce. If you know the difference between cilantro and parsley you are definitely girlyman material.

6. If you know more than six names of colors you might as well be handing out free passes to your ass. A real man doesn't have memory space in his brain to remember all of that crap as well as all the names of all the players in the Major League, NFL, NHL, college ball, PGA, and NASCAR. If you can pick out chartreuse you are a girlyman.

7. If you drive with both hands on the wheel, forget it. A man only puts both hands on the wheel to honk at a slow-ass driver or to cut the punk off. The rest of the time he needs that hand to change the radio station, eat a hamburger, hold his beer, or play with his honey in the passenger seat.

8. If you enjoy romantic comedies or French films you are a girlyman. The only time it is acceptable to watch one of those is with a woman who knows how to reward her man.

9. Only girlymen drink wine. Real men drink beer. Or just plain whiskey that doesn't cost more than $15 a bottle.

Well, let's see, let's grade Dad. How fun is this! Maybe I should wait and do it with Mom.

Cat? Yep, one check in the girlyman column. Sorry, Dad, but I know not only how much you love cats but also how much you hate dogs.

Peeing outside? Gross, but true. Even when he and Mom entertain on the patio, Dad will walk around to what he calls the "man box," a gravel area hidden by bushes along the side of the house.

Decaf coffee? Another check for the manly column. Dad says decaf is for wusses.

Knowledge of the kitchen: Total girlyman! Not only does Dad know the difference between parsley and cilantro, he used to grow cilantro in the basement under lights. In fact he's famous for his cilantro-pistachio pesto. I sure would like some of that now.

Does he know chartreuse? Ha! It's the main color in our living room. I can't count how many home-furnishing stores we've had to run into to look for chartreuse and "mocha" accents. My dad also has strong opinions on the recent color name changes in the jumbo Crayola box.

Driving with both hands: Always. In fact, he will not answer a cell phone while he is driving. I'm sorry, but wouldn't it look weird for anyone to drive a minivan with one hand? You never see anyone driving a minivan with one hand. I can't even picture Arnold Schwarzenegger driving the Man Van with one hand. It would look unnatural. Why is that?

As for romantic comedies, definitely not his thing . . . unless you count Reese Witherspoon movies. We own *Legally Blonde*. I love it, and so does Dad. I think he's probably seen it ten times, maybe more. Okay, multiple repeats of *L.B.* are definitely in the girlyman column. But wait. If he has a crush on Reese Witherspoon, couldn't this count more toward a manly man vote instead of girlyman?

28

Jessica

I don't know why I keep coming over here and sitting here in the dark in my car because he's never in that window anymore. It used to be that I could sit here and watch him for half an hour while he washed the dishes. Everything was dark except that lighted window. It was like my own personal movie screen, starring the most handsome man I have ever laid eyes on.

But these days she's doing the dishes—Josephine is. Or Violet. And some nights I drive by and just keep driving because his van isn't even there. One time I saw him leaving and followed him for a while, but I had to stop because he kept heading east, and the traffic started thinning out, and I know he would have spotted me.

Not that I don't want him to. But I don't want to scare him, either. I mean, I'm a little bit more aggressive than most other girls, and I've got to be real careful because some guys just don't like that. They don't know how to react to that. The secret is you've got to be aggressive but not look that way. My model for that is Julie Cooper on *The O.C.* That girl gets exactly what she wants from every man she wants, and they don't even know it until they're dead.

Anyway, he's home right now, his van's in the driveway. I just caught a glimpse of him walking past the living-room window in his blue jeans and a green tank top. I can't see his feet from here, so I don't know which boots he's wearing.

I reach over to the passenger's seat and pick up his socks that I took off their patio a few visits back. They're white boot socks with a day's living in them. They're rubbed in spots with the black dye from the leather. He's got big feet.

I smell them. There's a little bit of bleach, a little bit of leather, a little bit of his sweat, and a little smell from the Ziploc bag I've been keeping them in.

29

Violet

My dad doesn't go grocery shopping, he goes "marketing"—
that's what he calls it—which means instead of pushing
around a cart like everyone else he breezes into the grocery store
and picks up one of those green plastic baskets with the handle and
fills it with what he needs to make that night's meal. He says it's the
way Europeans do it, and I think it makes him feel superior. I love
my dad, but he can be truly insufferable at times. In the checkout
line he'll look at some poor working mom's huge cartload of
canned soups and frozen veggies and then look at me and raise his
eyebrows. When I was younger I just smiled back because it was always easier, but lately I've started challenging him on his nasty
little judgment calls. I mean, he needs to realize that not every
household has a stay-at-home mom or dad. These poor women
probably work as hard as my mom, and then they have to go home
and do all the cooking and cleaning, too, because their husbands
are so lame.

Anyway, somehow all the big-item things still make it into our
house, like cat litter and laundry soap, but I'm never with him when
he buys them. I think he goes out late at night for those things a
couple of times a week. It's like he doesn't want anyone seeing him

do it. Usually, all we need when we go to the store together is one of those plastic hand baskets.

So of course I'm surprised when we walk into the Publix, just like we've done a jillion other times, and he says, "Violet, can you get a cart, please?" He might as well have asked me if I wanted to drive the van home.

Of course, our first destination is the produce section, it always is. Most of the food we buy is fruits and vegetables. My dad has complained to the store manager more than once about how there's no coupons for produce, only the unhealthy food that comes in boxes and cellophane.

I actually love most vegetables, and I miss them when I'm away at camp in the summer. One of my favorites is Brussels sprouts, but only the way Dad cooks them, with lots of butter and lemon juice and bread crumbs.

But these days, Oh, God, the things he's doing to vegetables in that pressure cooker. It's as if Dad has started making his meals for people in a nursing home or something. What I'm missing are crunchy things.

"Dad," I say, "let's have some roasted asparagus. We haven't had it for such a long time."

"Takes too much time," he says.

"We can grill it," I say.

"Nah. Too much trouble. You want asparagus? I think it would be really good with lamb and some tomatoes, maybe some olives . . ."

"In the pressure cooker?" I finish.

He stops and turns to me so abruptly that I bump into him with the cart.

"Do you have a problem with the pressure cooker, young lady?"

Yeah, I want to say, and evidently you do, too. In fact, you're acting like one right now, Dad. You look like you're about to blow your top.

Instead, I say, "No. No problem."

"Because if you do then you yourself can certainly start cooking three nutritious meals a day for the entire family."

"I said 'no problem,' Dad."

"I've had to do it for almost fourteen years, and I've never taken shortcuts, not one single day. You and your mother have eaten like queens, and if I want to make things a little easier then that's what I'm going to do."

But I get the feeling it's more than that. He could cook better if he wanted to. This is the guy who made beef stew from scratch, even with the wine, over a fire during the first and last time we ever went camping.

And you would have never known it when lightning zapped the power plant near the house one time in New York. We didn't have electricity for three days, but he still made omelets on his crepe-station stove. He still made Linc pasta. So I don't know what's going on with this pressure-cooker infatuation. I just don't get it.

Normally I'd let this go, but he has been such a jerk lately. He has no patience with me at all, and I know he's not even listening to me most of the time. It's like I'm a radio station he's no longer tuned into.

For the first time in my life I'm finding out I can't always count on him. Last week he forgot to pick up me up after debate practice. For-got! My *dad*! He also missed the deadline for sending in my money for the eighth-grade trip to sea camp in the Keys. Okay, I did forget to remind him, but you don't understand—I've never had to ask my dad for anything more than once.

Last week I brought home a C on an Algebra Honors quiz. He said, "That's not very good, Violet, you can do better than that." But that was the end of it! No nasty e-mail to Michelle, my tutor, or Mr. Workman, my math teacher. He didn't make me add twenty minutes of math study onto my nightly regimen of homework like he's done so many times before. Nope. That was it.

So I guess it hasn't been all bad, this new dad. Instead, I'm suddenly thinking it's not such a good idea to push the pressure-cooker issue. No, I am going to take full advantage of this.

"Can we get some Diet Coke?" I ask, trying to sound very normal, like I've asked it a zillion times before. I hold my breath and look away, over toward the milk case, as he stops to think.

"Soda?" he finally says.

"Diet soda."

He breathes in really big, then sighs and kind of sags a little bit as he stands there, like some spirit has just vacated his body.

"Yeah, sure, I guess so. I'm not sure where the soda is, though."

My dad has always worked like antispam software in my life. Really. He pulls out everything that's bad for me: TV and Kool-Aid and Barney and polyester and glittery nail polish. And, now, suddenly, I'm feeling like a successful hacker, I've found a hole in the software. We don't drink soda in the house. We have never had soda in the house except for Mom's work parties. Of course I'm allowed to order it at restaurants now and then, and always with some kind of dad-scowl, but we rarely see it in our own home. Dad thinks soda is a scam . . . water dressed up in fizzy water and sugar.

"I think I know where it is," I say.

When I return I can't believe what I find in the cart. There is Green Giant frozen spinach and mixed vegetables and peas. A frozen pizza!

"Dad!"

"I'm tired of this place," he says. "I practically live here. This'll last us through the week."

I feel like someone has just pushed me and I've lost my balance. But this is what comes to my mind: Because of that stupid Harper Lee novel in English we've been learning about the civil rights era in American government, and right now I'm thinking of Martin Luther King's speech that I had to memorize . . . all of it, thank you very much.

"Let freedom ring from the snowcapped Rockies of Colorado! Let freedom ring from the curvaceous peaks of California! But not only that; let freedom ring from Stone Mountain of Georgia! Let freedom ring from Lookout Mountain of Tennessee! Let freedom ring from every hill and every molehill of Mississippi. From every mountainside, let freedom ring."

And now it rings for thee, Violet Anna Menner! From the top of Mountain Dew!

When Dad made me carry all the plants inside for the hurricane he made the worst mistake of the century. Not only was the whole hurricane scare a big joke, but guess what hitchhiked their way into the house? Lizards and toads, or, as my dad likes to correct me, anoles and Cuban tree frogs.

There must be hundreds of them in here now. When the sun goes down this house starts sounding like a rainforest. You never know when one of these nasty little things is going to pop up on your bed or in your book bag or your purse.

The other night, Mom was on the toilet when an anole dropped from somewhere, onto her leg. She screamed louder than I've ever heard her scream, and the argument it sparked between her and dad was, well, spectacular. I would describe it as a Category Three, at least.

I keep Tillie with me on the bed at night to keep the creepy little things off, but even that has some drawbacks. She'll eat the lizards all right, but evidently the frogs aren't the tastiest thing in the world. She bites their heads off and leaves them there. Isn't that glorious? And these Cuban tree frogs are not like the little African frogs I used to have in my aquarium. Those were the size of dimes, they were adorable. These are bigger, and they're ugly, scary-looking with yellowish skin. I have begged Dad to call Orkin or something to take care of the problem, but he says it would be silly to do that until the construction work is all done, which should be, by my own estimate, another sixteen zillion decades. Or longer.

Really, though, the only thing left to do to the house is the biggest project of all, other than raising the ceiling, and that's replacing all the windows and doors. The remodeling gods must hate us. The first batch of windows were on the way from Michigan or some place, and the truck crashed, and the windows were all destroyed. They had to reorder everything. Oh, joy.

So I remain here, a prisoner in Jurassic Park. Two months ago I was grounded for talking to my dear father in a bad tone, a capital offense if there ever was one. In the third month I lost my computer privileges because Mom caught me sneaking out the window. And I can thank lovely Miss Varnadore for the seizure of my cell phone.

I tried to tell Mom and Dad why I intercepted the midterm report—it was bogus, that's why. (Of course, my word is not worth much these days, I understand, and I guess I do deserve some of that.)

It's bogus because she's not grading me fairly. Everyone knows that a big chunk of an English grade is subjective. I ace my grammar and spelling tests, and I hand everything in on time. What she's grading me down on are my essays, and you know what? They're perfectly fine. They're better than fine. They're certainly better than anything she could do.

Dad has always told me never to be a victim. He loves that one comment from Eleanor Roosevelt that goes something like, "You are the only person in the world who can make yourself feel inferior."

I've challenged the grades, all of them. And Miss Varnadore says, "You're not working up to your potential, Violet. I hold you up to higher standards."

Now how fair is that? Getting punished for general excellence. I tried to tell this to Dad. He of all people should relate, but, oh, no, the teacher is always right and you, the student, are guilty until proven innocent. I think my dad is the only parent at Collier Academy who doesn't come to the school to fight his child's fights.

Hunter Johnson? You know what his parents did for him? He was flunking out of Spanish, which is a requirement—everyone has to take Spanish every single year—and after a little visit from his mommy and daddy all of a sudden he doesn't have to take any foreign language at all! Can you believe that? I think they gave some ADD excuse or something. My dad calls ADD, "BPD": Bad Parenting Disease.

Anyway, I've had it up to here with Miss Varnadore. She is increasingly creeping me out. The other day she asked me if my dad had been working out. Can you say "Ew"? When and why has my English teacher been checking out my father? I don't even want to think about it.

"Why do you want to know?" I asked her.

"Well . . ." When she says that word, it's almost, like, three syllables long, I swear. She stretches it like a piece of taffy: Way-oh-ell. ". . . My gym is raising its rates and I'm fixin' to find me another. I figured if he liked his then I might go take a look. Does he like his gym?"

"I guess," I said. "But it's a serious, manly weight lifter's gym, Miss Varnadore."

"Gold's?"

"No. Universal Gym."

It's after school, and I am banished here with no friends. They'll know if I've been online, so thank God for the cable TV. Dad's off helping Rod somewhere again.

The other day I told Dad my new toilet-paper holder was loose, and you'd have thought I told him he'd won the lottery. "I can fix that!" he exclaimed in a far happier tone than I've heard from him for quite a while.

He went to the pantry to get his tools. It used to be that the bottom two shelves were reserved for emergency food supplies, like for hurricanes and bird-flu epidemics. But since we have no garage Dad now uses the space to store his growing arsenal of tools.

Dad came out of the kitchen wearing a tool belt! I'm not kidding. Wearing a tool belt to fix a stupid toilet-paper holder.

He looked ridiculous, dripping with all those tools. He looked like those clunky Lunch-at-the-Ritz earrings Grandma Carol likes to wear for holidays. All he needed was a little screwdriver, but he certainly didn't have to reach far to get it now, did he? Thank God for that tool belt, Dad! You're the man!

I'm flipping through channels when I see Martha Stewart, and I stop. She has always intrigued me, maybe because I've heard my father compared to her so often . . . for as long as I can remember.

Honestly, my dad's better. He could run circles around her in the cool department. Martha's very traditional and boring, and Dad's more global and artsy in a cool way. He's more like Urban Outfitters. Martha's more like Talbots.

One time he set the table for a fancy dinner party in all grays and whites, and we bought this bag of flat river rocks of all different sizes and he set these around the table in random places, like someone had dropped them from some place up high. But here was the really cool thing: He painted one of the rocks bright, shiny red, and it was the only spot of color on the whole table. The guests loved it, some famous artist and his partner from Miami who were giving some big money to the hospital.

For Halloween one year, back before I cared when he did these things, he dressed me up as global warming. No kidding, he did this. We dyed a pair of pants and a shirt the color of seawater and then put yellow greasepaint on my face and neck and arms to represent sunlight. Then we made little signs and cut out some states and countries and pinned them all over me. I remember one sign said, "Has anyone seen Florida?" We had a picture of a lady in a grass skirt doing the hula dance in Nebraska or Iowa, which was the new tropics. And all over we had cutouts of hurricanes that looked like they were from a comic book, you know with faces, and they all wore one of those cheesy "Hello my name is" stickers. We wrote in different names, all of them the names of kids in the neighborhood. It was cool.

Martha has just prepared her house for a dinner party, and she's paid attention to all those details that Dad says people take for granted, and they don't notice them unless they're absent. The lights are all dimmed just right, and there's music playing and candles lit. All is calm, all is right, just like the Christmas carol says. It is very much what our house used to be like every single day.

I miss it.

Linc Menner's Handy Hints for
Caregiver Sanity

Hint #921

When your teenage daughter comes downstairs for breakfast and her face is dotted with white zit-zapping cream, pretend you do not see her. If you joke about it, you're dead. If you say nothing, but make it known you've seen her, she'll assume you're watching and judging her. So just avoid contact altogether. She knows it's there. Trust me.

30

Linc

I watch most of my TV at night, when Violet's gone to bed and Jo is still at work. I like TV Land on Nickelodeon. It's got all the shows from when I was growing up, but for some reason I get a bigger kick out of them now, especially the characters.

Archie Bunker takes no crap from anyone, and sweet Edith is the ever-adoring wife who thinks he can do no wrong. He never apologizes. He lets no one sit in his chair, even when he's gone. His word is final.

Andy Griffith, the sensitive man with the gun. In all these episodes, though, I've never seen him use it. That's probably more a statement on Mayberry than his manliness, though.

Mike Brady never has to do housework, never has to take the girls shopping or help Alice in the kitchen. The only thing he does in the kitchen is eat breakfast, which is served to him. When the girls get to chatting like magpies, Mike flees to the safety of his den, which is off-limits to everyone but Carol. I need a den.

Pernell Roberts on *Bonanza*. He's the dark-haired, kind-of-scary-looking brother who always wears black. He's got a territorial strut that is all alpha white-man, no wigger, as Violet would say.

Sam on *Cheers*. A former baseball jock revered by his patrons for his appetite for women. Sensitivity be damned. To Sam Malone, women are a tool of pleasure and intrigue with stress on the former. Of course, he loves Diane, but let's face it—most of the laughs come from him dancing around her attempts at dominance. You think he'd be with her if she wasn't good in the sack? No way, not Sammy.

Good Times. James, the father, with his chest perennially puffed out, he walks on this planet as if it's his, even if he doesn't own the ghetto-highrise apartment his family lives in. He's the bossiest, most bruiser-like of all the TV Land dads, and Florida, his wife, seems to like it just fine . . . in fact, is clearly attracted to that insensitive, cocky way about him.

Howard Cunningham on *Happy Days.* Soft and doughy like a woman and slow as a tortoise, he somehow remains king over his domain. Marion makes no decision without him. I like that coquettish look she gives over her shoulder when she's walking up the stairs, asking Howard if he's going to be long in joining her. (Wink, wink.)

It's very late, nearly midnight. Jo is still at work. The quarterly projections were horrible, so she's having to make decisions on cuts and report to corporate by noon tomorrow.

Star Trek has just ended. I turn off the TV, get up, and pour some food into Tillie's bowl before going into the bedroom.

I take off my shirt and jeans and stand before the mirror in my underwear. I like my white briefs. Glad Rod introduced me to them. I'd worn boxer shorts since I was a child. I remember getting them in my Christmas stocking as far back as age five. Boxers concealed my package as if it were something I needed to hide, like a drag queen taping his dick to the inside of his thigh before a show. With briefs, though, it's all out front. They scream, loud and clear, "Hello, male genitalia here!"

I flex my quadriceps, admiring the definition in my thighs. I then flex my traps and note that what was once a gently curving slope from bottom of neck to shoulder is now a straight line of taut muscle. I could rest a level on them if I wanted to.

My guns are looking good—they now have definition even when I'm not flexing—though I note that the rear delt-head still needs work.

I take a deep breath and look down at my chest as it expands.

"I could kick your ass, Ward Cleaver," I say.

31

Jessica

Usually on a Saturday night the Victoria's Secret at Coastland Center is crazy-busy, but there's a new mall that opened up in Bonita Springs this week, and everyone's decided that's the hot place to be, so that means life here is deader than day-old roadkill.

There are three customers in the whole store right now, two teenagers in Lely High School cross-country sweatshirts and a man who says he's looking for a nightgown for his wife, but if you want my opinion I think he's looking for himself because he keeps asking Rita if she has any size eighteens, and I'm sorry but I can't think of a woman that big who would even think of putting on something from our store. Victoria's Secret clothes shout, "Hey, boys, look at my body!" and when you get that big you just wanna forget about your body. You just kind of coast through life and not look in the mirror except at your face—I know this because of my dark days with the Beverly Hills Weight Loss program (thank you, Beverly Hills Weight Loss!)—and you buy lots of shoes because your feet, thank God, your feet don't get any bigger when the rest of you does. Most men have no idea that's why women like shoes so much, but that's the reason, plain as day.

All of a sudden I see Violet at the entrance with her mother, and just as I start to wave they come to some agreement and Violet leaves and goes on across to Wet Seal, and Josephine comes on into the store. She looks just like her picture on Google except with longer hair. Maybe she's growing it out.

Maureen starts heading over for the kill, but I stop her.

"Let me help her," I say. "She's a friend of mine."

It's pretty obvious Josephine's never been in here before. She looks a little lost and confused.

"Can I help you?" I say.

"Actually, no . . . actually . . . well, yes. But I'm not sure what I'm looking for."

I think to myself, "And this woman runs a whole hospital?"

"Is it for yourself?" I ask.

"Yes."

She starts to say something else but then bites her lip. For some reason this is hard for her.

"I'm going to be very frank with you," she says. "I want something sexy to wear to bed, and I don't even know where to begin."

"What does . . . your husband like? I'm sorry—are you married?"

"Yes. And I'm not really sure what he likes. I've never been one to wear these things. All I know is I need something to make him notice, perhaps to even startle him a little."

I'm stealing looks at her while she talks. She has a nice smile and pretty teeth but she looks tired. She's trim, I'll give her that, and her sandals—they look like something from Greece, strappy and natural-colored—they go nice with her jeans. Her wedding ring is a simple gold band, and there's no diamond on her hand. Her earrings are pretty jade cubes. I wonder if Linc bought them for her or if she picked them out herself.

"I've got some ideas," I say.

"Okay. I'm more than open to ideas."

I take her over to the back wall, near the dressing rooms, where our sexier stuff is. I point to a mannequin who's wearing a sheer, black form-fitting nightie and purple stockings with garter belts.

"No," she says. "I need something . . . softer."

"How about a teddy?"

"Sure, that would be nice."

"Well come on over here. I think we even have some on sale. . . . Here. This one is the perfect one for you."

She frowns.

"It's orange," she says.

"It's actually called tangerine."

"I'm not so sure I've got the right skin tone for that."

"Oh, your skin's perfect for this. Try it on. Go ahead."

She takes forever, as long as a teenager trying on her first bra. Finally, she says from behind the curtain, "I'm not sure this is right for me. I feel radioactive."

"You want a second opinion?" I ask.

"If you don't mind."

"Can I take a look?"

"Sure."

I poke my head around the side of the curtain and am very pleased with what I see. "No," I say. "That's definitely the color for you. You look real pretty in that. It's cute, real cute."

She cocks her head and looks in the mirror again.

What I'm finding interesting here is that this big-shot executive who probably knows real well that this color looks horrible on her is so insecure about lingerie that I can talk her into buying a teddy that makes her look like she's got leukemia.

32

Violet

I didn't think it would be possible to hate English class any more this year, but I was certainly wrong about that. Sensing that I am bored, which I am, Miss Varnadore has created a series of extra assignments just for me. I'm probably going to win the lottery next.

I already wrote about every pointless thing in my life for her: my favorite family tradition, the meals we have at home, my earliest childhood memory, the zodiac signs of my mom and dad, the worst argument I've ever had with a parent. She's even had me start an online journal of my perfectly boring life on a new myspace.com account.

"It'll be our secret," she said. "Don't worry, we won't let anyone else see it. . . . Upload lots of digital photos, too. Get some shots of your mom and dad doing whatever they do. I want this to be about the whole family."

"What's the purpose of this, Miss Varnadore?" I asked.

"To learn how to express yourself, Violet," she replied.

"And you really think I need help in that department?"

Is that the dumbest thing you've ever heard or what? I've got her for both semesters. You tell me how I'm ever going to make it through this year.

It's a good thing no one sees the MySpace account because my dad would surely kill me if he knew what I had on it. I'm kind of using it to vent . . . to get even with him.

When he got on me for not answering my phone when I was at the mall I posted a photograph of him reading the newspaper in his underwear.

Oh, that's not all. I've spent hours sorting through photographs on the computer, picking out ones that would be the absolute most embarrassing. A few days ago I posted a picture of him from the time he came to my fourth-grade classroom dressed up as Captain Underpants, dignified in a skin-wig and red tights.

I also found and posted a picture of him sleeping on a bench somewhere, and someone had written *loves cheese in a can* on the legs of his jeans. I think it was written with canned squirty cheese. I'm not sure where that one was taken, and I can't imagine Mom was there. Maybe it was during his trip out West, to his class reunion.

If that's funny to a forty-something-year-old then I surely want to die at twenty-nine.

33

 Jo

"Violet, it's Mom. Is your dad there?"

"What do you think?"

"Off playing with Rod?"

"Yes."

"Does he have his cell?"

"Yeah. He's pretty good about carrying it when I'm here at home, Mom."

"I work way too hard for you to be a latchkey child, Violet. I don't like you being home alone like this all the time."

"Mom, I'm fine. Really. This is like most of my friends. And those with moms at home don't speak to them anyway. . . . Wait, he's here. I just saw him pull up in the driveway."

"Let me talk to him."

"Let me talk to him, please," she corrects me.

"Please."

I hear his boots clunk across the wooden floor of the hallway, and the setting down of his keys on the countertop.

"Hey," he says. "What's going on?"

"You know, Lincoln," I say. "We need to hire someone to be home with Violet if you're going to keep going out with Rod."

"Okay," he says. "Why don't you put an ad in the paper? You know I hate to do that stuff. You know my bad history with that."

The one time we did hire someone to come into the house we soon discovered she was verbally abusive to Violet—Lincoln surreptitiously taped her while he was out—and her son ran some drug deals from the house. *Our* house.

"But the caregiving has always been your responsibility," I say.

"I'm busy, Jo. Just like you."

"Which leads me to ask, Lincoln . . . is he paying you? I like Rod as much as you do, but isn't he taking advantage of free labor?"

"I'm just helping him. We're working on an idea. . . . So what's up?"

"Have you been watching The Weather Channel?"

"Oh, is this about Dorene?"

"It is."

"Jo, don't worry about this one," he says. "Sartore says that trough from the north is going to keep it way south. That thing's headed to Guatemala."

"Still, I think we should prepare."

"Nah," he says. "Stop worrying like a dumb girl."

My instinct is to strike back, to deliver a good verbal smacking across his face, but I let the comment roll off my back. He is injured, I remind myself. He is not whole. Something is wrong—but what? . . . What!

"I have responsibilities here, Lincoln. I have patients to worry about."

"Storm's going to stay south," he says. "Trust me on this."

34

Violet

The quality of breakfast in this house has taken a dive, that's for sure. I eat a bowl of cereal just about every day now, and I know if I complain about it I'm going to sound like a spoiled princess, but you need to know that Dad used to make me wonderful things every day like omelets and oatmeal, fried peanut-butter-and-banana sandwiches and frittatas and egg burritos with chorizo and garlic and cheese.

Today things hit a new low in the culinary department at the Menner household. I ran out of vitamins. I have never run out of vitamins. Never. Ever. I mean it. Sometimes Dad would let the bottle get down to one or two, but then the next day he would have replaced it with a new, full bottle. Super Friends chewables or Flintstones or Looney Tunes characters.

Dad breezes through the kitchen, on his way from the patio to somewhere else in the house. He's wearing his stupid new tool belt. Why he has a tool belt is beyond me. He says he's helping Rod, but if you ask me it looks like he's doing nothing more than playing make-believe or something.

I shake the empty, white plastic bottle, exaggerating the movement so he'll notice. But he walks right on by like I'm some kind of beggar on the street.

Today will be the first day of my life that I will go to school without having taken my vitamin. I am not happy about this. Not happy at all.

35

Linc

Jo and I are driving home from a birthday party she put together for Marcie, her assistant. I did not want to go. I was mad
that she made me go.

Needless to say, we're not talking much as we head back south,
from Estero. The traffic is horrendous. It's always horrendous here.
Southwest Florida has more than a million people and no freeway
except those four measly lanes of I-75. Add two more hellish variables called tourists and old people, and you realize how very
screwed we are down here when it comes to getting from A to B. I
swear, every week there's a photo in the *Naples News-Press* of a big
old American sedan sitting in some store's showroom, the glass
from the window scattered about like confetti, because the driver
mistook the accelerator for the brake.

Oh, and then add another variable to this hellish mix—illegal
Latino immigrants who can't read the road signs because they
don't speak English.

"The left lane is for faster traffic!" I say. "If you want to drive
slowly then get your big fat ass into the right-hand lane!"

"Lincoln," Jo says, "calm down."

I have devised my own version of the Ten Commandments for
Drivers: Thou shall not drive slowly in the left-hand lane. Thou

shall not talk on the cell phone or smoke while driving. Thou shall not forget to use a blinker. Thou shall not drive gas-guzzling Hummers, etc., especially when you're a Collier Academy mom who never transports anything bigger than a table lamp. (What is it with women driving those big SUVs and trucks? Penis envy?)

Or, if the offender is driving too slowly, I will tailgate them so closely that I can detect whether the screws affixing the license plate are Phillips or regular. If they're polite they will pull over and let me pass.

I am not afraid to use the horn. Horns are a fabulous form of negative reinforcement. I use my horn as if it were a gun, shooting sound-bullets. The longer the beep, the higher the caliber.

When someone does something wrong, I scowl at them. Or I simply don't let them cut in if they need to turn. I am the Judge Judy of the Collier County roads system.

"Why did you honk at that man in the white car?" Jo asks.

"He threw his damn cigarette butt out the window. That's why. And he's being very inconsistent in speed."

"But he won't know why you honked!"

"Maybe not consciously, Jo," I explain, "but the honk is a form of negative judgment, and it'll make him scrutinize the actions he's taken in the past several seconds. It'll make him think about what he did wrong, and he'll feel bad about it, at least unconsciously. He'll go through this soul-searching process. My honks are very constructive, Jo."

She is quiet for a moment. Then, she says, "You're not taking the antidepressants Vernon prescribed—are you?"

I had been lying for a few weeks about taking them. Psychopharmaceuticals scare me. They're like hypnosis. They mean a loss of control.

"No," I confess. "I haven't. I haven't taken a single one."

"Why?" she asks.

"I know why you want me to take them," I say. "You want to take away my masculine edge."

"No, Lincoln," she replies. "I want you to be happier. They're called antidepressants, not emasculators."

The driver of the tan Honda Civic hasn't moved even though the cars ahead of him are long gone. And why? Because he's dialing some idiot on his cell phone.

I lay on the horn, not a tap, but one of those long beeps that makes you think the person has passed out and their forehead has fallen forward, onto the steering wheel.

He flips me the finger.

"Driiiiiiiive!" I scream out the window.

36

Jessica

My Daddy, God rest his soul, said if you wanted something in this world real bad you had to go out and get it for yourself. He said I shouldn't rely on some man to do it for me. He taught me everything I need to know to survive. Honestly, if the end of the world ever comes you want to be with me because there's nothing I can't do.

Last month I finally lost patience with my landlord and went and bought my own water heater at Lowe's and put it in myself, and I just deducted it from my rent. He actually was real appreciative. Most men like it when a woman takes charge. They don't know they want something until their lady does it for them, and then they're all happy.

My momma says I'm a fine catch, and she can't understand why I'm not married yet. It's not that I haven't had offers. I've been engaged three times—I don't know why I keep saying yes, but I guess I'm an optimist—and after every time I got a ring I found some other man and called it off. Isn't it funny how that happens?

Problem is all of these other men were married. Momma says I'm sick and that I'm trying to find someone to replace Daddy, but that's not it at all. I truthfully can say that I'm just more attracted to married men, and they just keep falling in my lap. Of course I had to be a little assertive, a little ugly sometimes because even if the man falls in your lap that doesn't mean his wife falls in there with him.

It's not that strange if you think about it. We're all attracted to certain types. Some girls like skinny guys, some others like muscles. Some girls like darker skin or tall guys or short guys or guys with big noses. I think married men are sexy because there's just some kind of a sadness about them, like they've just lost a ballgame or something. They make eyes at you without looking real hungry and scary, just little sideways glances because they know they're not supposed to be looking at all. They're real comfortable with who they are because the journey's over if you think about it, they got what they wanted, but there's also still a little bit of heartache inside of them. They remind me of dogs on leashes. They're out and about in the big world, they feel safe, but they can't go too far or get into trouble because of that silly leash. And we all know that dogs like to get away from their owners. Oh, they'll run as fast as they can, chasing something they want, but they're always happy to be caught again.

I just need to find me one who's gotten away and is still dragging a leash behind him. That's Linc. I can tell his wife is barely a ghost in that house. He needs someone who really, truly appreciates him. And I think Violet and I would get along real good.

She likes me a lot.

I figured he was the type who liked getting his workout done first thing in the morning. He just seems like a morning person, like he'd be the first one up to make coffee and bring me some in bed.

And yessiree, there he is over in the free weights. I knew that's where he'd be. I love the free-weight area. It's Man Land all the way, though the guys there usually ignore you—I don't care how pretty you are. I've always wondered if it's because bodybuilders are gay or just so into themselves that they can't see anyone else. I mean those mirrors are all over the place in the free-weight area. What's that all about? Guys just shouldn't be lovin' mirrors that much.

Linc won't be like that, I know. He's too aware of other people's feelings. I don't think I've ever seen someone who's so sensitive and so manly all at the same time. Let me tell you, he's perfect. I've never known anyone like him.

I pick one of the elliptical machines closest to the free weights, and I put on my iPod. I bought this leotard just for today. Periwinkle is most definitely my color, and I thought the black tights were slimming. I wasn't sure what to do with my hair. I got up at six to worry about it, and I couldn't decide what looked best, but I finally just put it up in a high pony because I thought it looked natural for the gym, and I liked how Paris Hilton looked when she put her hair up like this when she was doin' laundry in *The Simple Life*. He'll notice me. He'll see me. He's pretty focused right now, but he'll look over here eventually.

"Hey!" I hear him say, no more than five minutes later. Of course I saw him comin' from the corner of my eye but pretended to be into my music and watching the TVs up on the wall.

"Jessica!"

I pull the buds out of my ears.

"Linc!" I say. "I didn't know you belonged to this gym."

"I've never seen you here," he says.

"I usually come real late at night, after I'm done gradin' papers."

He's got on the same kind of gray T-shirt he's always got on with big sweat stains under the arms and in that spot under the chest. I haven't seen his bare legs for a while, he's been wearin' jeans most of the time in the pickup line. I am sure glad he gets out every day to help Violet with her bag. I found a better place to watch him, by the way. The band room is empty during last period, and it's got a big bank of windows overlooking all the cars, and I can click away with my camera to my heart's content.

"Do you come every day? I'm guessing by the looks of it you do."

He holds his arms out like Frankenstein and looks at them. "Five days a week," he says. "I work my ass off in this place."

"I can tell," I say.

"Thank you," he says. "No one ever tells me that."

"Oh, surely your wife says something."

"Not that much. Not that often. I think she digs my new look, but she just doesn't tell me those things. She never has. It's not like her to."

"Well you're lookin' mighty buff. . . . Can I touch?"

"Excuse me?"

"Your arm. Can I touch it? I've always wanted to feel muscles like that."

37

Jo

Dressed in cutoff blue jeans and one of Linc's old T-shirts, I'm working on the shower with a sponge and Scrubbing Bubbles while Violet is on her hands and knees, cleaning the toilet. I begged off the toilet. I told her I would dust the living-room bookshelves (normally her job) if she agreed to let me preserve my record of having not cleaned a toilet since I got my master's seventeen years ago.

The first thing I did after graduating from college was hire a maid service. And then I married Lincoln, who has always cleaned his own house because he says no one else can do as good of a job. And, frankly, he's right.

After Violet was born I suggested he hire at least a biweekly housekeeper, but he refused. He believed strongly that kids need to work in the household, and because he'd sold his landscaping business there was no place but the house in which to make her work.

Violet has been doing housework since she was about four. Linc had her start with dusting and moved her up from there as strength and motor skills grew. It is Violet who has had to teach me how to clean a house, which we've been doing more often these days because Linc just doesn't seem real interested in it.

Much to Violet's dismay, her father has started standing when he pees, rather than sitting to avoid making a mess, probably because he's not the one cleaning the toilets these days.

"This is so gross!" she says, wiping the porcelain rim. She crinkles her nose. "This toilet looks like a Jackson Pollock painting. Are all guys this messy when they pee? . . . Yuck! God, Mom, I need more allowance if this is the way it's going to be."

I change the subject. "How's Robert these days? He doesn't call much anymore."

"Oh, that's so over. He started to annoy me too much."

"How so?"

"He wanted to come over all the time. I mean he's nice and everything, but I need my space."

"He seemed nice," I say.

Violet stops her wiping and looks, contemplatively, at the new, azure, tiled wall in front of her. Though I'm not sure it was worth the wait, this really is a beautiful bathroom. Linc picked out one-inch tiles the color of the Caribbean, which run from baseboard to ceiling on all the walls. The floor is covered with one-inch tiles that are emerald-colored, except for a few random spots—islands, Lincoln called them—in which he had the tile man replace occasional green tiles with the blue tiles used on the wall.

"I think the only reason I liked him is because he liked me," she says. "No one's ever liked me before, Mom."

"Oh, that'll change, honey."

"I'm not so sure," she says, resuming her cleaning. "But that's okay. I scare boys away. They're terrified of me. I'm too bossy. I can't help it, but I'm too bossy."

"Your father would say you have a passion for excellence."

"Whatever."

We continue our cleaning as we listen to Violet's mix on her iPod, which she has set into the docking station in our bedroom. When we started cleaning she was wearing earplugs, but I said I wanted to listen along with her. Violet had been immersed in her own private world of music too often. It's too easy for today's teens to cut themselves off from their parents and environment in general. They bottle up. A potentially toxic fermentation can begin.

The docking stations take care of this. They're basically a set of speakers, and when you slip your iPod into a hole between them it turns the speakers into a boom box. I bought two, one for the kitchen and one that roams from room to room, though it's usually found in Violet's bedroom. I like her choice of music, lots of indie bands with sad-sounding male vocals that remind me very much of R.E.M. and John Lennon.

"Mom . . . can I ask you something?" she asks

"Of course."

"How do you flirt? I mean not you, but women in general?"

"Flirt?"

"Yes. Flirting. How is it done?"

I step out of the shower, close the door, and stand back to admire my work. I do like the immediate satisfaction that house-cleaning brings. Everything I do at the hospital, policy-making, benchmark performance, planning capital projects, all of that is long-range and intangible, and it's hard to gauge and savor your successes. But a streak-free shower door can be yours in just a few minutes.

"Oh, Violet . . . I'm not the one to ask about that. I've never been good at flirting."

"You must know something, Mom. You married Dad."

"Your dad's unusual. I never flirted with him. He thinks flirting is tacky. Girls with long fake nails and red satin jackets. That sort of thing."

"Well he sure doesn't seem to mind it when Miss Varnadore flirts with him."

"Miss Varnadore? Your English teacher?"

"He laps it up like a hungry cat. It's almost embarrassing."

"When is your dad in the classroom? He hasn't told me about that. What's he doing there?"

"She brings him in to talk about landscaping."

"In English class?" I say.

"We're reading British lit. There's always some garden in there somewhere. Right now it's *Lady Chatterley's Lover*."

"*Lady Chatterley's Lover*?"

"Yes."

"By D. H. Lawrence?"

"Yes. What's the big deal, Mom?"

"Do you think that's appropriate for an eighth-grade English class?"

"Yeah, it's pretty racy. The boys can't stop giggling. God, they're so immature!"

"And no one's complained?"

"You mean like a parent? Not that I know of. We've been on it for a week now. Dad came in to talk about the role of gardeners on English estates."

"How did she know he was a landscaper?"

"I don't know. Maybe I put it in an essay sometime. I can't remember."

"How does she flirt with him?" I ask.

"Oh, she gushes over him, I mean so much we just roll our eyes. She goes on and on about how Dad was the landscaper of the rich and famous. I swear she's got a crush on him."

"Very interesting," I say.

"What?"

"How I know nothing about your father volunteering at school."

Violet shuts the lid to the now-clean toilet, then gives the chrome flushing mechanism one last wipe.

"Mom," she says, "if you haven't noticed, he's not sharing much these days."

"Yes, I realize that."

"Why is that?"

Of course I have no answer. He's given us no indication of what's behind his new persona.

The strain of home renovation?

The stress of the hurricane season? As I've learned at the hospital they really can throw you into a fierce, focused survival mode.

Is it his new body?

His new friendship with Rod?

It seems what we have here is a different version of one of Lincoln's favorite shows on cable. Let's call it *Extreme Makeover: Man Edition*.

Linc is now getting a gun magazine called *The Blue Press*, which I mistook for pornography at first. Each month's cover features a scantily clothed woman with glossy red lips, holding some deadly firearm as if it's a sex toy. It is hard-core, to say the least. No hunters inside. No taxidermy ads. This is one for the mercenary crowd. It features pistol magazines and blue jeans with special built-in pockets for concealing handguns. Oh, and shooting mats as well. (Hey, why be uncomfortable when killing multiple victims? The Dillon Shooting Mat features a large, padded skid-resistant elbow pad area to provide the ultimate stable shooting space!)

And Miss Varnadore? There could be only one reason he has not mentioned her to me.

Linc Menner's Handy Hints for
Caregiver Sanity

Hint #75

How many times have you not sent a birthday or anniversary or wedding gift because you didn't have time to get to the mall, and by the time you finally bought something you were too embarrassed to send it because six months had passed? To counter this, keep a diverse supply of greeting cards in a file in your desk: sympathy, congratulations, birthday, anniversary, etc. This way you can shoot off a card that day, and if you don't ever get around to buying a gift at least it shows you were thinking of them. Actually, in this e-mail age, a real paper card with hand-penned message can mean more than a crystal picture frame.

38

Linc

Muscle and Fitness says I need two grams of protein for every pound of body weight. I weigh 236. A Taco Bell bean burrito has twenty-six grams. That would mean I need, at the very least, eighteen burritos every day. My metabolism is a raging furnace. I crave and down protein as if it's water and I'm on a daylong hike in the sun.

I don't argue with Rod when he chooses carnivore palaces for lunch, even though I wouldn't have been caught dead in such places just half a year ago.

Admission: I have supped on a blooming onion at Outback Steakhouse, which is an onion that has been slit and splayed to look like a huge flower in bloom, then battered and deep-fried in one piece. It comes with a spicy dipping sauce. This, of course, must be eaten with a rare T-bone and washed down with either whiskey or a beer.

Some things, however, haven't changed. I still refuse to drink watery American brews, and I've been successful in pulling Rod off his Budweiser and getting him to try some of the lighter Latin varieties that actually have flavor: Presidente, Sol, Modelo Especial.

Just one beer today, though, because we have to get back to work. We're eating lunch at the Hooters on Fort Myers Beach. I know this will sound like a lie—just like men saying they subscribe to *Playboy* for the articles—but we come to Hooters, first and foremost, for the wings. They're the best in town. I won't deny that the waitresses are attractive, but I have found that Hooters waitresses don't flirt any more than the waitresses at other restaurants, and I speak from experience.

Now that I am one of the labor class—okay, that I *appear* to be one of them—I am treated differently. There is a sort of secret, blue-collar fraternity. Both men and women belong. More guys will say "hey" to me now or acknowledge me on the road with a subtle raising of the index finger from the steering wheel. (This happens only when I'm in Rod's truck. These same guys do not wave to me if they pass when I'm driving the Man Van. A passenger van to a man is the equivalent of castration. I need a truck.)

Nowadays, female clerks are more apt to throw in one of their pennies if I don't have one. And waitresses talk and flirt with me like you wouldn't believe. It's perfectly acceptable, even expected. I'm not sure why, but it's nice. It makes you puff up your chest. It makes you feel desirable. It causes the blood to rush. Country-western lyrics don't seem so foreign and absurd these days. These working-class women remind me every day that I am a man, and that I should never, ever have to tuck my cock and balls between my legs and pretend they're not there.

We're sitting on stools at a high table in the corner of the restaurant. I flag down our waitress. Her name is Leesa. Unlike a lot of the Hooters girls she has short hair, a pageboy, and she's pushing the age limit for a Hooters waitress. I'm guessing she's working the final months of this job. Of course she's still very pretty, but there's something detectable on her body that you don't notice in Hooters waitresses: gravity.

Hooters waitresses defy gravity, both in flesh and personality, and I detect in Leesa a heaviness, a very subtle, downward pulling that most likely comes from the bittersweet burdens of motherhood.

"What else can I get you boys?" she asks.

"Could I please have more sauce for my wings, ma'am?" I say.

Not dropping her smile, she gives me an odd look, pausing for a second, then says, "Be right back."

"You did it now," Rod says.

"Did what?" I ask.

"What's that 'ma'am' stuff?"

"It's common courtesy," I answer.

"It's insulting to them," he says.

"It is not."

"Is so."

"Then what the hell am I supposed to call her?"

"Babe. Hon. Darlin' always works. . . . Sweetheart."

"No. *That's* insulting, Rod."

He shakes his head. "It's not. They like that. Especially the ones like her . . . the ones pushing thirty."

It's my turn to shake my head.

"I can't do that, Rod. I wasn't raised that way. Calling a woman 'babe' would be the equivalent of saying 'nigger' or 'cunt' or something like that."

Leesa returns with two plastic containers of orange-red wing sauce and sets them on the table.

"I want to ask you something," Rod says. "How do you like being called ma'am, like my friend just did?"

A smile slowly spreads across her face.

"Honestly?" she asks.

"Yeah," Rod answers.

"I don't like it much. Makes me feel old."

"Then what do you want to be called?"

"By customers?"

"Yeah."

She shrugs her shoulders and looks at the wall beyond us.

"I don't know. What you call me, I guess: babe. I don't mind babe. I kind of like babe."

"Doesn't that insult you?" I ask.

"Why would it insult me? Makes me feel young. Makes me feel pretty. What girl doesn't like that?"

"But isn't it sexist?" I ask.

She shrugs. "Maybe to Hillary Clinton. But not to most of the girls in here. Or in the whole U.S.A. for that matter."

Rod teasingly flicks my shoulder with the back of his fingers.

"Come on, man, try it out. Let me hear you say it: babe."

I grimace, shaking my head.

"Come on."

"Yeah, hon," she says. "Give it a try."

"Okay . . . May I please have some more sauce . . . *babe*?"

Rod rears back and hoots at the ceiling.

"You sound like a schoolteacher," she says. "Try it again. Try this: 'Can you get me some extra sauce for these wings, babe?' "

I repeat, "Can you give me some extra sauce for these wings, babe?"

This time, she laughs.

"Try 'hon.' " she says.

"As in . . ."

"Can you get me some more sauce, hon?"

Trying different words, we do this for a few minutes longer, and they both are laughing. I must sound like some monolingual Russian or Chinese man being goaded into repeating unfamiliar phrases in night-school English class, the unwitting life of the party. Addressing a woman in these words truly feels as awkward as wearing two right shoes.

39

Violet

I can't believe we're here, I mean I just can't believe it. I've tried
to get Dad to do this for two years now, but he has always refused. I'll bet Rod goaded him into it. He probably bet a beer on it
or something stupid like that.

You should see the traffic. I swear the entire county has come to
gawk. They're all slowing down to get a closer look at Dad and the
others. They've caused such a traffic jam that a police officer just
puttered in on his motorcycle a few minutes ago and is standing out
there among the cars, waving them on so they don't clog the highway too much.

"Come on, people, come on, come on, come *on!*" he says.

As my sign says, Dad is contestant No. 1. There are two others
participating in Z-ROCK 98.4's annual Dads in Drag contest. One
guy's wife is holding up his sign (No. 2) and another man's daughter is holding up their No. 3 sign.

When the drivers pass they're supposed to call the radio station
and vote for their favorite Daddy Drag Queen. The winner gets two
tickets and airfare to the Super Bowl in Minneapolis . . . like I
couldn't care less about that, but at least they've got that huge mall
there.

Contestant No. 3 will be easy to beat. He's not doing much to court the drivers, just kind of standing there with his arms crossed, all wobbly in his high heels. He shouldn't have picked three-inch heels, that was his first mistake. He's obviously not happy to be here. I wonder why he even agreed to do it.

The other guy is our serious competition. He's dressed in a short-length, sequined, aqua-colored dress. It's strapless and form-fitting and incredibly gross because you can see his bulge. He's got a blond wig on, and red lipstick and outlandish fake eyelashes. And, I have to say, he looks pretty comfortable in those high heels. He must have practiced walking in them. He's really into it, really hamming it up for the crowd.

Since nothing of Mom's would fit him, Dad and I got his outfit at my favorite consignment store. It took us a long time to find something that would fit around his back and chest, I mean, we were looking at things that were size 24!

There was a great, long-sleeve black dress, but Dad wanted to show his arms off—sorry: his *guns*, as he calls them—so we ended up with a white dress with straps, kind of like the one you see Marilyn Monroe wearing in that famous photograph where the wind is blowing up her skirt. He let me do his makeup, and he even let me shave his legs. We found a black wig that reminded him of one of Charlie's Angels. (An unbelievably lame show; I saw it on TV Land because he made me watch it with him. He called it a "classic," which is hard to believe.)

We used water balloons to stuff the cups of the dress, and I have to say that when he waves energetically they do seem to jiggle like the real thing . . . I mean real *fake* ones. That was my idea. I'm proud of it.

His tan makes it even funnier. Since he started working most days with Rod he's gotten very brown, but only on his forearms and neck and face, and right now they really stick out, compared to the white skin of his chest and shoulders.

The other good dad is getting lots of honks. Two men in a white pickup pass and yell, "Hey, baby! Whoooooaaa!"

"Come on, Dad," I encourage him. "Blow more kisses."

Two TV crews are here from the local stations. They interviewed us before we started, and now they're getting footage of the passersby. One of them is actually broadcasting live for the six o'clock news. Is that pathetic or what? Only in ultra-dead Naples would something like this get that much attention.

I hold the sign with one hand and continue to text-message all my friends, instructing them to call the radio station and vote for Numero Uno.

"Dad, can you do some booty dancing?" I ask him between texts.

He looks at me and frowns.

"No, Violet, I can't and I won't."

"You've got to be sexier. Put your hand on your hip. Put all your weight on one foot. . . . Yes, like that. Don't grab your crotch like the other guy. That's tacky."

"Then what should I do?" he asks.

"Look drag-queeny, try to be convincing. That's good. Look naughty. People like that."

"Violet!" he snaps.

"We're in an MTV world," I yell, though I don't think he hears me because as I say it an eighteen-wheeler putters past us, blaring his huge horn.

Suddenly, my eye catches a woman in sunglasses walking toward us. She's zigzagging her way through the three lanes of sluggish traffic as if they were a maze. She is holding a large piece of fluorescent-green poster board.

"Dad, look," I say, finally recognizing her behind her sunglasses.

(To my credit, she's wearing her hair up, too, a look I've never seen.) "Miss Varnadore."

"Hey, y'all," she says, waving. "I'm here for moral support."

She holds up the piece of poster board that urges drivers to vote for Dad. She must have written it in her car just minutes ago because I can still smell the Magic Marker.

"Whoo-hoooooo!" she yells to the cars, waving the sign in the air. "Whooooo-hooooooooo!"

"Miss Varnadore," I ask. "Why are you here?"

"To help the best man win," she says.

"But why?" I persist.

"Your daddy's been real nice to me, coming to talk to the class and all that. . . . Whooooooo-hooooo! Number One!"

It is hot outside, and the longer we stand there the sweatier and grittier I feel from the dirt on the road being kicked up by all the cars. I never realized how hard it is to stay so up and peppy for such a long period of time, and I have a new appreciation for the nauseating cheerleaders at Collier Academy and their puppy-dog enthusiasm.

My phone rings. It's Robert.

"Hey," he says. "I'm over here."

I look out, into the river of cars.

"Over here, stupid. Can't miss me."

"You're crazy," I say.

He's standing up in the seat of his mother's Lexus, poking up through the sunroof.

"Your dad's cool," he says. "We called and voted for him."

"I'm worried that other guy's going to win," I say. "He's getting all the honks from the pickup trucks."

Robert sinks back into the car, and they move on. I think the policeman is losing his patience. His voice has grown louder.

"Move on, people," he says, rolling his arm in the air. "Move on, move on, move on, move on . . ."

I look at Miss Varnadore, waving her sign in the air. I read it for the first time.

"Miss Varnadore," I say. "It's number *one*. O-N-E. Not number *won*."

40

Jessica

The first thing I do every morning is make my coffee and go online to read Violet's MySpace account, and today I'm up a little earlier because something extra special should be waiting for me. It's Monday, the sixteenth. Today's the deadline I gave Violet on her interview with her daddy. I told her to ask him about his childhood and get him to think about how he got to be what he is: Total Perfect Man!

There it is—thank you, darlin'. That girl is so responsible! A-plus for punctuality, girl.

Okay, I told her to download a photo of him when he was a little boy . . . and there it is. Oh! He is so cute! Look at those chubby cheeks!

Q: I know that you were fat as a kid. How long were you fat?
A: Let's talk about something else. This is stupid, Violet.

Q: I'm typing every word you say, Dad. Besides, you promised. Come on. Being overweight had to be tough on you. How long were you fat?
A: I don't know . . . from five years old to maybe seventh grade. Maybe eighth.

Q: What happened? Did you get sent to fat camp?
A: Very funny. Ha-ha. No, I started growing.

Q: So that would be what—eight years of chubbiness? Do you think that's why you're obsessed with your body now? Because you've never been fit?
A: I'm not obsessed with my body.

Q: Dad, you're obsessed with your body. This whole Arnold thing? Hello?
A: There's nothing wrong with being fit. You see all the moms doing it after their kids get to be a certain age. They're tired of being soft and out of shape. They get their hair colored. They join a gym. It's my turn to think about myself.

Q: Okay, next question: Which parent had more influence on your life—your mom or your dad? Your mom, right?
A: You're leading the witness, Violet.

Q: But Grandpa Donnie wasn't around much, right?
A: No.

Q: For the record, I will tell the audience that Don Menner is a car dealer in Bakersfield, California.
A: Right. Big Ford dealer. Biggest in the state.

Q: So you didn't see much of him. Why wasn't he home?
A: Because home life drove him crazy.

Q: How so?
A: (Interviewee sighs deeply and sits quietly for a few moments before answering.) We were always talking, I guess. And always redecorating the house. We always had some room torn up and in disarray.

Q: Sounds like your mom might have been looking for attention.

A: Maybe.

Q: Do you think staying home with kids could drive a parent to do weird things?

A: What kind of question is that?

Q: A good one, I think, but never mind. What kinds of things did you do with your mom? Did you cook together? Is that why you like to cook?

A: Yeah, we cooked a lot. We took food to little old ladies in the neighborhood. . . . She was always doing artsy things for people, like decorating for banquets and making costumes for people and stuff like that. I was always tagging along. I didn't have a lot of friends.

Q: Why was that?

A: I don't know. My mom didn't like any of my friends. She always found something wrong with them.

Q: Tell me the coloring club story again.

A: Violet, what does that have to do with anything?

Q: Come on, Dad. Please. I think it's interesting.

A: Okay, okay. . . . When I was in second grade I decided to have a coloring club on Mondays after school, but it didn't last for long.

Q: It lasted for, like, ten minutes, right?

A: Right. And don't say "like."

Q: And why was that?

A: You know the answer to that.

Q: But I need you to say it for this interview.

A: R.L. and David and Matt didn't color neatly enough, so I immediately disbanded the club and sent them all home and colored by myself every Monday from that day on.

Q: I'll bet that didn't make you very popular.

A: No, it didn't.

Q: You didn't play sports as a child. You didn't get into trouble like other boys do. You were kind of a Goody Two-shoes, right?

A: I guess so.

Q: And you had a doll, didn't you?

A: Yeah.

Q: Did other boys call you a sissy?

A: No. But I was big. I wasn't strong, but I looked strong.

Q: That would help.

A: I guess so.

Q: But you're strong now.

A: What are you getting at?

Q: I don't know. Maybe that you didn't get to be much of a boy so you're doing it now as a grown-up. Do you think that's true?

A: Did your mother tell you that?

Q: No. These are my own opinions.

A: Well thank you for your insights, Dr. Freud. Are we finished now?

Q: I don't think so. Not yet.

A: Oh, no, I think we're finished. I'm very busy.

I am just shocked that such a hot guy could be fat and weird as a little boy. That is real interesting, very interesting.

I've never heard of a boy having a doll before. I wonder if it was a real baby doll or something like a little stuffed doggy. That would make more sense for a boy. Maybe it was a G.I. Joe. That's probably what he meant.

The phone rings. I pick it up and look at the caller-ID screen. It's Momma. I'm not gonna talk to her, she'll just lecture me again. She's been calling at least four times a day. Maybe someone died back home.

I don't know why I still keep sharing things with her. My personal life is none of her business, and she was just way out of line telling me I need professional help . . . way out of line. I mean you just don't say those ugly things to your own daughter.

41

Jo

It is Sunday, and when I woke this morning I decided that I would cook a real meal, something I've never done, largely because Lincoln has been so damned territorial in the kitchen. But now that he has abandoned ship, I have moved in and claimed it, just as a rattlesnake claims a badger's empty hole.

"Do you like it?" I ask.

"It's great, Mom."

"Very good," Linc says. "You should do more cooking."

"You're just being nice," I say.

"No, really," he says. "It's good."

I made Chicken with 40 Cloves of Garlic from Martha Rose Schulman's *Mediterranean Light* cookbook. Violet is happy that the chicken was actually browned on a stovetop rather than thrown into the pressure cooker, raw.

What they don't know is that I ruined four chickens over the five hours it took me to make the meal, despite the cookbook telling me it should take only forty-five minutes. Apparently, to make things brown you must have the heat turned up high—but not too high, I learned, or the smoke alarm will weigh in on the situation.

"What do you guys have going on for the rest of the day?" I ask.

"I really should go into the office. We're having a hurricane-prep meeting."

"Wasting your time," Lincoln says. "It's not a big storm. It's nothing."

"Maybe so, but I can't take any chances."

"Can Robert come over?" Violet asks.

"Only if your father's here."

"Can't," Linc says. "Ted and I are going fishing."

"Ted?" I ask. "As in Ted The Stucco Guy?"

Linc nods.

"Since when did you become friends with an inept service provider? Didn't you refer to him as part of the Evil Empire just last month?"

"He's not that bad," Linc answers. "I had him all wrong."

"Well then, can I go over to Robert's house?" Violet asks.

I look at Lincoln and wait for him to quash this with one of his questions, but he says nothing. He picks up a chicken thigh and starts to eat it. God, where is my husband with the brooding, authoritative scowl, the one who normally presides over the family as if he's at Zeus's throne-on-high?

"Will a parent be home?" I finally ask.

"Yes. Probably."

"I need to talk to his mom."

"Why his mom?" she asks. "Isn't his dad good enough?"

"Yes, his dad would be fine. But I need to talk to one of them."

Violet gets up to fetch more milk. She reaches to open the refrigerator door but stops short.

"What's this?" she says.

"What?" Lincoln asks.

"This on the door. *Men's Rules.*"

"That is your father's contribution."

"I got it from Pete," he says.

"Pete?" I ask.

"Pete at the True Value Hardware store on Glades Road."

Violet retrieves the milk from the door of the refrigerator, pours herself a glass, and returns to the table with the printout, which she begins reading out loud.

1. Men are NOT mind readers.

2. Learn to work the toilet seat. We need it up, you need it down. You don't hear us complaining about you leaving it down.

3. Ask for what you want. Let us be clear on this one: Subtle hints don't work. Strong hints do not work. Just SAY it!

4. Come to us with a problem only if you want help solving it. That's what we do. Sympathy is what your girlfriends are for.

5. If you won't dress like the Victoria's Secret girls, don't expect us to act like soap opera guys.

6. Christopher Columbus did not need directions and neither do we.

7. If you think you're fat, you probably are. Stop asking us.

8. You can either ask us to do something or you can tell us how you want it done. Not both. If you already know best how to do it, just do it yourself.

9. If we ask what is wrong and you say "nothing," we will act like nothing's wrong. We know you are lying, but it is just not worth the hassle. Besides, we know you will bring it up again later.

10. If it itches it will be scratched. We do that.

"These are hilarious," Violet says.

"There's truth in every one of them," Linc says.

"In most houses, maybe. When was the last time I asked you if I was fat?"

He swallows, then gives me a look of incredulity.

"Like two nights ago? For the Cancer Ball?"

"The one you didn't attend with me?" I say.

"My tux doesn't fit."

"You had three months to buy and get another one altered."

"I've been busy, Jo."

"Busy doing what? Playing contractor with Rod? Jesus, Lincoln, what's next? Firefighters' school?"

Violet clinks the lip of her empty glass with her spoon. "Objection, objection," she says. "We're off topic here."

"Violet . . . sweetie . . . can you please leave us alone?" I say. "We need to talk here."

She shrugs, picks up her plate, and stands up.

"Okay, but I'm taking all the sharp objects off the table. And, Dad . . . where's your gun?"

"Cool it, Violet," he says.

"Okay, okay, I'm gone. Can I eat in the TV room? . . . Dad?"

"Get the Clumsy Cloth."

The Clumsy Cloth, made by Linc's mom and presented to us at Violet's birth, is a soft, vinyl, white tablecloth on which Carol drew with permanent markers pictures of spilled juice, splattered watercolor paints, a plate of spilled spaghetti, and the words *Clumsy Cloth* in the middle. We pull it out at least twice a week. It's been used for snack time and eating in front of the TV. Linc also spreads it out and sits, cross-legged, on it to polish my shoes—or at least he used to. We've made science-fair projects on it as well as messy Valentine's Day cards. Tillie gets her nails trimmed on it. Linc repots houseplants on it. It's the most versatile item in our household.

In our move from New York to Florida we thought for a while that the movers had lost it, and you'd think that one of us had perished in some fiery car crash. Weeks later we found it crammed in the platform-drawer of the clothes dryer, and that night we ate a feast on it. Linc fashioned the messiest meal possible, celebrating the importance of our fine fabric friend and breaking all household rules of nutrition in the process. I remember potato chips and peel-

and-eat shrimp, watermelon and spaghetti with meatballs. Cornbread, too.

Violet disappears into the family room, and after a few moments I hear the sound of the TV, loud at first but then it melts into muffled conversation.

"I'm actually surprised she asked for your permission to eat in there," I say.

"What do you mean by that?"

"I mean, Lincoln, that you're not an authority around here anymore. It's as if you've died or run away."

"You're just mad because I forgot to pick up your dry cleaning yesterday."

"No," I say, shaking my head. "It's more than that."

"Are we done now?"

"No, we are not done."

I get up from my chair.

"Do you want something to drink?" I ask. "I'm going to have another glass of wine."

"Some Jack. Straight up. It's under the sink."

"Yes, I know. I almost used it to clean the dishes the other night. Why is it down there? Why not up with the other liquor?"

"I don't know. I just like the idea that it's kind of hidden."

"Hidden from whom?"

"God, Jo. What bug's up your butt?"

I start walking over to the counter.

"Why don't you drink wine anymore?" I ask. "You used to love wine."

"I'm over wine."

"You're over wine," I repeat.

"It's overrated. Too expensive, too."

I pull a crystal tumbler from the cabinet, but he stops me.

"No, no, not crystal," he says. "Just get me a juice glass. No one drinks bourbon from a crystal tumbler."

I sit down, refill my glass with cabernet, and take a drink. He pours a finger of whiskey into the glass, throws it back in one swallow, then slams it back onto the table. I'm guessing he has learned this from watching *Gunsmoke* or *Bonanza* on TV Land.

"Whiskey. The boots. The new gun. Lots of changes these days," I say.

He shrugs.

"It was time for a change."

"A change from what?" I ask.

"I don't know—the same old stuff."

I reach across the table, take his hands into mine, and stare intently in his eyes.

"Lincoln," I say, "it's very common for people to reinvent themselves. Violet's going through it right now, this infatuation with being pretty and tossing everything of substance aside. I hope it doesn't last, but that's another matter. Sometimes we have to become someone else, someone different for a while so we can look back and see who we are from a different perspective. Am I making sense here?"

He refills his glass and says nothing.

"Do you remember two years ago when I started having my hot flashes? . . . and I bought the BMW and started wearing skirts and jewelry that were too young for me and I didn't even know it?"

"Cut to the chase, Jo," he says.

Damn him! This is what I get for trying to delicately traipse around his weird, male vulnerabilities. Fine! You want direct? Direct it shall be, mister!

I yank my hands away from him and bring them back into my own camp.

"Listen, buster, and listen to me good," I say. "In your desperate and bizarre attempt to find your inner man you have completely dropped the ball as a parent. You're out playing *Home Improvement* with Rod while Paris is burning."

"Paris isn't burning."

"Paris is burning, Lincoln. We are using tissue paper for toilet paper. The light in my closet has burned out. The van has a burned-out headlight. My white bras are now pink. Tillie needs hairball medicine. Violet is eating Cheetos and Ho Hos for breakfast. Paris is burning, Lincoln. Feel the heat. I have budgets due in another two weeks, and I do not have time to spend an hour haggling with the flood-insurance people on the phone like I had to today. This is not a single-parent household. Life should not have to be this difficult. . . . You'd better start picking up the slack, Bucko, or I'm going to do something drastic."

When I stop talking I realize just how loud my voice has become, and my hands are shaking. I take another drink of wine.

"You just want to keep me barefoot, in the kitchen," he says.

"What!" I scream.

"You heard me."

"What did you say?"

"You were happier when I was your domestic slave."

"Slave?"

"Yeah, I don't get paid for what I do around the house."

I slam my palms on the table.

"Who spends $600 on a case of French wine, buster? Who spent $7,000 on an Italian leather sofa that he was going to die without? Who never has to bargain shop at Wal-Mart? Who likes staying at five-star hotels whenever he leaves town?"

"I don't do those things anymore. I work now. With Rod."

"Then let me see that paycheck, Mr. Construction Man."

"I'm an apprentice right now."

"Apprentice to what? What in hell are you planning to do?"

He leans back in his chair and folds his arms across his chest, stealing a glance at them in the process.

I take a few deep breaths so I can calm down. "Listen," I say. "I thought we agreed that you'd be home, running things here, while

Violet was growing up. I didn't ask you do to that. You offered—remember?"

"But I'm sick and tired of it, Jo."

"I don't like working eighty-plus hours a week, either, but I do it because my family depends on me. And I depend on you here at home, Lincoln. I truly depend on you. I need help here."

I top off my glass again, not because I want the wine but because I need a moment to muster up the courage to say what's next.

I throw my trump card on the table. "That's why I'm going to find us a full-time maid," I say.

I lean back in my chair and await his reaction, but there is none. He fills the glass with another finger of whiskey, drinks it, then sits there, looking down at the table.

"Did you hear me, Lincoln? I'm getting a maid. An intruder in your kitchen. Don't you even care?"

There is a long pause.

"You know," he finally says, "there are some people who like the new me."

"The new you?"

"Yeah, the new me. Chicks dig it."

"Chicks dig it. . . . I'm guessing that's a word you learned from Rod. And what do the chicks like, Lincoln?"

He raises his chin and gives me a teasing look. "I don't know," he says. "What do you like?"

He is wearing one of those gray T-shirts that clings to his chest and drapes over that new flat belly of his. I will admit that this new, albeit foreign, construction-guy persona is kind of sexy. He navigates his world differently now. He walks with an honest-to-God strut. He appears taller than he's ever looked. Part of it is the boots, certainly, but he also has this new relationship with the physical world around him, which must come from manipulating that physical world all day with tools and his own hands. I think of the unused orange negligee. I tried it on at home that night and relegated it to the Goodwill bag in the hall closet. But right now? Right now I am so mad at him that I just might spit in his face.

"The chicks, as you call them, don't have to live with you," I say. "And living with you these past several months has been nothing short of hell. I'm tired of it, Lincoln. Tired of this phase, whatever it is."

"It's not a phase," he says. "It's the new me."

He puffs up his chest and brings his arms up into a flexing position. "Don't you like it? I thought you'd like it."

"What I like is order, Lincoln," I answer. "I need some order. I need a port in the storm."

Linc Menner's Handy Hints for Caregiver Sanity

Hint #168

Tired of waiting so long for mashed potatoes or whipped cream? No problem! Simply attach one of the beaters from your handheld mixer onto your power drill, just as you'd attach a drill bit. That beater will oscillate faster than you've ever seen it go!

42

Linc

Rod has finally talked me into going with him to Peepers, a strip club in Fort Myers. Naples doesn't have such things—the zoning laws are too strict—so, evidently, the average man has to drive north into Lee County for a good lap dance.

We cut off work early and get there about five o'clock. I'm surprised to find the parking lot full at this hour.

Inside is a mix of guys, most of them white and working-class but also a few in cheap suits and ties. They're almost all drinking beer, specifically Budweiser products, which I can't stand, so I settle for a Heineken, which must be distributed, if not owned, by Budweiser because it's everywhere you find Bud. It is an acceptable import. Not good, but acceptable, its flavor dumbed down for the American masses.

We sit at a deuce near the stage ("deuce" is waitress slang for table with two chairs, so my waitress friends say) and we wait for the show to start. The marquee outside promised us a performance by a woman named Delilah. Rod says she's well-known among the NASCAR crowd as a sort of pinup girl for Ford, I think, or maybe it's Dodge. At any rate, she's relatively famous, and I'm guessing this is why the place is packed while there's still sunlight outside.

Rod and I drink one beer, then start another. I want to talk to him about my absence of pay and how I think it's time he started giving me something for all my help, but I still am reluctant to do so because I fear he'll drop me and I'll be stuck at home, once again. I'm having too much fun these days and don't want to ruin it. So I sit and let him tell me about his visit to the new Bass Pro Shop out on the Interstate.

Finally, the lights above the stage come on, reflecting off the two chrome dance poles erected in the middle of the stage.

A man comes out with a mic to announce an act different from Delilah. Evidently strippers also have warm-up performers to whet the audience's appetite.

"I know, I know . . . y'all came here to see Delilah," he says, "but before she comes out we're gonna bring out Sharri, who comes all the way from Dubuque, Iowa. She auditioned with an act that involved a corn cob, and let me tell you . . . made me wanna turn vegetarian!"

"Is this supposed to be funny?" I say to Rod.

"Shhhh," he replies. "Just sit back and enjoy the show."

The man leaves the stage, and the lights go dark. Some kind of techno-beat music starts throbbing through the place, loud enough that I feel it vibrating on the floor and even through the air. It seems to settle on and permeate the skin on my face like fog.

Lights go up and there is a twenty-something young woman, dressed in a pair of tattered overalls with legs cut off and a straw cowboy hat. Remember, this is southwest Florida, and though we're a tourism destination we still have plenty of rednecks, which means there are plenty of men in here right now who can—and do—erupt with genuine yee-haws.

I'd always heard stories of strippers being long in the tooth and heavy in breast, but this young woman was so perfect she appeared to be robotic . . . like one of the Fembots from the Austin Powers movies.

Over the next few minutes she grinds at the pole and twists about, gyrating her hips with a fluidity that seems double-jointed.

She soon is naked except for her G-string. Her breasts—and, I'm sorry, but despite all of Rod's coachings I still can't call them "tits"—must have been enhanced. They are saucer-round and perfect, ignorant of gravity.

At one point, someone tosses a coiled rope on stage, and she proceeds to wrap this around her torso and limbs, in the process attaching herself to one of the poles, and soon she is giving the appearance that she's been tied up by some lover and is writhing against her bonds which conveniently lie across the top and bottom of her breasts, leaving them to bounce and tremble, both of them slick with sweat.

It turns me on. And the second I realize this I feel guilty, and I look around the room to see how all the other guys are reacting. Several are unconsciously licking their lips, I kid you not, and Rod is one of them. I wonder if I, too, have been licking mine.

For a moment I imagine it is Jessica up there on stage, dancing for me, which she basically does every time I see her on the weight floor of the gym. She's over the top with her flirting—she must be because it's got to be ramped up pretty high before it hits my radar. I get nervous every time I spot for her when she's doing bench presses. I have to stand over her, my crotch hovering over her face.

"I've always wanted to feel a pair of those," I yell to Rod.

He shoots me a bewildered look.

"I mean fake ones," I elaborate, pointing at the stripper.

"What? You've never had a pair of those in your mouth?"

"Not ones like that."

"Whoo, you're missing something, man. Fake tits feel as good as they look. Man, they're fun to play with."

Rod's wife is trim and, though not gymnast-flat, has small breasts, nothing like this. If Rod has had breasts like this in his mouth he has strayed from home to get them.

"But you're married, man," I say.

"Yeah . . . duh!" he says.

I look at him for the longest time, a little disgusted, frankly. Finally, he catches on and peels his eyes from the stripper, back to me.

"So you can honestly tell me you haven't made it with your schoolteacher chick yet?" he asks.

"No!"

"Thought so."

"No. I meant, no, I haven't had sex with her. Jesus, Rod, I'm married."

He looks back up at the stage and takes another draw of beer.

"Yeah," he says, "aren't we all?"

"You're a jerk," I say.

He shrugs his shoulders and turns his attention again to the woman onstage.

I've never been this tired, not physically tired, anyway. I've been more sleepy-tired before, like the time when Violet was a toddler and she had that vomit bug and was up all night, and the next day all she did was walk around the house and puke like Linda Blair in *The Exorcist*. I swear she must have thrown up fifteen times. I couldn't even clean up the spots fast enough, just threw towels on top of them. No, the tired I'm feeling now is different. It's pure physical exhaustion, like how you feel after a long day of downhill skiing.

It started this morning with a ninety-minute back-traps-shoulder-ab workout and ended this evening with me and Rod moving a client's furniture from the garage, back into the living room that we'd just finished. I would have been home earlier, but after we got everything into place I made some suggestions to Roslyn, the homeowner, on how she could make the room more attractive. I rehung pictures and a big-honker mirror, and we moved furniture back and forth a few times as I tried to find the right combination.

In the end she was thrilled, and we were whipped, too tired to even go out and get a beer. All I want now is to go to bed.

I turn onto Jacaranda and see a small red car in our driveway. Who could be at my house? Jo's car's not there. One of Violet's friends, maybe? Does she have friends old enough to drive?

I pull in next to the Dodge Neon, which has a set of wooden rosary beads hanging from the rearview mirror.

I walk inside, stomping my boots a little louder than usual to announce my arrival and claim my turf. I walk into the kitchen and find a short, older Latino woman in my kitchen, stirring something at the stove that smells like . . . like cumin and pork?

"Hello," she says. "You are Mr. Menner?"

"I am—and who are you?"

"I am Marta."

Violet has heard my arrival and comes into the room.

"Violet, who is this?" I ask.

"She told you. She's Marta. . . . Marta that is smelling really, really good. What is it?"

"Pork," she answers, and she turns to the stove again. She pays me no attention. It's as if I hadn't even come in.

"Why are you cooking in my kitchen?" I ask.

"I am making dinner," she says, not even turning to look at me.

"Why?"

The woman gives me a look of confusion, as if I've said something in a language she doesn't understand.

"I don't think Mom told him about you," Violet says to her. She then turns to me.

"Dad, Marta's our new housekeeper. She picked me up from school. She's awesome. She's already done the laundry."

"How did you get in here?" I ask.

Marta stops stirring, reaches into the pocket of my *Chez Panisse* apron and pulls out a key.

"*Mi llave,*" she says.

I pull my cell phone from its leather holster on my belt and speed-dial Jo.

"Marcie, I need to talk to Jo. . . . No. . . . Now!"

As I wait for her I take inventory of the changes this woman has already made in my kitchen. She has folded dish towels and draped them over the oven-door handle, which is a Betty Crocker look I despise. The layout of the blown-glass vases on the windowsill has been changed so there is the same exact amount of space between each one, instead of being artfully, randomly arranged.

"Where is my pressure cooker?" I suddenly ask.

"What?" she says.

"My pressure cooker. It was on the stove."

"Ahh, *si,*" she says nodding her head. "I put in the garage."

"Why?"

"Too big. No room to cook."

Jo finally answers.

"Lincoln, this had better be good. What is it?"

"What the hell is this whole Marta thing?"

"I told you I was going to get extra help. I need it because you're gone all the time. We talked about this. It should not surprise you."

"She's not living here, is she?"

Marta interrupts: "I have a very nice house! I own my house!"

I turn to Marta. "Thank you very much for that useful information," I say. "Jo . . . we don't need this."

"Yes, we do. It's a done deal, Lincoln."

"But it's not safe. What do we know about her?"

"She's a cousin of Gonzalo Perez, who works in my purchasing department. She used to take care of his kids."

"She's been frying things," I say. "I can smell the oil in the air. You know how I don't like people frying in my kitchen. I always do that on the grill, outside."

"Then you'll have to take that up with her," Jo says. "Anyway, when did you start taking such an interest in your kitchen again?"

"I don't like this one bit."

"Just sit back and relax and accept it as manna. Apparently she's a really fabulous cook, and you know you love ethnic food. I'll be home within the hour. We'll talk then."

"I have sixty minutes to fix this situation," I say.

"Don't you dare sabotage this, Lincoln. I mean it."

I hang up and walk over to the sink, where she is standing.

"I need something from under there," I say.

She doesn't budge.

"Excuse me," I say. *"Por favor!"* I add, louder.

She moves the bare minimum, maybe six inches—this most certainly does not bode well for our future—and I crouch down and pull my Jack Daniels from amongst the cleaning supplies. Seeing what I have, she cocks her head and raises her eyebrows in motherly judgment. But I do not cower. I lower my own eyebrows in a territorial scowl and reach for a juice glass.

I'm playing checkers with Mort because he asked me, and he asks me because he knows he can beat me. And that's okay, it's all a trade-off. Mort probably doesn't get laid much anymore, and winning at checkers is the seventy-six-year-old's equivalent of a hellish orgasm, and if I can give that to him then good for me.

It's easy to lose at this game. I get too caught up in the shapes and colors of the board and the playing pieces, and I don't pay any attention to strategy, as I should. Checkerboards are beautiful things. The round pieces on squares, sometimes matching, sometimes opposites. I like the sound they make when you stack them, the ridges hugging each other in that negative-positive way. They're doubly mesmerizing to me because black and red were my high-school colors, and whenever someone brings out a checkerboard my mind wanders off, onto a trip down Memory Lane. I start thinking of Joan Jett and the Go-Go's.

We have the TV on, tuned to The Weather Channel, of course, because this is southwest Florida and it's the end of September. I've taught all the guys to chant "Mike, Mike, Mike, Mike!" whenever our man, Sartore, is on the screen, but the taste of that word is a little bittersweet at the moment.

I was right about Dorene—she blew to the south and slammed into the Yucatan. There was another, Earl, that twisted and turned north before it hit Florida, up near Cedar Key. Jesus, there's one of these every ten days! Fiona hit Galveston as a Cat One, not much damage there. Germaine came ashore in Honduras. Haley is the one we're watching now. Big time. She is a Cat Two and about five hundred miles off the coast. And our man, Sartore, is again standing right at the foot of Naples Pier off Fifth Avenue.

"God, wasn't he just here?" I say.

"You get your new windows in yet?" Ben asks.

"Hell no," I answer.

"How long can it take to make new windows?" Mort asks.

"The first batch got in a wreck somewhere in Tennessee," I explain. "They had to make them all over again."

"That's a darn shame," he says.

"Nahh," I say shaking my head. "This whole hurricane-prep thing's overblown. Rod says Home Depot is behind it all to make some money on plywood and batteries."

"So you're not gonna put up plywood this time?" Mort asks.

"Nah. And I'm not dragging everything inside again. Man, it took me a week to recover from all that work last time, and all for naught."

"Are they saying when landfall's gonna be?" asks Phil Dougherty, a relative newcomer to Hoyt's Barber Shop. Phil is from Erie, Pennsylvania. They just bought a house in Pelican Bay.

"Day after tomorrow maybe," I say. "Won't be bad, though. This one formed in the Gulf and they're never as strong as the ones that start way out in the Atlantic. . . . This your first hurricane?"

"Why do you think I'm here? My wife is driving me crazy with things to do around the house. It's just gonna be a little windy though, right?"

"Yeah," I answer. "Nothing big. Right, Ben?"

"If you say so, Linc."

"Why is it circling like that?" Phil asks. "Do they always do that?"

"No, I've never seen one do that," I say. "It is pretty interesting, though, isn't it? Even the great Don Maley is scratching his head."

"Don Maley?"

"Dr. Hurricane on The Weather Channel."

"Category One, Category Two, Category Three," Mort says. "It's like it can't make up its mind what it wants to be, just going round and round in circles like some woman in a department store."

We're all very talkative this morning. I realize now it's me who has done this to the atmosphere of Hoyt's Barber Shop. I have raised the level of chatty. No one seems to mind, though, and, depending on the mix of guys and whether there's any pressing news out there, we still have times when we don't say much at all.

Ben, scraping the chin of a man I don't know with a straight-edge, has been quiet for the most part during the shave. He finally stands up straight, wiping the lather from his blade.

"Things always take a path," he says. "Sometimes it makes sense, sometimes it don't."

43

Jo

It's hard to believe I am sitting on a green-and-white Collier Academy bus, zipping across Alligator Alley, but here I am, on the way to a field trip in Miami. I'm surprised they didn't reschedule because of the pending storm.

Though I'm thrilled to be here I also feel guilty, as if I've decided to skip class and drink beer all afternoon. Of course I never did that in college, but I think in retrospect it might have done me some good.

Violet called me at work at the last minute, asking if there was a chance I could come along as one of the parent chaperones.

"Mrs. Jenik didn't show up," she said. "It's rumored that her plastic surgery went bad."

"What about your dad?" I asked.

"No," she said. "I'm asking you. It's a tour of the Art Deco district on Miami Beach. I thought you'd really like it."

Of course, South Beach architecture would be more of Lincoln's thing, but I was so pleased—shocked, actually—she called that I agreed on the spot. I had Marcie cancel all my afternoon appointments. Everything. Even the conference call with the finance guys in corporate. "Tell them it's a family emergency," I said. Marcie stared at me as if she didn't hear correctly, her mouth actually gaping in surprise. "You're really going, aren't you?" she asked.

Violet has been reaching out like crazy these past few months. E-mails. Phone calls. Requests to go shopping. I will be there for her.

Last week, after Violet offered my name as a volunteer, the school called me to help with something called the Sensitivity Awareness Workshop of Southwest Florida. It was run by a woman named Lisa Cronin, who brought in her lovely, developmentally disabled daughter, Rachal, to help teach the kids how to be open to those who are challenged in some way. It was truly transformational, and I even hired her to come and present to the ER staff at the hospital. The ride home that day led to a great, deep discussion between Violet and myself about reproduction . . . everything from abortion to cloning. It used to be Lincoln who had these discussions with Violet. Now, it's me.

Obviously, I now recognize the whole "quality time" claim is a hoax designed to assuage the guilt of parents like me. You learn most about your child not during a special trip to the zoo but rather from the accumulation of comments and conversations that bubble to the top while you're stuck in traffic, shopping for groceries, and cleaning the house. Your child's personality may seem like a certain color from a distance—Violet, in my opinion, is true to her name—but only when you spend enough time with her do you discern all the different colors of threads that meld together to make that color that other people see.

God, my emotions!

Regret: for not realizing all this earlier.

Thankfulness: because I learned it now and not four years from now when she's gone.

Anger: because I let ambition distort my values.

Guilt: because what allowed Violet to become so wonderful are the sacrifices made by my formerly selfless husband.

On the bus to Miami, I am the only mother not sitting at the front, where the four others, dripping in designer jewelry, are chattering about amongst themselves. (And my husband is right—chattering women do sound like excited turkeys.) They've done nothing to bring me into the fold, and that's okay. They don't know what to make of me. I don't know what to make of them, although I do know a little more now than I did four or five months ago.

About twenty miles into the trip, Violet sees that I am still sitting alone. Much to my surprise, she gets up and leaves her friends and comes and joins me.

We talk for a few minutes. She gives me a kiss and goes back to her friends. At least something good has come from this wobble of Linc's—Violet and I are closer than I ever thought possible.

Composing e-mails on my phone, I ride the rest of the way to Miami, alone.

44

Linc

For dinner, Marta has made a potato pie with minced beef, raisins, and olives. I'm fairly certain there is a touch of nutmeg in the potato crust, but when I ask her she refuses to tell me. I don't know if it's because she's guarding some family recipe or that she has no respect for me. I'm guessing it's the latter. Actually, I think she hates me. She acts like she has no idea that I know how to cook and clean. Any time I even attempt to do something domestic around her she is on me immediately, waving me away as if I were some dog getting into the raw hamburger on the counter.

I have stopped arguing with her about the food. She is a decent cook, and the school lunches she makes for Violet are healthy and interesting. Violet especially likes the raw jicama sticks that come with a little Ziploc bag of cumin-and-garlic-infused mayonnaise.

Her cleaning, however, sucks, so it is the source of most of our arguments. She seems to focus on only two things: scouring the tile grout on the backsplash over the kitchen counter and plumping up the throw pillows around the house. Honest to God, she can't pass a couch without picking up and plumping every single pillow. It drives me crazy. I've told her that if she spent even one-tenth of the time dusting that she spends playing with the pillows this house would be as clean as an OR at the hospital.

It's the cleaning agent she uses that I despise the most, some Latin product called Fabuloso. She favors the green-apple scent, which means our home smells like a ten-year-old's perfume bought at Wal-Mart.

"I don't think it's antibacterial," I say.

"It cleans *todos*," she replies. "Everything."

"Yes, I know. That's not the point. What I'm saying is that it doesn't kill germs."

Again, she waves me off like some bothersome mosquito and walks away.

"You a bad man."

It did not help matters that she saw me on television in the Dads in Drag contest, which we did not win, by the way.

"Marta!" I yell. "You just can't walk away from me like that."

"I work for Josephine," she says, pronouncing it in the Spanish way: hoe-sae-feen-uh. "You are not my boss man. You can't say what I do."

"The hell I can't. This is my house. What I say goes, and I want you to use lemon-scented Lysol on those counters—comprende? This house, my family, has a signature smell, and part of that is lemon-scented Lysol."

Violet walks into the kitchen.

"Are you two at it again?" she asks.

"Where's your mother?" I ask.

"Pensacola."

"Is she coming home tonight?"

"Tomorrow."

I turn to Marta. "You can leave early tonight," I say. "Go ahead. Go on home."

She shakes her head in an exaggerated way, like a little girl resisting command. "I work until seven o'clock. I must clean the kitchen."

"You must be mistaken because you do not clean the kitchen," I say. "You never clean the kitchen, you simply redistribute the dirt. This fabulous new kitchen is the dirtiest kitchen I've ever had. It sickens me."

"Dad!" Violet cautions.

"You are a bad man!" Marta blurts.

I walk over to the roll of paper towels on the counter and pull one off. I crouch down and swipe the area of the floor beneath the overhang of the cabinets.

"Look," I say, showing her the dirty towel. "Do you know what this is? This is grime. It's from using a damp mop instead of washing the floor on your hands and knees. All damp mops do is push the dirt around from place to place."

"Dad, you're really out of control here."

"Butt out, Violet!"

"Gosh, cut her some slack. She made flan today."

"None for you, bad man!" Marta says.

"I don't want your stinkin' flan," I lie. "I want you to vacuum the cat hair off the Persian rug in the hallway. That's what I want."

"She's going to tell on you, Dad. You'd better apologize."

"For what?"

"For being rude."

"She resists me, Violet. She ignores me. She treats me like some chauvinistic Latin man who doesn't know anything about domestic duties, and we most certainly know that is not the case."

Violet takes my hand in hers and pulls me from the kitchen, into the living room.

"You want to sit down?" she asks.

"No. I'm too hoppin' mad right now."

"Listen," she says. "You may not like hearing this, but you need to hear it. Marta is very important to me and Mom—and even you, Dad. She's holding this family together."

"You've been brainwashed."

"No, Dad, we need someone to take care of us here at home.

You're too busy now. You're never here. I know Marta's not perfect. She can't cook Italian or Thai the way you do, but she's not the devil."

I hear her turn on the TV in the kitchen, one of those soaps on Univision with the porn-star-like women and the coiffed guys who all look gay. I hear water sloshing in the sink and then the *click, click, click* of the stupid sponge mop being pushed back and forth across the floor.

I don't like her. I am envisioning her demise.

45

Jo

Marcie comes into my office, waving a CD in her hand.

"Marc Sutphen from NBC-2 dropped this by," she says. "He had a devilish smile."

"Do you know what it is?" I ask.

"One way to find out."

She walks over to the media center and pushes the disc into the player, then takes the remote and points it at the TV hanging from the ceiling in the corner of the room.

At first, it appears to be a report on some horrific logjam of traffic on U.S. 41, and then it looks like a protest of sorts . . . people with signs . . . and then I recognize my husband's voluminous calves! And my daughter, who is holding a sign that says *No. 1*, pumping it in the air as if she were embroiled in some angry protest.

"The Dads in Drag contest," I say, and I smile.

"Did you know he was doing this?" Marcie asks.

I nod. "Violet told me all about it. . . . He didn't win, though."

"Might be his choice of dress," Marcie says. "That thing's awful."

Another woman stands alongside my husband and daughter,

her back to the camera. She waves her own sign, screaming "Whoo-hoooooooo!" She's wearing a denim miniskirt and a skimpy, clinging, low-cut tank.

"Who is that with them?" Marcie asks.

The woman puts down her sign, walks up behind my husband, and proceeds to give him a backrub as he waves to the passing cars. Linc seems to enjoy the attention, rolling his neck to stretch it out as she massages his shoulders.

Marcie looks at me, her eyebrows raised.

"Yes," I say. "Damn good question. Who is that?"

As if on cue, the cameraman then moves to the left, revealing the young woman's face. I scrutinize it, fairly certain I recognize her, but I'm not sure until I hear her talk. Yes. The Southern accent.

I grab my BlackBerry and dial Violet. She answers on the second ring.

"I'm watching a video of you and your father in the Dads in Drag contest," I say.

"Wasn't he great?" she says.

"Yes."

"Isn't it hilarious?"

"Yes. Very funny. But why is a clerk from Victoria's Secret giving your father a massage?"

"Victoria's Secret?"

"Yes. She works there."

"Mom, I don't know who you're talking about."

"The sign with the spelling error?"

"Oh!" she says. "Miss Varnadore."

"Miss Varnadore?"

"Yeah. Miss Varnadore. Why? What's wrong?"

I forget for a moment that Marcie's in the room with me, and I cut the conversation short.

"Nothing. Never mind. But Violet . . . don't tell your father we talked about this."

"Why?"

"Just don't. Please."

46

Linc

Rod needs me, that much is very clear. He's taken me on the last seven bids, and it has been my input, my insights into what makes a good house great, both in aesthetics and practical design, that gets us some plum jobs: put the washer and dryer on the main floor and only on the main floor; give the person who has to wash dishes something nice to look at from the kitchen window; minimize the path from car to kitchen so that unloading groceries isn't such a pain; use a European door lever rather than a round handle on the garage door because you generally have your hands full from errands and it's easier to push down on something than twist it. Much to the architect's ire, we usually make these suggestions after the blueprints have been delivered, but the customers like my ideas so much they ask to have them incorporated.

He now offers a free landscape plan for those who sign up for major work. He's paying me now, too, though it's not very much. I've even lied to Jo about the amount because I know she'd have a fit. I'm fully aware that I'm getting screwed in a huge way, considering everything I bring to the table.

We have just left a meeting with a woman in the SunTrust Tower in Estero. The president of the region's branch offices, she has relocated here from Ocala and wants a five-bedroom, four-bath home on a lot in Pelican Point. Knowing her proclivity for things Japanese—she and her family spent three years there in the 1980s—I pulled out the Zen landscape plan I did years ago for Shirley MacLaine. She loved it so much she signed on for a full landscaping plan and decided to supersize all of the windows to maximize the views.

We leave the meeting feeling good and full, a signed contract in hand. It will be the biggest residential job Rod has ever had. It's now a few minutes after five o'clock, and we're joined at the elevator by the woman's good-looking secretary, whom we tried to chat up while waiting for our appointment. Rod was especially enamored with her. He tried to flirt with her numerous times in the twenty minutes we waited for our client, but she was as cool and impenetrable and tough as a refrigerated spaghetti squash. It was very clear she does not like him at all.

The elevator door opens. The three of us get on, and Rod pushes the button for the first floor. I feel my stomach rise toward my heart with a tickle as we begin the downward fall, and all is quiet except for a slight rattling sound.

Five seconds later, the light suddenly goes out and the elevator comes to a sluggish stop, as if we have run into one of those walls of dense foam they spray onto a runway to help stop a plane that has had to land without its wheels.

It is pitch black. Eerily silent.

"What the hell?" Rod says. "Power outage?"

"Must be," I answer. "But aren't these things on generators?"

"Don't be frightened, hon," he says to the woman.

She is silent. Rod is oblivious to the fact that this woman feels extremely vulnerable right now in this dark, contained spot with two big men, one of whom has made no secret of his desire for her.

"Ma'am?" I say, hoping the word somewhat eats away at the edges of her fear. "Has this happened before?"

"No," she answers. "Not that I know of."

I pull my cell phone from its holster and flip it open. "What's your number upstairs?" I ask.

She tells me, and I dial, though it does no good because it rolls over into voice mail.

"Do you know the number for building security?"

"No."

"I guess we can call the police. . . . Rod?" I ask. "Are you still there?"

"Yeah, I'm here," he answers.

"Tell me these things don't fall anymore—right?"

"They're not on cables anymore, if that's what you're asking."

"No, I want to know that we're in no immediate danger."

He says nothing for a few moments and then, finally, "These things are hydraulic now. But the same power that's holding this in place should also be powering the lights, so I'm not sure."

I wonder, even doubt, if he truly knows what he's talking about. I hold my open cell phone up to the control panel, illuminating the buttons with the faint blue light emanating from the keypad.

"I thought elevators had emergency phones," I say.

"Guess not," Rod answers.

I hear a stifled whimper from the woman. I can tell from the position of her voice that she has crammed herself into the far corner of the elevator, as far away from us as possible.

I dial 911 and talk with a dispatcher. She first chides me for using the emergency number for such a call and then puts me through to a dispatcher. I explain our situation, give our address, and she promises to notify building security.

"Nothing else we can do now but wait," I say. "I'm sitting down."

I hear Rod sigh and then the popping of his knees as he joins me on the floor. After a few moments, I hear the woman's suit sliding down the wood-paneled wall as she, too, decides to wait it out in comfort.

Suddenly, I remember that I'm due to pick up Violet from a Model United Nations meeting at school in five minutes. I speed-dial her cell phone and tell her I won't be there, that I'm stuck in an elevator.

"Yeah, okay, no problem," she says, obviously not believing me. "Marta can pick me up."

I hang up and sit there in the silence.

"How long do you think we'll be here?" asks the woman.

"Not long," I say. "Don't worry."

"Would it be okay if I borrowed your phone? My daughter has mine."

"Absolutely. Here."

Our hands clumsily brush against each other in the darkness before her fingers close around the end of the phone and take it from me. When she flips it open and looks at the lit keyboard I can see that her eyes are moist with tears. She dials a number, but there is no answer. At the sound of a beep, she leaves a message.

"Meaghan, honey, this is Mom. I'm going to be late picking you up today. I'm . . . stuck in an elevator right now, if you can believe that. Go to Ms. Cromwell's room and wait there with her until I can get there."

She pulls the phone away from her face and looks my way. "Can I leave this number for her to call?" she asks.

"Absolutely."

"Call me on this number if you need anything," she says. "Don't worry. It's not a big deal. This has happened before. Bye honey. Love you. See you soon. Bye."

She closes the phone and is swallowed again by the darkness.

"I thought you said this hasn't happened before," Rod says.

"She said that so her daughter wouldn't worry, stupid," I say. "Ms. Cromwell . . . that's not Joyce Cromwell at Collier Academy is it?"

Judging from the details of this woman—the bubble-gum hue

of her lipstick . . . the faux Louis Vuitton purse with its vinyl edges rubbed raw . . . her status as a secretary . . . and the clingy, love-drenched tone of her good-bye—I surmise that the girl on the other end of the line is an only child, like mine, and most likely very bright because she probably is on full-tuition scholarship.

"Do you know her?" she asks.

"Seventh grade, right?"

"Yes."

"My daughter had her."

"She goes to C.A.?"

"She's an eighth-grader. What's your daughter's name?"

"Meaghan."

"Mine's Violet. . . . And I'm Linc. Lincoln Menner. I'd shake your hand but I might poke your eye out. Your daughter must be sharp. Ms. Cromwell gets all the bright ones. I think it's a seniority thing."

The minutes stretch to a half hour. Sometime during this, Rod nods off to sleep and leans against the wall in the corner, snoring. We laugh when we hear it and continue talking, finding those strings we have in common in the fabric of our families' lives. Maybe the biggest thing we share is that we both feel like outsiders in the Collier Academy culture, I being a stay-at-home dad and she being from a class that doesn't know the airline hubs with direct transatlantic routes. We note how the bitchy women in designer sunglasses rarely yield for those of us in lesser cars, and how we're never asked to contribute anything at a school function. "I think they're afraid I'm going to bring crackers and Cheez Whiz," I say.

After an hour, I call the police again and discover that the dispatcher had completely forgotten to call building security. Evidently, the other three elevators in the building met the demands of the rush-hour crowd with no problems, and we have hung here, unnoticed and unneeded.

By the time the fluorescent light blinks on again and the hum of electricity fills the aural landscape, we have dissected each teacher's personality and made our guesses as to which parents have had plastic surgery. We've compared the clothes at Gadzooks and Limited Too and shared ideas on what we do to keep our daughters feeling good about themselves in this awful Kate Moss culture. We've shared cooking shortcuts, something I haven't been open to in the past. (Evidently, sometime in the past year they've started packaging fresh green beans, already snipped, in a bag that you simply set into the microwave.) I'm especially impressed at how this very busy mom manages to work full-time and still cook what I consider to be nutritious, perfectly acceptable meals, and I make a mental note to buy her bible, a cookbook called *Working Moms' Kitchen Companion*.

I also realize that, if her daughter had been Violet's age or older, this conversation would have been very different. I would have had little to offer. I'm working with an outdated caregiver database, living in the past and commenting on the present with no bona fide, current knowledge, like some octogenarian MD telling someone she needs to take up smoking to help combat frequent head colds.

Later, Rod is driving me home.

"You sure as hell can snore," I say.

"You sure as hell can be chatty. You guys lost me in the mall talk."

"We talked about a lot more than that. Women are cool—they talk about things that matter."

Rod gives me a frown that says "yeah, right."

I start gathering my thoughts, like scattered sticks on the forest floor, so that I can build a fire to enlighten him, but I decide it's not worth it. He wouldn't understand, couldn't understand because he has not been as tightly tethered to another human as I have.

I usually see Jessica at the gym only on Saturdays because I come in the morning, during school. But there she is.

I hop onto the adjacent cross trainer. There's a free one next to her.

"You playing hooky?" I ask.

"Just taking a day off," she says. "Like a beauty rest, only I'm fixin' to have some fun."

"Doing what?" I ask.

"I'm going shootin'."

"You shoot?".

"Course I do. Why do you look so surprised? Can't pretty girls shoot?"

"Yeah, I guess, I don't know. Schoolteacher thing? Maybe that's it?"

"Are you calling me an old maid?"

"No, sirree. That's the last thing I'd call you."

"Well then I guess you're safe for now."

"What do you shoot?" I ask.

"Everything. Right now I'm shootin' combat handguns. . . . Forty-fives."

"You shoot a forty-five?"

"Yep."

"Wow. I've only shot a thirty-eight. I'm just starting, though."

"You want to shoot a forty-five? I'm going right after this workout."

"I can't. I don't have time."

"Now how many times are you gonna get an offer from someone to teach you how to shoot a forty-five?"

I look at my watch.

"Can we finish by four?" I ask.

"Depends."

"Depends on what."

"What time we finish lunch. Because that's gonna be your pay-
ment for me teaching you."

I love the .45. I'm hooked. I want one. I'm buying one after the
storm passes.

A .45 is so powerful and cool-looking I'm almost embarrassed
that I got such a kick out of shooting a .38. With the .45 I feel like
Clint Eastwood. With the .38 I feel like Festus on *Gunsmoke*.

Jessica is a first-rate marksman, definite professional sniper material here, and while she might suck at teaching English—that's
what Violet says, anyway, though I'm sure she can't be that bad—
she's a helluva good firearms teacher. At the end of the morning I
was hitting within the three inside rings just about every time.

We're now sitting in Ruby Tuesday, which was her choice, of
course, not mine. I have finished my plate of ribs. She has barely
touched her salad.

The waitress arrives and sets down Jessica's third Cosmo, and
she takes a sip. She's getting all willowy in body language, and she's
starting to have trouble with the delivery of consonants.

"You have a pretty healthy tolerance for hard booze," I say.

"Oh, I'm an Amazon woman," she replies. "You've never seen a
woman like me."

I can tell she's drunk because she's trying to look seductive, and
it's coming off about as well as if an eight-year-old were doing it.
She cocks her head, clumsily licks her lips with eyes halfway closed.

"You probably should eat something if you're going to drink that
much," I say.

She sets down her drink, rests her chin on her fists, elbows on
the table, and leans toward me.

"I've got a secret," she says.

"Yeah?"

"Yeah. . . . I think you're one sexy man."

"Really?" I deadpan. "I had no idea."

"Oh, yeah, I've been watching you all year," she says, my sarcasm eluding her. "I got a question."

"What?"

"Your wife's out of town a lot, right?"

"Yes."

"Don't you get lonely?"

"No. I've got Violet."

"No, I mean lonely for . . . you know . . . lonely for a woman."

"Yeah, a little maybe," I say. "We've had some ups and downs, Jo and me, but we've got a long history. She puts up with a lot of crap from me, I put up with a lot of crap from her."

"Are you happy with her?"

"Yeah. I am. . . . I think you should probably work a little on that salad, Jessica."

She looks down at her plate with a look of confusion, then picks up her fork, clumsily, as if she's Frankenstein's monster, and stabs a cherry tomato slathered in ranch dressing. She brings it to her mouth and proceeds to run it across her lips, slowly, back and forth then in a circle, coating them with the greasy dressing. From the corner of my eye I notice an older couple at a nearby table, watching us and frowning.

"You're drawing attention to yourself," I say. "You're making people uncomfortable."

She sucks the tomato from the tip of the fork, and it disappears into the cave that is her mouth. Staring at me, she purses her lips, pushing the red orb back out with her tongue, but she loses control, pushing too hard, and it pops out like a cannonball and falls directly into her Cosmo with a plunk. Almost instantly, the grease floats to the top.

The waitress breezes past me, and I stop her and ask for the check. She looks at Jessica.

"She's not driving, is she?" she asks me.

"No," I answer. "I'll be driving her home."

"She shouldn't be driving. It's my responsibility to tell you that."

"Are you driving me home, you sweet man?" Jessica says, though I'm surprised she even heard me because she's been drifting in and out of this reality now for about twenty minutes.

Her arm around my shoulder, I guide her to the van and strap her into the passenger's seat. All is fine until somewhere near Vanderbilt Beach Road, on U.S. 41, where she unbuckles her seat belt, crawls onto the floor, then starts trying to unbutton my blue jeans.

"Stop it, Jessica."

"Oh, com'on . . ."

"I said, 'stop it'!"

She persists, giggling, her hands fumbling at my crotch.

I pull over and stop on the side of the road.

"Get back in your seat and put your seat belt on!" I yell.

She gives me a startled, hurt look, then the features of her face stretch outward, squinting, pinched into a sob.

Instead of sitting back down in the front seat she flees in embarrassment, squishing her way through the cleavage of the two front seats and crawling into one of the backseats. She curls up into a fetal position and starts to cry.

"Jessica!" I yell back at her. "Seat belt! Now!"

Unable or unwilling to open her eyes, she paws, blindly, in the air for the shoulder strap. I get out of my seat, open the back door, and strap her in as if she were a TV or something bulky and big that I'd just bought and wanted to protect for the ride home.

When we get out to her apartment, I help her to the front door and unlock it. The second it opens she tumbles inside and onto the carpet of the living room. My phone rings, but I ignore it. I know Jo's home with Violet, so anyone else can wait.

I pick Jessica up, throw her over my shoulder like a rolled-up carpet, carry her into a bedroom—I'm guessing it's hers—and dump her on the bed. She sings something unintelligible, then stops and says, "Linc . . . Linc."

"What?" I answer.

"You're best for taking care of me, and I just wanna have you take care of me, and I'm gonna be right here and you're gonna be right there, okay?"

"Yeah, whatever, Jessica," I say. "Get some sleep now. Sleep it off. Have I told you tonight you're a fabulous role model?"

"No I'm not hungry but you're sweet for askin' . . ."

As I'm leaving, I hear her start to vomit on the floor in the dark. I entertain the thought of going in to help her clean up and put her to bed, but I'm a little freaked out by all of this and worried about taking her clothes off and what that might provoke. I can tell from the sound that she's on her stomach, spewing downward, so the chances of her choking are nil. I turn the lock on the door handle, close it, and leave.

On the way home I pull into the parking lot of Hoyt's Barber Shop even though I know he's been closed for more than two hours. It is dark except for the lit Coca-Cola clock hanging on the wall over the door to the bathroom. There's only one bathroom at Hoyt's, and the sign on the door says *Gentlemen*. I learned last week that Ben keeps a sign that says *Ladies* in the cash register drawer, which he brings out and tapes beneath the *Gentlemen* sign when the health department decides to stop by.

I sit there for a while, looking inside. I need to get home. I've told no one where I am.

47

Violet

My dad always taught me to be nice to the janitors. You never know when you're going to need them, he said. They hold immense power. And he was right.

Ms. Varnadore is gone today, out sick, I guess, and I need my entry for the Collier County Veterans Association poetry contest. I told Ms. Hutchinson it wasn't a big deal, they could just enter the runner-up, but she insisted I go and try to find it in Ms. Varnadore's desk.

Of course, it's locked. Oh, joy! So I have gone in search of Lawrence, my custodian friend.

Lawrence is very cool. I stop and talk with him frequently even though my friends all think I'm weird for doing it, and I get teased. He's really interesting. He and his two kids and wife moved here from Haiti two years ago. He's an artist, a painter. He believes that the world is inside out, and that we live on the inside of the planet. Or something like that, I'm not sure.

Thank goodness, he does have one of those magic keys that fits all the desks in Collier Academy.

We find the poem in the bottom right-hand drawer, but something continues to bother Lawrence.

"What's wrong, Lawrence?" I ask.

"That top drawer should open along with this one," he says.

"But we don't have to get in there," I say. "I've got my poem, Lawrence. Thank you."

"No, it's a security issue," he says. "All these locks are supposed to open."

He pulls at it again, rattling it hard.

Lawrence is a big guy, so when that drawer finally does break free it comes out like a rocket. Lawrence loses his balance and falls on his fanny, and the contents of the drawer scatter about the floor.

There's a pink photo album sitting open . . . with a picture of my dad in it!

"Lawrence—that's my dad!"

He looks at it. I look at it. Then he looks at me.

"We probably shouldn't pry," he says.

"Are you kidding me? That's my dad. My *dad*!"

I pick it up and start leafing through it.

There must be forty pictures here, and every single picture is of my dad. And of me with my dad. Almost all of them were taken in the pickup line at school.

"Lawrence," I say. "This is really random. I'm creeped out."

"Uh-huhh," he says, nodding his head and giving a concerned look. "I think you had better take that to Ms. Hutchinson."

"I need to call Mom first," I say. "I knew Ms. Varnadore was crazy. I just knew it. Psycho."

48

Linc

I wake up and discover that I've fallen asleep in my van, out-side the barbershop. I look at my watch. It's almost ten o'clock. I've been here, what . . . three hours?

I pull my phone from its holster and discover that it's been turned off. Did I do that? No . . . no it had to be her.

I turn it on, and it rings immediately. I have missed sixteen calls. All of them from Jo, either at work or at home.

I call her. She answers in one ring.

"Linc!" she almost shouts into the phone. "Where the hell have you been?"

"God, man, chill," I say. "I fell asleep at the barbershop."

"The barbershop?"

"Yeah."

"The barbershop is closed, Lincoln. I called there."

"It's a long story. I'll tell you when I get home."

"I called the health club and they said you'd gone shooting."

"Yes. I did."

"With Jessica Varnadore."

I pause for a while. "Yes. No big deal, Jo. She's almost a profes-sional. I learned a lot from her. She's an incredible shot."

"That's not something that gives me great comfort to hear right now."

"What's going on?" I ask.

"She's dangerous, Lincoln."

"Jo, you're jealous. You're overreacting here."

"No. While you were out shooting, the janitor at Collier found a photo album in her desk . . . a photo album filled with stalker pictures of you."

"What?"

"And then I find out from Violet that she instructed our daughter months ago to keep a MySpace diary of our family. Lincoln, there are pictures of us . . . mostly pictures of you . . . and personal anecdotes that I know you would not appreciate anyone knowing about."

"Jo . . . I don't know what to say. Do we call the police?"

"Been there, done that, buddy. I can't believe they haven't found you yet. Or her. Where is she now?"

"At home."

"Lincoln, you have to be seriously sure about this. We could have a *Fatal Attraction* situation here. . . . I'm scared. Are you sure she's home right now?"

"Yes. I'm sure. She has no car. She passed out. I had to drive her home."

"Come home," she says.

"I'm coming."

"Now!"

I'm awakened at about 2:30 by wind and sheets of rain whipping at the jalousie windows so hard it sounds as though they're being sandblasted. The windows have started weeping around the edges—I've never seen them do this—and the water already is pooling on the yellow-tile windowsills. Tillie is on the bed, a forbidden zone, meowing nervously on top of Jo's back. She is beginning to stir. The ceiling fan is still, so I know we've already lost power. Finally, a direct hit on Naples.

"Hey," I say. "She's here. Haley. And she looks mad."

Jo reluctantly crawls into consciousness. As she stretches, lying on her side, I lean over to the bedside table and pull from the drawer a transistor radio I put there just for this moment.

The announcer tells us that Haley blew ashore about fifteen minutes ago, and that she's a strong Category Three. No Katrina, for sure, but trees will be all over the place.

"We are so screwed," I say. "I'm sorry, Jo. I was so wrong about this storm. The windows are crying. Look at them."

"But as long as they leak like that . . . doesn't that mean there won't be as much pressure building up on the outside?"

"Maybe. But what if a missile strikes them?"

She laughs.

"Not funny, Jo. We're screwed if the structure loses its integrity. One hole, wind gets in and lifts that roof right off like the lid of a shoebox."

" 'Loses its integrity,' " she repeats. "Is that Rod talk?"

I feign a frown.

"Hey," I say, changing the subject. "There's something we need to talk about. He wants me to be a partner. I mean a full-fledged partner."

"That's long overdue."

"I know. He's kind of been a jerk about using me for free labor."

"Do you want to do this?"

"Yeah, I think so. Honestly, I'm tired of Girlyland, Jo. And I'd be good at this, working with Rod. I have good ideas. I mean, I'm a caregiver. I know what looks good. Rod doesn't know what looks good. He only knows how things work. Rod has his limits."

"So you are a caregiver?" she asks, raising her eyebrows.

"Of course I'm a caregiver. . . . Okay, so maybe not much of one lately."

"You've been absent for several months, Lincoln, both figuratively and literally."

I look away from her, at the tumult outside the window. The street has become a river, and the seawall has disappeared beneath several inches of water. For the longest time I say nothing, then I feel my bottom lip tighten, and my eyes start to tear up. It's been a long time since I've cried like this.

"I'm sorry, Jo," I say. "I don't know what happened. Are you totally hating me right now?"

I know I am a man of extremes, uncomfortable with the gray regions. I often imagine myself as a person in miniature, grasping onto the end of a grandfather clock's pendulum as it swings from side to side, howling like Tarzan as I sail from one side to the other. We all are on a pendulum, it's a natural movement that feels very good. (Consider rocking chairs and cradles.) Each of us chooses a different spot on which to ride.

I'm out there on the end of the pendulum, experiencing the greatest degree of change, the arc from left to right so great I can actually feel the wind in my hair as I swing back and forth.

Jo tends to ride the pendulum at the very top, where it connects to the mechanism that makes it run, where the arc from left to right is barely perceptible. Her swings aren't wide, aren't scary, so she can keep focus on what's important, and she's always there for me when I swing too far in one direction or another. She asked me if I had slept with Jessica. I told her no, and she believed me. I know I complain a lot, but lying is not something I do, and Jo knows this.

Things could have turned out much worse while I was checked out. Violet could be piercing her ear cartilage in multiple spots, or her nipples and tongue for that matter. Or she could be wearing black lipstick and shopping at Hot Topic. She could be obsessed with observing anniversaries related to Kurt Cobain. She could be getting Fs in school and torturing the cat and pooping out babies every ten months.

But overall, things are okay. My family did fine. A thirteen-year-old is pretty much like a bowl of freshly made Jell-O, still steamy-hot inside the refrigerator. All the ingredients are already there, everything's properly mixed and dissolved. There's really nothing else you can do at this point to change the outcome. All you have to do is sit back and watch it gel. At this point, it's going to take a lot to mess it up. So you can't be too mad at me, Jo . . . right?

We are lying side by side, facing each other. I reach up and stroke her cheek with the back of my hand, mainly because my hands these days are cut up and calloused.

"Do you hate me for what I put you through?" I ask again.

She touches my cheek. A tired but serene smile forms on her face. She begins to shake her head.

"We missed you, but we're fine," she says. "You lost something. You had to go find it."

Incredibly, the jalousie windows held. We had no penetration of the house. We lost one large oak, but it fell into the bay instead of the house. It cracked the cap of the seawall, but that can be fixed. In fact, I think I'll try fixing it myself.

The hospital lost part of the roof of the ER drive-through, but other than that it escaped major harm.

"We need to check on Marta," Jo says.

"Why?" I ask.

"Because she lives alone and because she's part of this family."

"I don't like her, Jo. I just don't like her."

"I know that, Lincoln."

"The only reason she's still here is because I'm not chained to this house anymore."

"Precisely. That's why we have her. Now . . . you and Violet take that fancy new chain saw of yours and go over and see if she needs any help with debris."

The phone lines and electricity are down, of course, so we drive on up, unannounced, to her home in east Naples.

When we pull up she is outside with some neighbors, looking at an immense royal palm that has been pushed over by the wind. But instead of crashing through—and that's exactly what one of those heavy bastards would do—it miraculously stopped just a few inches from the edge of her roof.

She is surprised to see us. I am introduced not by name but as "Josephine's husband."

"We've got to get that off the house," I say. "It could go at any time."

I have the long rope in my van that Rod used to tie up my Porta-Potty for Arturo. I drive up onto the lawn then tie one end of the rope to my chassis, beneath the bumper, and then I climb onto the roof and tie the other end around the trunk, which is nearly two feet in diameter. Ted has taught me how to tie lines on his boat, and this new knowledge comes in very handy right now. I'm amazed at how simple all this manual-labor stuff is. It's only rocket science if you don't take the time to stop and look at how things work. That said, you also need the right tools for the job. It's really not much differ-ent from a kitchen—you can't cut crusty bread with a meat knife, not without ruining the bread, anyway.

Before I get into my van I do exactly what Rod would do . . . I stand back and survey the situation, making sure there is nothing in the tree's path, no matter which direction it might fall.

"Everyone, go stand in the street," I say. "Get out of the way."

I get into my van and start to slowly inch forward. The tree be-gins to creep upward, to its original upright position, and when it is perpendicular to the ground I put the van in park, get out, and yell to the men who are standing in the street with Marta and Violet. They are short and Hispanic, but they appear to be strong.

"Guys, I need your help," I say, pulling my knife from my pocket. "Okay, you, sir, you take this knife and cut the rope when I say so . . . And you and I," I say to the other man, "you and I are going to push this toward the street, right in that direction over there, toward that turquoise house. . . . Okay, we're gonna push, that's it, push hard, man, yeah, that's right . . . okay, now cut that damn rope. Now! Cut it!"

The rope severs and snaps off the trunk. And after standing there for a second, as if it can't make up its mind, the tree starts leaning in the direction we are pushing, then gains momentum and comes crashing down into the street.

Marta claps her hands and smiles. *"Que bueno!"* she says.

"Mas trabajo," I say. More work.

I go to the van and get my chain saw, and over the next half hour we dissect the trunk into pieces, which the two men and Violet and I roll off the street and onto the curb.

I am exhausted and sweaty, and as we get into the van I see Marta coming my way, across the grass, and I realize I've forgotten to say good-bye.

"Linc," she says, stern, not smiling, which is the usual look I get from her. Great, I think, I've done something wrong again. But she did call me "Linc." She has never addressed me by my name, and I am perplexed.

To my surprise, she takes my hand in hers and pats it.

"You are a good man," she says. "Flan for you."

Mr. Burkert, the headmaster, has called and wants to talk with me. School's out while repairs are being made—there won't be classes for at least another week—so I offer to meet him at The Red Croissant, which is a post-drop-off breakfast spot popular with Collier Academy moms.

"No," he says. "Let's have a beer somewhere. Fifth Avenue's got power back. Do you know the Irish pub downtown?"

"Yeah."

"Let's meet there. Say . . . three-thirty?"

We sit in a booth, talking for a while about the repairs and renovations on campus, and then he changes his tone to one more serious, as if I'm a student in trouble.

"That's not the reason I wanted to talk with you," he says.

"What, then?" I ask.

"It's about Miss Varnadore," he says.

"I know. She scared the hell out of my wife. And the photo album? I think you should fire her."

"That won't be necessary," he says.

"No, really, I think it would hold up in court if she sued. There's valid reason for terminating her."

He shifts in his seat, then takes another drink of beer.

"Miss Varnadore was arrested last night."

"Arrested?"

"Transported back to North Carolina."

"What for?"

"Failure to show up in court."

"For what? Do we know?"

"Firearms possession."

"Yeah, but she's a marksman," I explain. "She's crazy about guns."

Mr. Burkert starts to shake his head. "No," he says. "There's more."

"What, then?"

"It's a small town up there. Everyone knows everyone. I called the superintendent of schools. The charges were filed by some woman, presumably someone's wife. Evidently, she had a thing for married men. . . . It appears that you and I, Mr. Menner, have escaped great calamity."

"But we don't know if she would have done anything drastic," I say. "We don't know that."

"No, we don't," he says. "There is only conjecture."

He raises his glass in a toast.

"Here's to our good fortune, Mr. Menner," he says.

"Call me Linc," I say.

"Linc."

I raise mine. We clink glasses and take a drink.

"Do you know the roster of names for this year's storms?" I ask.

"No, I'm afraid I don't."

"The storm named for J this year?"

He cocks his head in curiosity.

"It's Jessica," I say.

TO: Headmaster@CollierAcademy.org
FROM: LincolnM@AOL.com

Mr. Burkert:

It was great meeting you for beers. Thanks for the request to help you in your hurricane repairs. It is my pleasure to be of assistance.

Now, in these past several days on campus I have noted some potential improvements we can make to the campus.

First of all, those signs that you love so much have become thriving mosquito breeding grounds. If you haven't noticed, the kids love stealing the decorative PVC caps off the tops of these posts, leaving the hollow posts open to gallons of rainwater. RECOMMENDATION: Replace caps and this time use PVC cement to keep them in place. The stuff is amazing. It actually chemically melts the PVC material, creating a bond that simply can't be broken.

Also, now that the royal palms are all knocked over and dead from the storm, I think we should replant with native sabal palms. I realize

they are messier looking, and all the chit-chatty tennis moms probably won't like them as much, but they harbor wildlife better than most
species of palms. Perhaps we could even build a canopy around one
of them so your science classes can observe the birds and reptiles
and bugs that live within these remarkable trees.

On another note, thank you for granting me permission to take Violet and her friends to help clean debris on Sanibel Island.

I will see you at the Model U.N. Awards Dinner. I'm bringing my famous pasta picante and Marta's (my housekeeper) incredible red
snapper in coconut-lime sauce.

One last question: Will there be serving spoons provided or
should we bring our own? I will bring several, just in case. It may
sound weird, but I keep a set of basic kitchen utensils in the storage
bin on my new truck. Some wooden spoons, grater, rolling pin, paring
knives. You'd be surprised at how handy they can be in construction
work. One man's spatula is another man's putty knife.

Sincerely yours,
Linc Menner

acknowledgments

I could not have written this book without the friendship and teachings of my good friend, Hans Wilson. Also thanks to Matt Steele for his construction know-how and to Roman David Garay for introducing me to firearms.

Thanks to Rose O'Dell King and Karen Feldman for their undying, loyal enthusiasm and help in critiquing my writing.

Thanks to Anne and Bud Pagel: Anne, for introducing me to the artist-in-residence housing in Lincoln, Nebraska; Bud, for all his writing wisdom over the years; and both, for their friendship and support of my career.

Thanks to my good friends, Kevin and Cindy Pierce, who are my utmost companions when my wife is out of town and working late.

Thanks to my editor, Signe Pike, who understands marketing and packaging better than most editors twice her age. Thanks to my agent, Wendy Sherman, who has grown to be not only my negotiator but also my friend. Thanks to Allison Dickens and her pleasant, crucial guidance these past several years. And thanks to Kate Collins, who helped to push this book over the finish line.

Lastly, thanks to my wife, Carol, for her insights, patience, and hand-holding. And thanks to my daughter, Haley, whose keen analyses and observations of humanity not only made this book possible but also help make my life as a parent enriching and enjoyable.

man of the house

Ad Hudler

A Reader's Guide

a conversation with
Ad Hudler

Ad Hudler sat down with his seventeen-year-old daughter, Haley, to discuss their lives and the characters from *Man of the House*.

Haley Hudler: *Man of the House* begins with Violet Menner's entrance essay to Collier Academy. You say that I was your inspiration for Violet. That is the biggest understatement I've ever heard in my life. Dad, I know you fancy yourself a fiction writer, but I mean, come on. Violet *is* me, down to the "Oh, joy," exact dialogue stolen from my preteen years. What was it like for you writing from my point of view? How did you have to change your writing style to do it?

Ad Hudler: Because I spend so much of my time with you, it really wasn't that difficult. I have spent hundreds of hours driving teenage girls around in the van, so I've certainly got the dialect down. Honestly, Haley, I did have to dumb Violet down a little bit; you have a better vocabulary than most English teachers, but I didn't think that would be believable to the average reader.

HH: *Man of the House* is set about ten years after its prequel, *Househusband.* In that time many important things happened to the Menner family. How did you fit all of this background history into the first few chapters of the book without making it seem contrived to those readers who didn't read *Househusband?*

AH: That was the challenge, indeed: making *Man of the House* a stand-alone book without testing the patience of all my readers who read *Househusband.* It helped that my editor read *Househusband,* so she could spot any over- or under-explaining. In retrospect, though, I realize I should have reread *Househusband* before writing the sequel because there were some things I forgot. For example, I was speaking at a convention, talking about the sequel I was writing, when one woman in the audience said, "Hey, what happens with Violet now that she has a sibling?" I thought, "Holy crap!" I'd forgotten that Jo was pregnant at the end of *Househusband,* and I'd already written 80 percent of the book without the second child. A quick mention of a miscarriage solved the problem.

HH: Knowing that he could have made life much easier for his family by moving out of the house while it was under construction, why do you think Linc Menner insisted that they stay there?

AH: Two reasons: First of all, Linc, as I do, has this inexplicable masochistic streak; he likes to test himself all the time. He is definitely not a path-of-least-resistance kind of guy. Second, the novel would have been much more boring if they had been staying in a condo somewhere. Lots of the household tension comes from the family having to live in a construction zone.

HH: I remember that as you were writing the chapters from Jessica Varnadore's point of view, you were worried that she sounded over-the-top, almost unbelievable. However, bizarre, abnormal characteristics are common in the characters in your books. What personality traits did you give Jessica to make her a believable character?

AH: I think it helped that she wasn't drop-dead gorgeous, just attractive. I also think talking about how she'd been engaged three times showed a volatility and zaniness that made her actions believable.

HH: I have noticed that in almost every single one of your books, you like to add in parenting tips and advice. Is this your passive-aggressive way of correcting the child-rearing skills of others?

AH: Guilty as charged! No, in all seriousness, I think a lot of parents can be too absorbed in their own lives, and they try too hard to be their kids' best friends. Parents negotiate with their young children too much. It's perfectly all right—in fact, necessary—to tell a kid, "Because I said so!"

HH: Yes, but you frequently terrify my friends by attempting to parent them. This goes along with your whole philosophy that you voice in *Man of the House:* It takes a village to raise a child. How has that been working out for you in real life?

AH: I'll admit it pisses off some parents, but that's just too bad. I've also noticed that, in your older teen years, Haley, the kids have stopped hanging around this house.

HH: I was happy to see that you included my viewpoint on Harper Lee's *To Kill a Mockingbird*. I am sure that looking back on her book, there are many things she would have liked to change about it. After writing the sequel to *Househusband*, are there any things you would like to change about the first book?

AH: I wish I would have made Jo less one-dimensional. I wish I would have fleshed her out more. But, overall, I still really like that book. I think it's funny, and I think it says some really important things about gender behavior and relations in our culture.

HH: Throughout the book, Violet begins to rely on her father less and less. In fact, she wants to exclude him from certain parts of her life. For example, when Linc takes Violet and her friends to the mall, rather than having him come to the stores with them as she usually would, she asks him to stay behind on "The Man Bench." I know that I, for one, felt guilty reading these parts of the book because I know that I did do things like that. Was it hard for you to relive those moments as well?

AH: Actually, no, Haley. You've been so much better than most other teenagers in that department. You rarely appear to be embarrassed by me or your mother, and you generally show us great respect, and we really appreciate that. You didn't even mind when I dressed up in an adult diaper and posed as a baby for your friend's high-school photo project. It takes a cool, confident young lady to weather something like that.

HH: In real life, you began to develop your new masculine tendencies at around the same time our house was under construction and the hurricanes came. How curious. Response?

AH: I suppose the book is a little autobiographical in that way. I have undergone some kind of finding-my-inner-male-redneck metamorphosis, and I think it's due to several factors. Those hurricanes did bring out the protector in me. Also, you going through puberty and your mother going through menopause have left me scratching my head several times, accentuating my maleness simply because you were experiencing things I could not relate to. But perhaps the biggest influence in my metamorphosis was my good friend Hans. We are a good fit, Hans and I. He not only is in touch with his female side, but he also embraces all those very fun guy traits that I had all but forgotten in the years of being a caregiver. We have cut down trees together. He has taught me how to think like an engineer. We eat at Hooters. The scene in the book where Rod coaches Linc on how to address waitresses as "hon" and "babe" happened exactly like that, with Hans. Oh, one more thing: my boots. I bought my first pair of work boots about three years ago. I'll tell you what . . . putting on a pair of boots changes a man. You're two inches taller, and you just start to naturally swagger. I've also discovered power-lifting in the last three or four years, and I've gained thirty pounds. That, too, has changed my personality somewhat because people react to me differently now that I'm a bigger man. All these changes have kind of fed one another.

HH: Well, the reason I brought that up is because I noticed that the language associated with hurricanes, like "Cat Five" and "cone of uncertainty" seemed to correlate directly with your newfound sense of masculinity. Why would this be? Is this because hurricanes are powerful and unpredictable? Or am I reading too far into this?

AH: You're reading too much into it.

HH: You frequently complain about the huge lengths we had to go to in order to protect ourselves from the hurricanes. However, in the book you almost seem to look back on these days fondly. You seem to actually enjoy putting so much time and effort into maintaining a stable environment during a disaster. Why is that?

AH: I'm one of the most anal-retentive people I know. Preparing for impending disaster appeals to my need to control my environment. I also have this weird feeling that if I overprepare for something horrible, then it won't happen. It's like, "Oh, great, now I've wasted all that time worrying about something." It's as if by worrying about it I can will it not to happen. In a similar way, I personally keep the plane from crashing whenever I am flying. You all need to know that it is my constant worrying while airborne that keeps us in flight.

HH: In *Househusband*, the book was entirely from Linc Menner's point of view. Only he got a say in what was told to the reader. However, *Man of the House* is from four points of view. Why did you do this?

AH: People cannot see themselves change as much as those around them can. I couldn't have Linc talk about his metamorphosis because he himself doesn't understand it. I needed other characters, those people who were close to him, to observe his actions and comment on his transformation.

HH: Throughout the book Linc tries to hide the small changes he is making in his life, almost as if he's ashamed of them. For instance, he hides his muscle magazines from Jo. Why does he do this? Why is he ashamed of changing?

AH: I'm not sure. I think maybe he feels like a traitor for abandoning his female traits that he's practiced for so long. Does he feel as if he's moved over to the competition? But hiding the muscle mags . . . At first glance, they do really kind of look pornographic, all that bulging, bare skin and all on the covers, and the photo spreads of nearly naked people. I think most people would agree that the magazines look like they need to be hidden beneath the mattress.

HH: In chapter 22, Linc uses the phrase "she has a great spirit" to justify his reasons for liking Jessica Varnadore, who happens to be wearing Daisy Dukes when he comes to her apartment. A euphemism, perhaps?

AH: I had to be careful in showing that, despite Linc's metamorphosis into manliness, he also remained a caregiver in a woman's world, and by having him notice her "spirit" as well as her boobs, I was able to show he was a man who saw the world both from the female and male perspectives. Also, I'm not sure my female readers would like him to be all locker-room-talky about her. You notice that I never use the "t" word for breasts, even though most men use that word when referring to them.

HH: Well, now that we've finished up this question and answer session, I'm curious about something. How does it feel to be interrogated by your own daughter?

AH: It's a pleasure, Haley. And I want to say "thank you" because I know it's hard to have a father who writes so intimately about his family. I know you must feel very exposed at times, and I appreciate your maturity and self-confidence. And I'm sorry that I admitted to the listeners of National Public Radio that the poop scene from *Househusband* was real—I just couldn't lie to a national audience like that. Some day, long after I'm gone, I hope these books give you comfort and help you to remember me.

reading group questions and topics for discussion

1. The characters in *Man of the House* are all trying to find an inner balance between masculinity and femininity. Linc is attempting to break free from his feminine role as a caregiver and to get in touch with his masculinity. Jo is a woman who has a profession that usually belongs to a male. As Violet is going through puberty, she begins to become more of a teenage girl and less of a companion for her father. Jessica is a femme fatale, but has the aggression of a man. How does the mixture of characteristics from both genders affect each character?

2. How does the popular saying "Be careful what you wish for" apply in this novel?

3. How does Linc's transformation affect his marriage with Jo? What are the positive changes? What are the negative changes?

4. Women who have read *Househusband* frequently say that they want a househusband of their own. However, throughout history women have generally wanted the typical masculine man as a mate. Which of these types of men is the most appealing and why?

5. As the book progresses, Linc begins to forget small details he usually pays close attention to. What are some of the things he forgets? What are some of the small details that get forgotten around your household during hectic times?

6. Explain how Jo's "intervention" with Linc and the foreboding Hurricane Arturo foreshadow disaster ahead in the novel.

7. Everyone knows that kids change with puberty. However, Violet goes through some very big personality changes. Can some of these be blamed on puberty? If so, which ones?

8. The construction at the Menner household makes it so Linc is surrounded by macho men every day. How did this contribute to Linc's metamorphosis?

9. Discuss Jessica Varnadore's progression into a stalker. What does she start out doing that hints to trouble later on in the novel?

10. In chapter 9, after Violet gets her braces off, Linc wants to call someone and share his emotional moment. However, he has no one to call. Why do you think male caregivers often feel so alone? Do they forge relationships as women do? Why or why not?

11. Judging from Linc Menner's experiences, what can men bring to caregiving that women cannot?

about the author

AD HUDLER is a stay-at-home dad and novelist who lives with his wife and daughter on the coast of southwest Florida, where he frets over impending hurricanes. Raised in a four-generation newspaper family in Colorado, he has written three comic, controversial novels: *Househusband, Southern Living,* and *All This Belongs to Me.* Now that his daughter is old enough to drive, Ad has traded in his Man Van for a Ford F150 truck. Visit his website at www.AdHudler.com.